Tangled LIES

KAREN E. OSBORNE

Black Rose Writing | Texas

The author grants the final approval for this literary material.

Second printing

This is a work of fiction. Unless otherwise indicated, all the names, characters, businesses, places, events, and incidents in this book are the product of the author's imagination or used fictitiously. Mount Kisco, NY, the Mt. Kisco police station, and Northern Westchester Hospital are real. However, the author created streets, businesses, and incidents. Any resemblance to actual persons, living or dead, or actual events is purely coincidental.

ISBN: 978-1-68433-732-3
PUBLISHED BY BLACK ROSE WRITING
www.blackrosewriting.com

Printed in the United States of America
Suggested Retail Price (SRP) $19.95

Tangled Lies is printed in Georgia

*As a planet-friendly publisher, Black Rose Writing does its best to eliminate unnecessary waste to reduce paper usage and energy costs, while never compromising the reading experience. As a result, the final word count vs. page count may not meet common expectations.

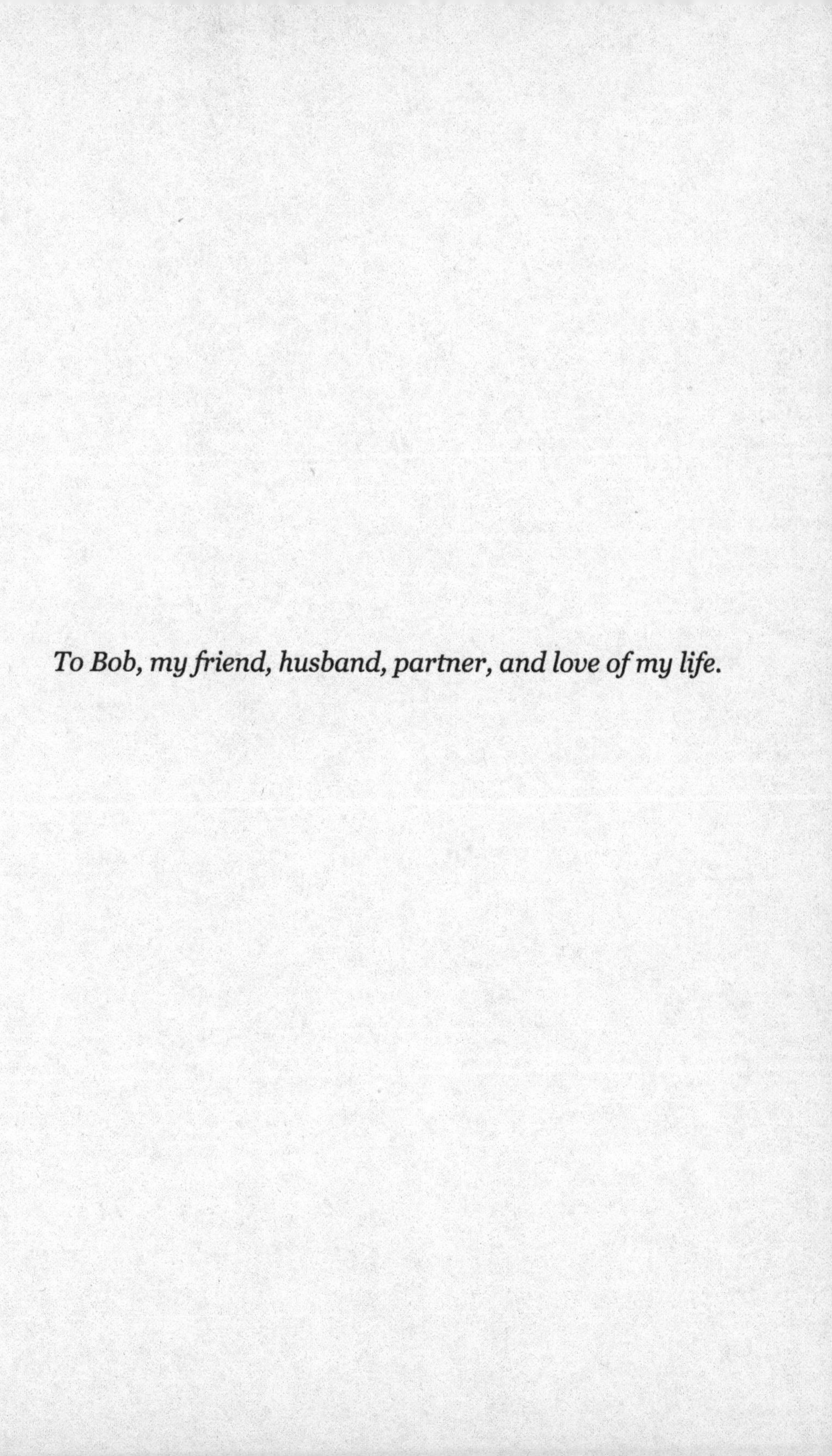

To Bob, my friend, husband, partner, and love of my life.

Tangled
LIES

Chapter 1

Vera

Disquiet hung in the air. It filled Vera's lungs, traveled down her spine, and spread by tingling nerves to her limbs, fingertips, and toes. She stood still and concentrated. Wintry gusts chilled her cheeks. She listened. Nothing.

She hoisted her re-usable grocery bags and struggled across the parking lot, careful to step around the ice patches from the recent February storm. The cold converted her breaths to fog-puffs.

Already low in the sky, the pale sun made it around four. She promised Charlie dinner by seven — chicken again, but she planned to dress it up. Glazed carrots, scratch biscuits, and brownies for dessert. All three of her adult children loved chocolate.

The unmistakable stench of fresh urine assailed her nose. Vera pressed the elevator button. *What a place.* Her late husband, Vincent, would be sick if he saw her here. With the fat of her thumb, its cuticle ragged, she pushed again. Something else she gave up. No more manicures or pedicures. No more trips to the hair salon to straighten her curls.

Charlie had to find a proper job soon.

Six months without steady pay, only a contract here and there. He paid the rent and insurance, but Vera's Social Security covered everything else. Charlie apologized for how and where they lived and sometimes, she hated to admit, for the unsavory-looking people who dropped by.

What could she do? She was a guest with no options.

A positive person, she focused on the minor pleasures of her life instead. Dancing in the living room to Motown, *The Brian Lehrer Show* on public radio, and novels she borrowed from the library. Although Charlie decorated the apartment using inexpensive pieces he scavenged, he had made room for some of her favorite things — the walnut bookcase, her hand-knotted Persian rug, an antique floor-length mirror, and two wing chairs covered in plush mocha. There were days, however, when she cringed at the trash-edged grass and the hall's vexing brown stains.

For the third time, Vera hit the elevator's up-button. *Please God, send it down.* She stopped. How selfish to pray for a working elevator while children starved in Somalia. She took the prayer back and waited. No creak or bang. The super had promised to fix it more than a week ago. *Never mind.* She was not too old to climb four flights. She started up the narrow staircase. By the time she reached the third-floor landing, her breathing became audible. *God created elevators for a reason.*

She pushed on and made it to her front door anticipating comfort and peace. She imagined the lavender scent of her bath, heard the water's undercurrent, and the soundtrack provided by Smokey and Gladys, easing tired muscles before she turned her attention to dinner.

One bag still in her hand and the other on the welcome mat, Vera inserted her key.

The door swung open. Silence.

"Charlie?"

Brandy's yelps pierced the eerie quiet.

Cold air stung her ankles.

Charlie's writing desk lay crippled, almost halved, wood splinters scattered across the Persian rug. Her treasured bookcase sat face down next to the desk. Papers, books, and shards of glass spiraled out from the epicenter. The grocery bag slammed to the ground. Coffee and canned tomatoes thumped onto the hardwood floor. A dozen eggs puddled around her feet, oozing over a bloody footprint.

She stepped inside.

Brandy, her bark almost a human wail, strained against her collar and leash, bound to something outside the opened living room window. Blood smeared her matted coat.

Angling around the debris, right hand pressed against the wall, Vera followed the blood smears to Charlie's bedroom.

The stench of raw meat, vomit, and feces filled her nostrils. A metallic taste made her gag. Splattered blood streaked the walls, dark red, almost black.

His head faced her on a blood-soaked mattress. Huge brown eyes, always amused, stared opaque and blank. His opened mouth seemed to call to her. Cocoa-brown skin stretched over sunken cheekbones. Her legs sagged. A weight crushed her chest.

She forced her gaze away from his.

Only then she saw the rest of his body, two feet away, severed from his head.

Chapter 2

Dani

Preparations complete, Dani dressed in black yoga pants low on her hips and a faded Save the Children T-shirt for the long drive. She laced up her Nikes. Her favorite movie star sunglasses muted the squares and triangles of sunlight on the walls and floors. The platinum blonde wig, left over from last year's Halloween party, might be overkill. Costumed as Marilyn Monroe with red lips, a circle skirt, fitted sweater, and padded push-up bra, Mirko, her used-to-be-boyfriend, told her she looked hot. Goodwill received the clothes, but not the wig. Now it made her scalp itch. As an extra precaution, she'd parked her yellow Chevy several blocks away.

The scents of damp air and dogwood blooms barely registered as she leaned out the side window and scoured the alley. Empty. She checked the view from the front. A couple made their way across the asphalt lot, climbed into their mini-van and backed out. Dani stretched her neck. No sign of Alice or Pete. Six days a week, Dani's landlords returned from work at five-thirty, making now Dani's last chance to escape.

For the past eighteen months, Dani lived on the third floor of a low-rise walk-up in Mount Kisco, a suburb of ten thousand, thirty miles north of The Bronx, New York border. It was an economically and racially mixed town, home to politicos, financiers, movie stars, shop owners, government employees, and many Latino gardeners and house cleaners. Dani blended in. She worked hard at being unobtrusive, spoke quietly, smiled, and said *please* and *thank you*. That way, people let things pass, like shaded truths and late payments.

Her crammed suitcase stood open by the door. Packed-away bracelets and earrings her mother left her shared space with pictures of her brother Bogie and his three girls, a softball trophy from Dani's last high school and prints from Paris, Prague, and Ireland, places she loved but never visited. Everything else landed in the trash or in the bag tagged "Goodwill."

The stuffed animal collection from Mirko lay lumped in the donation bag. Every month on their anniversary, he presented her with a new one — an elephant, bunny, teddy bear family, and a fat panda. No room for them now. *Banish the memories, close the door, and move on.* Something else her mother gave her. Except Dani wasn't giving up on Mirko.

After a last sweep to ensure she remembered everything on her to-do list, she ended the quick tour in the kitchen. She had planned to leave in the morning, but sorting, packing, and cleaning took much longer than she had expected. Plus, she fretted about her meager cash supply. Only eighty-five dollars remained of the kiss-off money from her job. Shredded bits of the layoff notice mingled with the remnants from last night, her private going-away party. Only Dani, a Diet Coke, and cupcakes from Stop & Shop. She'd eaten the iced tops of all six and chucked the bottoms.

Two-hundred-dollars from Bogie and fifty-dollars from her errant father made up the rest of her paltry reserves.

Bogie also concerned her. Well, not Bogie as much as his wife, Sally. An email informed Dani about the money. She twisted her mouth right and left, her feet shuffling in sync. Deft fingers searched for the message on her iPhone, its cracked screen still readable.

"Sally and I can't wait to see you. The girls keep talking about Auntie's visit. Can you still stay for two weeks? Sent you dough for gas and a motel room. Aim for Ohio on day one and Kansas City by dinnertime on day two. We'll go out for barbeque.

When are you leaving? Call me on my new cell. I texted the number to you.

Love you, Big Bro Bo"

When she first told Bogie about her visit, she felt confident at least one of her job applications would be a winner. Seattle sounded perfect for a new life — booming with tech companies and thriving nonprofits. According to Googled articles, spring weather came as early as February and stayed until the fall. Indeed.com, an online job-finding site, listed tons of positions and Dani submitted applications for seven that kinda-sorta spoke to her skill set. She liked the phrase skill set. A few fudged facts plus puffed-up work history, and a downloaded template, helped her create a promising resumé. She looked good on paper. The few who responded, however, emailed polite rejections. Most ignored her. Thus, a longer stay at Chez Bogie.

It would piss off Sally. Bogie too, but only at first. To make things right, Dani planned to babysit the kids, shop, clean, and become indispensable. She'd crash on the sofa or get a sleeping bag and tuck away in the den, practically invisible.

Quick thumbs double-checked Bogie's new number in her contacts.

Next, she retrieved the envelope and card from her father crammed with fifty dollars in wrinkled ones and fives. *Who sent cash in the mail?* Her father's cluelessness was legendary. It arrived on February 28, a week *after* her birthday. For over two months, she ignored his scribbled note, but as she mapped out her escape, she opened it. No need to re-read it since she remembered every damning word.

Happy twenty-fifth birthday. Hope this is your best year ever, better than last year, anyway. LOL. Thought you'd like this picture. I was cleaning out a junk pile and there it was.

Love,

Pop

P.S. Missy sends her love. She wanted me to tell you half the money is from her.

There was a photo of the three of them, her dad, Missy and Dani, an ancient shot taken weeks before one of Dani's many escapes and a weird but typical thing for her father to include. Missy, his girlfriend for the past fifteen years, five-feet-six-inches tall, the same as Dani, displayed purchased breasts bulging over a scoop neck tank and out the sides of the armholes. Missy *claimed* to be thirty-two. The truth was closer to fifty, plus ugly and mean.

A sweat-stained John Deere cap perched high on her father's head. Rubber bands held his mixed-gray ponytail. An unsmiling Dani, only twelve years-old and her mom dead for a year, stared into the lens. Black-Irish, dark hair so thick it took an hour to dry, hid most of her pale face. One could barely make out her eyes' distinctive shade of violet, lighter when she wore blue, darker during arguments. Mirko said he saw layers of colors worth studying to discern. She didn't understand, but she liked the way it sounded.

She'd left her father's money in the envelope with a vague notion of returning it. No explanation. *Yeah, right.* Dani retrieved the bills, ripped up the card and picture, and dumped them in the garbage with her severance notice and cupcake bottoms — perfect companions.

Better hurry. It had been time to go hours earlier, and every minute offered opportunities for things to go wrong.

Her backpack and donate bag in one hand and a cooler filled with two peanut-butter sandwiches and six Diet Cokes in the other, Dani moved through the apartment. Despite skipping out on two months' rent, she left the place spotless. She'd emptied and scrubbed the refrigerator, scuff-freed the walls, stripped the kitchen shelves, and replaced the more abused linings. Besides, she intended to pay Pete and Alice as soon as she landed a job in KC or Seattle. Patience stretched to a snapping point, two weeks ago they said pay or leave.

"Water under the bridge; the ship sailed; the barn door is wide open, and the cows ran off." Her mother's clichéd answers to every forgotten promise.

Dani sat on the suitcase. After several tries to zip it shut, she removed Lefty the panda, the only gift from Mirko that made the cut. She hesitated. Pete and Alice helped her move in, held packages for her despite a "We're the building managers, not your delivery service," sign in the lobby. When Mirko had dumped her, Alice came by carrying a six-pack of beer for herself and Diet Cokes for Dani. For the last two months, they believed her when she said, “I’ll pay you next week.” They deserved better.

Dani balanced Lefty on top of the suitcase. She walked back to the kitchen and ripped off a sheet of paper towel. The ballpoint pen tapped on the tabletop as she pondered her message. She landed on,

“I know I owe you $2,400 and will pay soon. Have a great new job in Seattle. I’ll send the address when I arrive. Thanks for everything and, hey, I’m really sorry.”
Dani Gerrity

Now a legal document, unless the white lie invalidated it.

Chapter 3

Vera

Vera tried to listen, but the remembered blood and smell saturated her senses. Fingers interlaced, she squeezed her hands together until the color drained away. God would not give her more than she could bear, but the weight of her grief buckled her soul.

"Mom, are you okay?"

They were loading leftovers from Liza's yard sale into the Saturn hatchback, more things than Vera thought prudent. Stuffing old things into a smaller place would create a cramped feel and add to Liza's distress. Her divorce had become final a few weeks earlier, sending her into another funk. Her husband's insistence on selling the house piled it on.

"I am able to manage," Vera said, using the formal syntax she had cultivated and paid a social price for since her teen years. Children could be cruel. Black children accused. *"You act so white."* White ones condescended; their voices filled with surprise. *"You speak so well."* As if Black folks do not or cannot speak the English language correctly. No matter. As in all aspects of her life, Vera persisted.

"Wait." Liza, visibly perspiring, helped her mother hoist a blond-wood bookcase into the back of the car. "People are unbelievable. Did you hear the last man dickering?"

Argh. "It is not important."

"To you."

"The best pieces sold." Vera attempted to avert the sure-to-follow rant. "The set of African masks seemed to find a suitable home."

"Cheap people make me nuts. Would it kill him to spend ten dollars for something I bought for one-hundred?"

Liza found fault with everything and everyone. Vera gave it another try. "Let's load these items." She hefted one corner of an end table.

Liza lifted the other end. She was a carbon copy of her mother, tall and busty but not fat, high cheekbones under caramel-colored skin, hazel eyes, full lips, and short hair (Liza's dyed and straightened, Vera's a silver curly afro).

"He started at one dollar. Did you see how many pieces of the banana bread he devoured?"

The table landed hard. Vera shoved it over to make room for two folding chairs. Sometimes the grief took over so completely, she found it difficult to follow conversations. At first only a thought, longing for a drink became urgent.

"Plus, creeps showed up, like the guy with the horrid complexion hanging around and not buying one thing." As if to underscore her point, Liza gave her body a shudder.

Vera had noticed the pimply faced man's sidelong glances, saw him touch too many things. Every time Vera looked his way, he put his phone to his ear as if speaking to someone. "You locked and armed the door. We were safe enough."

"He kept looking at the house like a crook casing it." Liza glared at her mother. "It's your fault. I told you there'd be trouble from the rally."

So much work, too few people. The need to do something, anything, spurred Vera to enlist friends, neighbors, and her church members to rally for Charlie.

"Dangerous. All that personal attention."

Who Killed Charlie Moon? signs bobbed along the road from Vera's apartment complex to the police station. After it ended, people milled about for a few minutes but soon dispersed and returned to their lives. Charlie forgotten and still no clues. "No harm done," Vera said. The sting of disappointment layered on top of her grief.

"Public grieving. Everyone still looking at us. The family of the..."

"Stop. Do not speak it."

Liza froze, blinked hard. "It was embarrassing."

"So what?" A dull throbbing at Vera's temples moved to her forehead. "There is a killer out there." Her tone was thin and shrill.

"Not this again." Liza threw up her hands. "It's not your responsibility."

"It is."

"You never let go of anything. Ever."

Vincent called it doggedness when the trait annoyed him and grit and perseverance when he admired it. Maybe she *should* steer clear, but the police were not making progress. Just another dead Black man soon forgotten. She had hoped the rally would jog a memory and uncover a witness or pressure the police to dig deeper. She needed an alternative plan.

In a slower cadence and at a lower register, Vera said, "Let's not fight. We will finish and get on our way." Grunting, she hoisted a chair. "Where will you store all this junk?"

"Junk?"

"Poor word choice."

"Too bad *your children* missed out on your pricey tastes and queen-of-the-kingdom ways."

Is that how Liza saw her? Did Penny and Charlie? "I meant... your apartment is smallish."

"If you'd helped me afford a decent condo, co-signed or even given me a loan, I'd have plenty of space."

"My credit rating is no better than yours." Should she inquire about alimony? "You will be fine."

"How can you still live there?"

Argh. "I am tired of explaining." The urge for a glass of wine flooded her mind again. She never used to drink, not even a nightcap with Vincent. It made her head fuzzy. But now she required more. Dulled, fogged.

Through congested nostrils, Liza pushed out air.

"Whatever you blame me for, whatever you think I did or failed to do..."

"*You know*."

Yes. Of course. A flush rose from her breasts, to her neck, and cheeks. It happened years ago. Vera tried to make amends. What was the statute of limitations on deserting your family? At what age are your children responsible for their lives and choices? Why continue to blame Vera for every cloud?

"I'm sorry." Her one-hundredth apology. She scrubbed her face with both hands. "And I'm tired." She thought about Charlie again. The youngest, and a toddler, her disappearance hit him hardest. Did he ever forgive her? Why didn't she ask him?

"Mom, I'm talking to you."

Vera raised her hands and hiked her shoulders in apology. "What were you saying?"

An audible huff. "I said, some of his crap is still in my basement." She paused. "Not mine anymore." She looked around with a wistful expression.

"I will put them in storage when I have the strength." Every day a paltry amount of energy seeped out leaving her depleted.

"Probably hot."

"No." Her voice trembled. "He never stole." The police implied as much. Yes, Charlie had friends and visitors who made her nervous, but he lived an honest life. "Your brother was *not* a criminal."

Vera angled the second chair until it fit snugly against the first. She reached for the next item. In an emotion-ladened silence, the two women continued to fill the Saturn.

Liza spoke first, her tone softer. "Are they still working on the love-triangle theory?"

"No angry husband so far." The detective thought the murder scene denoted intimacy-fueled rage. As opposed to what?

"Any fresh scenarios?"

"Using Charlie's machete, a weapon of convenience, and the mess in the apartment gave them another thread. Perhaps a robbery gone wrong, but the..." The word stuck in her throat. *Decapitation*.

"So, you've told me. I'm asking about *new clues*."

"Nothing missing."

Liza's voice rose. "You're not listening to me again, still."

"Do not yell at me."

"I want the killer caught as much as you do. I'm grieving too."

Of course she was. It wasn't right for Vera to measure grief, a mother's weighing more than a sister's pain. And yet...

"They say if you don't catch a murderer within forty-eight hours, you won't." Liza tied the hatchback door to the bumper with a rope, leaving the bookcase legs sticking out like forlorn leftovers. She grabbed the faux Tiffany lamp from its place on the thatched grass. "Let's go." She climbed into the passenger seat, the lamp on her lap. "They're never going to solve this one." Sadness, bitterness, and defeat laced her words.

Before joining Liza, Vera counted to ten in her head. She pulled the seat belt across her chest and clicked it into place. She started the engine, backed out of the driveway, and shifted to drive.

"You're wrong," she said, in a barely audible voice. She had failed at so many things — wife, mother, grandmother, businesswoman, losing her flower shop and her home. Not this time. "I *will* find Charlie's killer."

Chapter 4

Dani

Dani pulled her Chevy in behind a red Jeep Wrangler parked in one of the six slots at Javier's Gas Station and Garage — three spots on each side of the pumps. She hustled out.

At first, Javier appeared not to recognize her.

"Hola. ¿Cómo estás?" She poked him in the ribs.

"Dani?"

She laughed.

"Like your new hair." He shoved the gas nozzle into the tank of the Wrangler, and Dani started filling her car's tank.

Main Street, a narrow two-lane road filled with slow-moving traffic, curved through the town. A hospital anchored the in-town end to the south, and the Metro North train station denoted the other. The full-service station repaired and inspected many of the gardening trucks, taxis, and delivery vans driven by the Latinos who serviced the upscale residents. *Bogie wisdom: "Fill up where the taxi drivers go; best price, best service."* Since arriving, she only patronized Javier's gas station and tried to help when she could.

Dani adjusted her sunglasses, tugged on the wig's ends, and patted the top. It made her feel — she searched for the right emotion. "New city, fresh look," she said. Both feet moving from side to side, she screwed the gas-cap closed and replaced the nozzle. Dani always had trouble standing still. As a kid, she watched television doing cartwheels. Jogged in place during conversations. Her mother nicknamed her, "The Whiz-Bang Kid."

Using a squeegee, Javier cleaned the red Jeep's windshield. "You're acting jumpier than usual. Worried about the drive?"

Last week, Dani and Javier mapped out her route. He loved road trips, made several cross-country and shared good places to stop, rest, and eat.

The wig hair stayed still when Dani shook her head. "It's not that."

She *was* edgy but not sure why. Not because she ran out on Alice and Pete, nor the expected confrontation with Bogie and Sally. In a flash of insight, she realized she enjoyed living in Mount Kisco and hated leaving.

Three buildings made up the complex where she lived. High on a hill overlooking Route 117, she'd made her one-bedroom home. She enjoyed her job at the Party Store, helping people find the perfect decorations and celebration paraphernalia. New friends also made her want to stay, especially Alice, Javier, and Mirko. This escape felt different, sad, and a little scary.

"I'm good." She moved forward and back, touched Javier's shoulder, rubbed both hands against her thighs. "Time for a change." Anyway, things would work out. *Bogie wisdom: "Think positive, act with purpose."*

"How come you're so late?" He glanced down at his oversized watch. "It's already five. I thought you wanted an early start."

She kept finding things requiring more time and work. "Lots of loose ends."

Two more cars arrived. Javier approached the Mercury Marquis, *Tony's Taxi* stenciled on its sides with a lettered message "Download our app or text us for a ride." The taxi's not-so-brilliant answer to Uber.

Javier called to Dani, "Can you get the other one for me?"

If she left now, she could make it to Pittsburgh before midnight. "Sure." She skipped to a battered pickup truck. "What will it be?"

"Fifteen-dollars, regular."

Dani put the nozzle into the gas tank, imagining the conversation with Bogie once she confessed. He'd probably worry about Sally's reaction and come up with an excuse just like before. "Sally's pregnant again so not enough space." In truth, Sally disliked Dani. Jealous. Too bad. Bogie and Dani were a team long before Sally — the two of them against the world, not to mention their miserable parents.

Javier straightened up and wiped a dipstick with a rag. He told the driver, "You're only down a half a quart; check it next time you fill up." He grinned at Dani. "Don't worry, I'll share the tips."

"I bet you tell all your girls that."

Javier's laugh rose above the sounds of cars, trucks, and an ambulance siren. Dominican, with black eyes and hair and stocky legs, his smile always made Dani grin back.

A Camry pulled in behind the pickup truck.

"¿Qué te puedo server?" Javier asked the driver. Then, turning back to Dani, "How's Mirko taking things?"

"He's cool. No worries." She shifted left and right.

"You're gonna miss him." His tone teased.

"After I'm settled, he'll join me." Dani had a plan. Once in Seattle, things *would* work out. Mirko dumped her, but not for good. Was he the reason she took so long to leave today?

"Your brother must be excited about you coming to live with him, help with his kids and all."

"Yeah, until his wife recovers." Not a *total* fabrication. It would piss Sally off to the point of illness once she learned Dani planned to stay awhile.

Despite being finished some time ago, the red Jeep idled at the pump. The driver, an over-weight, thin-lipped man wearing a tan safari hat crushed low, appeared to text, or deal with email on his phone.

Dani raised a thumb in the Jeep's direction. "What's with him?"

Javier shrugged.

A guy with ravished skin and a mustache that looked as fake as Dani's wig banged on the Jeep's passenger window. Dani tried to watch without staring. Something felt off. The driver opened the door. Angry voices muffled by distance and steel followed.

"They're arguing," Dani said.

Javier peered at the Jeep's occupants. "Better not do anything here. I don't want any trouble."

Then it was over. The passenger-guy climbed out and walked away. Dani watched the driver shoot the retreating man the finger.

"Storm passed," Javier said. "Tell me about your going-away party. Big fun?"

"Oh sure, lots of speeches."

"Any crying?"

"Nope. They gave me nice presents and a cake, all chocolate and gooey."

"Not even a tear?"

"We couldn't eat the whole thing." She pictured the mangled cupcakes. "It rocked."

Movement to her left caused her to swing around. The previously idling Jeep shot out of the gas station into the traffic and T-boned a southbound black sedan. The sound of crunching metal filled the air.

Chapter 5

Vera

Vera continued south on Main Street, her mind still on the argument with Liza, whose bitter words rang in Vera's head. Shame washed over her.

A car honked, startling her. The light shone green. Still deep in thought, she pulled ahead.

"Liza..." She wanted to ask the searing question that hung between Vera and her children all these years, the question she never had the courage to ask. *Do you forgive me?*

Before the words came out, Liza screamed a thundering sound filled with terror.

A red Jeep Wrangler and black sedan, smashed together, came speeding at them from the right. The driver of the Jeep stared at Vera with cruel eyes.

Vera pulled the steering wheel hard to the left. The Saturn fishtailed across Main Street into the northbound traffic. An oncoming dirty-white truck blasted its horn before slamming into the Saturn, spinning the car around.

Liza shrieked again. Vera tried to get the vehicle under control. She remembered her lessons from long ago. Turn into the skid. Instinct took over. For a second, she felt the car righting itself. For a second, relief flooded her body. For a second...

The Jeep coupled with the sedan smashed into the passenger side of the Saturn, jerking Liza forward. The airbag on Vera's side deployed, crushing her chest.

She could not breathe.

Everything went quiet and dark.

Chapter 6

Dani

Dani saw a Saturn hatchback heading south in the left lane and the still moving red Jeep and black Sedan almost in its path.

An oncoming dirty-white truck blasted its horn as its brakes tried to grip the asphalt. The truck slammed into the Saturn and spun it around. The screech of metal crunching metal rang out followed by a second thud as the sedan, coupled with the red Wrangler, smashed into the Saturn's passenger side.

Dani yelled to Javier, "Call 911."

Javier tugged his phone from his back pocket, punched in the numbers and spoke into the phone. He lowered his cell. "Cops and EMTs are on their way."

She yanked Javier into the street. "We have to help."

People poured out from the neighboring shops, gesturing and talking on their cells, some clearly taking pictures of the wreck. Javier joined another man in the middle of the street. Together, they stopped traffic, directing cars to side streets, away from the accident.

Dani approached the Saturn. Mr. Kim from the cleaners, leaned forward and peered into the shattered car window.

"They not moving," Mr. Kim said in a heavy Korean accent.

Two African American women occupied the front seats, crumpled and deflated airbags no longer cushioning them. The air smelled burnt. Talcum-powder-like dust drifted down and settled on the women's hair. The younger one lay bent on the passenger side, her body twisted at an odd angle. A fractured glass lamp lay against her chest.

Dani tried to remember her long-ago Red Cross lessons. "Are you okay?" she asked the driver. She scanned the car for something warm, found a rug in the back, tugged it over the seat, and draped it around the older woman.

"Please help my daughter."

Mr. Kim slipped out of his sweater and handed it to Dani.

She covered the younger woman.

The man with the bad skin and fake-looking mustache approached. "Are they conscious?"

Dani said, "One of them is, but she seems woozy." She eyed the newcomer. He'd been arguing with the man driving the Jeep that hit the Saturn. She bit her lip, trying to decipher what she witnessed.

The older woman moaned.

"Come on, let's try to pull them out," the florid-faced man said.

Dani raised protective arms over the driver. "What if they have broken bones or internal bleeding?" She peered over her shoulder. *Where was the ambulance?*

Ignoring Dani's arms and cautions, the man grabbed the older woman's shoulder.

This time she moaned louder.

"You're hurting her."

An ambulance wailed its approach. Florid Face stopped. *Thank goodness*. Three patrol cars pulled up. Within seconds, police and EMTs took charge of the scene. Florid Face back-pedaled.

"Help's here," Dani said to the woman.

The woman reached for Dani's hand.

"What's your name?" Dani asked.

"Vera."

"I'm Dani."

An officer approached them. "Step back and let the EMTs do their jobs."

Dani eased her hand out of Vera's grasp. She clutched at Dani's escaping fingers. "Did you see it?"

"Yes." Flashes from the crash jumbled together.

An ambulance technician said, "Let us through."

"I have to go," Dani said.

"Help us." Vera blinked hard, as if trying to dislodge something in her eye. "They cannot find him."

"Who?"

The EMT wedged between Dani and Vera.

"Stay safe," Vera said through blood-caked lips.

At least it sounded like *stay safe*.

Heart rocking, Dani joined Javier on the sidewalk and examined the scene. After relieving Javier and the other Good Samaritan, a tall police officer directed traffic. EMTs tended the truck driver. The black sedan sat empty, its left side a deep V.

"Where's the red Jeep and its driver?" Dani asked. "And the guys from the sedan?"

"You saw them?"

"A blur. Silver-haired-man in the back and someone else driving."

"Took them to the hospital?" Javier suggested.

"Something isn't right."

Vera had begged Dani to help her. No one ever asked Dani for anything important. Most people doubted her follow-through. Not from lack of desire or trying her hardest. Things flew out of Dani's control. Mirko knew. As of this morning, Alice, her ex-landlady, did too. Only Javier and Bogie still trusted her.

"I don't know why she said, *they can't find him*."

"Probably in shock. People say crazy things."

"Do you think she meant the person who hit her?"

"How could she be sure he's gone missing? Which we don't know he has."

Why warn Dani to be safe? She observed the faces of the sizable crowd. Near the Saturn, the florid faced man who tried to drag out the women still hovered, his phone mashed to his ear. "The Jeep driver was arguing with that guy." Dani pointed her finger. "And he kept pulling on Vera." Dani shook her head. "The whole scene seems phony."

"What..." Javier asked, his raised arms taking in the tableau, "doesn't appear real to you?"

"Messed-up, right?" Dani turned toward the gas station on the opposite side of the road, her yellow Malibu still parked by the pump.

It would be hours before the police cleared the streets and let traffic move again. No sense driving tonight. "Did the woman in the Saturn look familiar?"

"Not so much."

"Like someone famous?" Mount Kisco and the surrounding municipalities were home to many celebrities who lived in the upscale suburbs but worked in New York City. In addition, the man trying to oust the sitting governor, a rich mogul named Lavender, lived there. Dani enjoyed reading the gossipy parts of the news.

"This is a movie and we're gonna be in it?"

"When the Jeep hit the sedan, the man in the safari hat..." She tried to envision his face, but nothing came to her. "His body leaned forward, kinda determined, focused, and aiming for the sedan except he faced left, toward the Saturn." Dani played the tape in her mind again. "I watch too much TV."

Javier stayed quiet, as if weighing her words. "You gonna tell the cops?" He lifted his chin towards the officers questioning onlookers, notebooks in hand. They'd reach Dani and Javier soon.

"What would I say?"

That's when she noticed a man in a navy-blue-and-white striped suit. He limped, favoring his left leg. Locks of silver hair covered his forehead and hung below his shirt collar. Another man, dressed in black, hooked his arm around the elbow of the silver-haired man, and tugged him along. Together, they plowed through the still-gathering crowd. As they came to the edge of the chaos, the man doing the pulling looked straight at Dani. His malevolent stare caused goosebumps on her arms.

Then she remembered she was still wearing her Marilyn wig and movie star sunglasses.

Chapter 7

Vera

Vera held Liza's hand, watched, and waited for the emergency room doctor to return.

Black and blue eyes above bloodied cheeks stared back. She groaned.

A petite woman entered their cubicle. "I'm Dr. Ginny LaSalle." Her voice hinted at the lilting tones of the Caribbean. She put out her hand. "You are?"

"Her mother." They shook.

Dr. LaSalle glanced down at the chart at the foot of Liza's bed. "Another physician already examined her."

"Yes, he called me. I'm a surgeon." She gave Vera a reassuring smile. "Let's see what's going on." With a penlight, she peered into Liza's swollen eyes. "Liza, can you hear me?" Swift fingers probed the glands in Liza's neck, then moved down her chest to her abdomen.

Another pained whimper.

"Is her stomach extended more than usual?" the doctor asked Vera.

"I'm not sure." Perhaps her guilty remembrances distracted her. Did she cause the accident?

Dr. LaSalle depressed Liza's tummy again.

Liza groaned louder.

"I'm sorry." Once more, she studied the medical chart before making a few notes. "I'll be back shortly. Press that...," she indicated the button on the wall, "if anything changes." The doctor's gaze swept over Vera. "Has someone examined you?"

"Yes." She lifted her arm and pulled back the jacket to show the bandage. "Nothing broken, just banged up." Vera licked her bruised lips. Because she had blacked out, the intern ordered a scan to check for bleeding of her brain. But Vera could not leave Liza.

Dr. LaSalle made a small empathetic noise in her throat. "I won't be long." She bustled out.

"Mom?" Liza's weak voice rasped.

"Yes, sweetheart, Mommy is here."

"You called Sam?"

Darn. "Not yet. As soon as they figure out what happens next."

"Is Penny coming?"

"I left her a message." Three, in fact, but no need to share.

"These are the worst belly cramps ever."

"The doctor will be back soon."

"I'm going to die."

"Do not say that. You'll be fine."

"Sam would want to know, right?"

"Yes." A harmless prevarication meant to comfort.

"Have you met his girlfriend?"

Stop torturing yourself. Vera made sure her voice conveyed none of her thoughts. "Rest now, my darling. You need your strength."

"Is she young?"

Vera suppressed a groan as loud as Liza's during the examination. "*You* are young."

"Not anymore." Ragged breaths filled the room. "You were younger than I am when you left us."

Her words slapped Vera. "Yes."

When Vera took off, Liza was eight, Penny seven, and Charlie three. Vincent worked all the time. They hardly made love. Their children demanded every ounce of her attention. The flower shop struggled to make a profit. Anxiety and unhappiness piled up in equal proportions. These were not excuses or even explanations for her terrible, unforgivable mistake.

She took off with another man. Deserted her babies. Abandoned her life.

It took one month for her to realize her folly. She crawled back to Vincent and apologized a thousand times. Bitterness, anger, and pain stoked every conversation. He did not, would not understand. She begged him to go to couple's counseling, to let her return home and see her children. He said, *"No. Your choice, your consequences."* She considered divorcing him, suing for custody, but all she wanted was her family back.

Two years passed before Vera and Vincent mended their marriage. The girls adjusted, at least on the surface. Charlie openly struggled. He wet his bed and started sucking his thumb again.

It was difficult to remember, much less talk about. "Shall I read something to you?" Vera fished out her Kindle, a present from Charlie.

Liza shifted under the thin sheet and let out another low moan.

***

The emergency room waiting area of Northern Westchester Hospital thrummed with activity. Two police officers spoke with a nurse. A pregnant woman called after a doctor dashing by. Groans, quiet conversations, and snuffles filled the room.

An African American officer approached Vera.

"Ms. Moon?" The short, curvy cop stood inches away. "I'm Officer French. May I ask you a few questions?"

"They are admitting my daughter suspecting a ruptured spleen."

Officer French sat down. "I'm sure she'll be fine."

A wall-mounted television silently shared the news of the day. White words outlined in black rectangles streamed at the bottom of the screen as the anchors' mouths moved.

"What makes you sure?"

She gave Vera a puzzled look.

"Why are you confident my daughter will be fine?" People said things they did not mean. "*We'll find the killer. Don't worry. We'll bring him to justice.*"

"I apologize. What I meant to say is the docs do an excellent job."

The officer's voice soothed, and kind eyes added to the sense of empathy.

"Have you met Dr. LaSalle?" Police officers must run into many of the medical personnel. "Does she enjoy a great deal of respect?"

Officer French's eyes shifted away from Vera's face. "The hospital's reputation is strong."

"Oh."

When Dr. LaSalle returned, she announced the need for more tests and possibly exploratory surgery. She told Vera to go home and get some rest, but Vera declined. She also did not go for the ordered brain scan.

"I came here a few months ago because I fainted or something akin." Her legs gave way for no reason unless one attributed it to Charlie's murder. "They treated me well."

Officer French's pen flipped from finger-to-finger. "You're Charlie Moon's mother, right?"

"Yes. Had you met him... before...?"

"No." In a tiny movement, she tipped her head forward. "I'm sorry for your loss."

The air whooshed out of Vera's lungs. "How can I help?"

Her face once again composed, voice professional, Officer French sounded relieved to be back on task. "Tell me what you remember about the accident, as many details as possible. Take your time."

"*What do you remember?*" The same question the detectives had asked Vera. Her purse, the cell phone tucked inside, still lay on the entrance floor. She had crawled to the house phone, pulled herself up, and dialed 911. The police arrived within minutes.

"The smell." Sometimes at night, as she drifted off, the raw meat and feces stench invaded her consciousness. Sleep slipped away. "His eyes." They held all the secrets, all the answers to her questions, locked away forever.

"Excuse me?" Officer French frowned. "The smell? And what about his eyes? Whose?"

Vera sucked in a deep breath. "A red Jeep ran into a sedan, like one of those cars people hire. I tried to avoid them but slammed into a truck or it ran into me." Vera still heard Liza's screams. "I thought perhaps..." Her words trailed off. She touched her bruised lips. Tears gathered.

The man in the Jeep stared at her as he hit the sedan. She had been sure. Now, it all felt preposterous. Charlie's murder made her paranoid.

"You thought, what?" Officer French handed Vera a tissue.

"Thank you." Tissue in hand, Vera said, "Forgive me. It has been quite a day." She longed to go home and drink a few glasses of wine until the pain dulled.

Officer French nodded as if she understood, her smooth mocha skin marred only by a smattering of tiny moles on her left cheek. "Did you witness the Jeep hit the sedan?"

"Yes. It plowed right into it. The Jeep came from the gas station." Vera blew her nose. "What is it you are trying to determine?"

"The facts."

At the police station, the detective had asked Vera to describe what she recalled. "Notice anyone suspicious?" "Who were Charlie's friends?" "Who would want to hurt him?" "Why keep a machete in the house?" "Did you two get along?"

"Sometimes the smallest detail can help."

Vera raised her eyes to the level of the officer's round nose. "It happened quickly. Everything is a blur."

Sometimes, the detectives' questions made Vera feel like a suspect. During other conversations, they tried to make it Charlie's fault. He caused his own murder. At least that is how the questions landed, spiked with judgment. Vera wondered if they treated white bereaved mothers the same way.

"How long have you served on the police force?"

Officer French let several beats go by before answering. "Five years."

"Do you encounter much racism?"

She ignored the question. "Did you see the driver's face?"

"I ask because the investigation does not seem vigorous."

"We've just started."

"It's been three months, and my son's murderer is still free."

"I'm not asking about that case." She sounded miffed. "I can assure you, however, we're all committed to our jobs." She took an audible breath, the kind that conveys disapproval. "My question concerns the accident."

"Big guy, thin lips over bucked teeth, wearing a hat."

The officer wrote a notation in her pad. "Do you remember the license plate or anything about the Jeep?" She shifted in her seat, head up, chin tilted in Vera's direction. "Decals, dents, something that distinguished it?"

"I'm confused. The driver left the scene?" The machete disappeared. Charlie kept it on the wall in a sheath, a decoration. He had bought it on Amazon. The police searched the house, the grounds, and nearby dumpsters and lowered men into the sewers. No murder weapon.

"We haven't been able to locate the Jeep or the drivers of either vehicle."

"No one recognized them?"

"If you remember anything else, please call me." She handed Vera a business card, a firm white-and-blue rectangle, the town seal in one corner and three different phone numbers centered below. It was like the one the detectives gave her, accompanied by the same words.

Vera tried to picture the Jeep's driver. No more images came forth.

Officer French pushed herself up from the chair.

"Any new leads on my son's murder?"

The officer faced Vera, flipped opened her notebook and clicked her pen. "Do you believe there's a connection?"

"Do you?"

"Thanks for your time." She closed the notebook again and clipped the pen to its side. "I hope things go well for your daughter."

"What are you not telling me about Charlie?"

"You know what we know."

And that summed up the problem.

Chapter 8

Dani

Humiliated, Dani sat in her car in front of Mirko's building. Javier offered his living room floor. His wife, and their eighteen-month-old daughter, plus a visiting nephew, lived in a two-bedroom apartment. She declined. The local Holiday Inn cost at least two hundred dollars. Decision made. Ashamed but desperate, she waited.

Her eyes darted, surveying the street, lobby door, and sidewalk. Maybe he'd found someone else. Mirko and his new girl would walk by holding hands. That would be worse than bad. On the positive side of possibilities, he might be away on vacation. Escape, ghost — like her mother before her, Dani's first instinct when things got difficult or painful. Of course, he wasn't hurt. He'd arrived late for their movie date. She knew the minute she opened the door what he'd say. Countless men saw the same expression on her mother's face — determination tinged with guilt. At least the ones she bothered to tell. Sometimes the three of them, her mom, Bogie, and Dani, hit the road. Her mom's getaway theme song filled the car. "*Fifty ways to leave your lover. Slip out the back, Jack. Make a new plan, Stan.*"

Still, Mirko sounded sad. Dani understood. She wasn't easy to love.

The rap on the window made her flinch. Mirko peered at her through the glass. She rolled down the window.

"What are you doing here?"

He looked yummy. Shaved head, small regular features except for a longish nose; his blue-gray eyes crinkled in concern.

She hadn't thought through her story. "I witnessed an accident."

"Are you hurt?" He opened the car door. "What happened?" As if checking for damage, his gaze roved her body.

Dani eased out of the car. Jiggling her entire body, she said, "A Jeep deliberately mowed down two women. The bad guys might be after me." This came out in an unedited rush. Dani usually practiced her stories. "The woman, Vera, begged me to help her." Again, Dani searched her memory but couldn't identify a time when someone asked her to help with something consequential. Nothing she worked at or experienced mattered.

"The pile-up on Main?"

"Yeah."

"Lots of folks talking about it at the store."

"I could be in real danger."

"Is this one of your fantasies?"

A reasonable response. After all, Mirko and Dani had lived together for many months. She gave him her earnest best. "I stopped to fill up my car before heading to KC."

"I thought you were moving to Seattle." His tone accused.

"To see my brother *before* starting my new job." Once in KC, she planned to apply for more positions, thus erasing the lie.

"Okay. Then what?"

"The driver of the now *disappeared Jeep*, plowed right into a sedan, spinning the women's car into on-coming traffic and then a truck hit them."

Mirko lowered his raised eyebrows. "Gus told me the police are searching for at least three men."

Before the breakup, Dani and Mirko often ate breakfast at Gus's diner. Back then, Mirko shared his writing ambitions and his worry that his skills weren't good enough. As time passed, he stopped telling her his secrets and only spoke when she initiated.

"I saw them, and they saw *me*. The woman inside the hatchback *begged me* to help her." Vera's identity came to Dani. "Oh, wow."

He gave her a questioning look.

"Remember the guy who got his throat slit with a machete?" The story had run in the papers for weeks, first on the front page and after a few days on the lower right corner before landing on a back page.

"Sure."

In a blur of movement, she stepped close, touched his arm, and stepped back. "His mother..." Her arms flew in the air. "Got hit today."

"For real?" They stood next to Dani's car, Mirko still, Dani in motion. A strong breeze from the west gave the May day a March chill. Spring leaves swayed with the same rhythm as Dani. Mirko zipped his jacket.

"They splashed her picture on the local news. It's her." Dani nodded her head with vigor. "I'm sure. And now, I don't know where else to hide."

"What?"

"Like I explained, one of the perps..." That's how they said it on television. "...saw me." She decided not to mention the wig and sunglasses, discarded under the backseat before driving to Mirko's place. "I need time to make a plan."

He frowned, collapsing his face muscles in what Dani perceived as skepticism.

They'd been here before. At first, he believed everything she said. After a while, he figured her out. It wasn't his fault, but he rarely believed the truth either.

"The guys in the crash are bad guys and they're after you?" He sounded the way his face looked.

"Yaaaa."

After several beats, he said, "Come in."

Relief swept through her. She opened the trunk and retrieved her backpack, cooler and suitcase. Mirko took all three. Although they weren't visible under his jacket, she knew the bulge of his biceps, the ripples of muscle under his skin. He kept a set of free weights in his apartment and jogged or rode his bike almost every day. She imagined his naked body. Heat moved through her.

He swung the backpack over his shoulder, gripped the cooler in one hand, and carried rather than pulled the roller-bag in his other.

Lefty, the panda, lay alone in the trunk. Dani picked him up. "I appreciate this. I won't be in your hair for long."

His mouth almost smiled.

"Figuratively," she said, grinning back.

***

They sat side-by-side on the convertible love seat in Mirko's living room. Jazz played in the background, something off-kilter and hard for

Dani to follow, but Mirko loved it. Panda Lefty lounged against a decorative pillow Dani had bought Mirko from Kohl's. She tried not to make a big deal of it, but she noticed his refrigerator still chilled several Diet Cokes, her personal addiction and something he disliked.

With noisy enjoyment, she slurped down her soda. He finished a glass of Weihenstephan — too bitter a beer from Dani's perspective. He wiped the foam from his mouth with the back of his hand.

Everything about the apartment was deliciously familiar. Dani put her feet up on the leather ottoman next to Mirko's and soaked it in. Books piled high in every corner, stacks of papers by his computer and printer on a table against the far wall. Yellow Post-Its marked various articles in each of the magazines stashed on shelves above his computer table. In his spare time, Mirko wrote. Once, he showed her one of his short stories. She'd read it several times, told him how much she loved it. He'd shrugged it off, but his expression telegraphed pleasure and pride.

He also planned to become a golf pro. He worked at a cool day-job, a local golf shop helping "duffers" choose clubs, clothes, balls, and gadgets. A full golf bag stood next to his bike — its seat wrapped with an anti-theft chain.

The apartment felt like her "could-be" home. She almost cried remembering the happiness that filled her, the sense of belonging that colored each day. Six months of contentment, a record for her.

After telling him her story twice and answering his probing questions, they watched re-runs of *Law and Order, and NCIS,* ate pepperoni pizza for dinner, and listened to music.

Mirko downed his third beer and rose. "I'll get clean sheets."

Dani jumped up. "I can do it." She moved toward the chest of drawers in the hall. "Do you have an extra pillow? If not, no problem." She hoped he'd ask her to make love. Fat chance.

"I'll get it."

Dani put Lefty on the end table under a lamp and opened the bed. She shoved one corner of the pebbly, worn-thin mattress cover into the fold of the fitted sheet. Mirko grabbed the other end. “Lefty looks well fed.”

“Ever loyal, so I try to do right by him.”

Mirko grinned a genuine smile for the first time all evening. They finished making the bed.

“I’ll clean up and turn in,” Dani said.

Both of his hands pressed the mattress up and down. “It’s kinda lumpy,” he said.

Instead of saying something flip, Dani covered her mouth.

He stared at her. Finally, he said, “If you want to sleep in my bed...”

His gaze was so hard and steady she glanced away.

“I’m okay with it, if you are,” he said, finishing his sentence.

How to respond? The invitation didn’t sound “loving,” or passionate. His voice lacked the enthusiasm she craved. Should she decline or show joy, be coolly accepting, grateful, surprised, or offended?

This time, she opted for the unvarnished truth. “I’d like that.”

***

After weighing several options, Dani put on her sleeping tank top and matching drawstring sweatpants. Toothpaste tingled her mouth, her skin soft from her moisturizer. Heart rocking, she approached the bed. Mirko swung the covers back.

The first time he invited her home, they stayed up until 3:00 a.m. each unsure of what to expect. Finally, Mirko pulled her close and kissed her. Dani recalled her surprise and pleasure at the deep kiss, hot, soft, awash with a mixture of emotions — fear, happiness, arousal, and uncertainty. Mirko had leaned back and Dani opened her eyes. “Is this okay?” That question clinched it.

Dani still felt the same. She climbed into the bed and Mirko drew the covers over them.

“Good night.” He rolled unto his left side, knees drawn up, his back to her.

Unexpected tears sprang. “Sleep well.” With her face mashed into the pillow, she added, “And thanks for letting me stay.” Someone always dumped Dani. Her father, her mother. Bogie, too. For no good reason, she thought Mirko was different.

“Dani?”

“Hmmm?” She rubbed her face in the pillow to get rid of the moisture on her lashes and cheeks and rolled onto her back.

He turned toward her, so Dani completed her 180-degree. He had a funny expression on his face, one she couldn’t decode.

“This wouldn’t change anything.” A frown creased his forehead. His usual baritone came out a bit high-pitched. “It won’t mean we’re together.”

Dani tried not to show her shifting emotions. Why didn’t he sound more excited? Probably a one-night stand. Where was her pride?

“You don’t have to.”

Making love might remind him of happier days, and how much she cared.

He reached out his hand and stroked her cheek. “Okay?” His voice sounded choked.

“Yes.”

He kissed the tip of her nose, her cheek and nibbled his way down to her neck. Little shivers rippled along her arms and legs. With gentle hands, he pulled her on top of him. A stifled moan. His dick, thick and hard, pulsed against her. The tiny ribbons of electricity increased in speed and force. Using both hands, he massaged her butt. Dani drew her top over her head and off. He kissed and sucked each of her nipples. They ached; she ached.

The nightlight in the bathroom let her see just enough. He closed his eyes. She kicked off her sweatpants and slipped off his briefs. Silky chest hairs stroked her face. She took his dick into her mouth. Tasted the cool liquid droplets seeping out.

He lifted her head away. “Now you.”

She loved the way his tongue swirled against her clit. Licking, sucking. Heat shot through her.

He slid up her body. She smelled her scent on his breath as he eased into her.

At first, he moved slowly. His back slightly arched, resting on his elbows; his mouth busy kissing her lips and breasts.

Dani lifted her hips, meeting his tempo.

Mirko moaned.

Everything went fast after that. Pushing, thrusting. She opened her eyes to see the remembered joy on his face. He gasped, long and slow. She let her own release come surging through her.

So good.

Even if nothing else happened between them, at this moment, Dani savored the joy and love engulfing her.

Chapter 9

Vera

Sunday morning sweat streamed down Vera's face. Nightmares filled with stalkers and flashes from the murder scene lingered after she awoke. She willed her heartbeat to slow before attempting to sit up. Three months of this. Too long.

A few days after the murder, the police declared the apartment no longer a crime scene. On an overcast Wednesday, windblown snow making it hard to maneuver, Vera returned. Liza and Penny protested. Still mourning Charlie, both hated being in the apartment. When they spoke of the murder, they sounded horrified and embarrassed as if it tainted them.

They begged Vera to move. "How will you get closure?"

Not easily. Since then, Vera kept Charlie's room locked and never ventured in. Until the insurance money came, she had nowhere else to go. Living with her daughters was not an option. Not that they offered. Liza and Vera would fight, and Penny's oldest girl coughed and sneezed around Brandy. Slashed and left to die, Brandy and Vera were a package deal.

The building's super surprised her when he told her Charlie paid the rent for twelve months in advance. Stunning news since Charlie did not have a job. Still, it sealed it for her. Painters removed the bloodstains from the walls and floors and applied fresh coats of off-white. Liza helped discard the smashed furniture. They tried to salvage the Persian rug with no luck. The place looked better. But, on too many days like today, that awful Thursday haunted her.

Brandy leapt onto the bed and nuzzled Vera with her wet nose. The dog wanted breakfast and needed a walk to boot. Vera sat up. A wave of dizziness and stomach rumbles made her nauseous. She waited and counted in her head until it passed. Yes, too long. Finding Charlie's killer surely would end it.

With Brandy at her heels, Vera padded to the front door, opened it, and grabbed *The Journal News* from her welcome mat. Paper in hand, she shuffled into the kitchen and lit the kettle burner. Tea and dry toast — a remedy for the nausea at least. She poured *Purina* and water into Brandy's bowls.

While the water for tea boiled, she scanned the paper. Her accident made the front page accompanied by a recap of Charlie's murder. Once again, they made Charlie sound like a crook. She stuffed the paper into the recycle bin. Then she recalled all the puzzles she liked to do and retrieved it. No sense letting other people's ignorance steal one of her few pleasures. As soon as she figured out who killed him and why, the public would learn the truth about her son's character.

People judged, even people who loved you.

Would they print retractions and set the record straight? *Ha.* She poured the water into her mug and dipped an English Breakfast tea bag. One step at a time.

Last night, she had dragged herself home at four in the morning. After a nightcap of Cabernet, she tumbled into bed. Time to shake it off. Church. She hadn't been in weeks. Gospel music would lift her spirts.

The praise music filled the apartment. Mood brightened, Vera popped a slice of wheat bread into the toaster oven and set it for dark. Morning plan — eat, take a quick trip around the building, plastic bag in hand for Brandy's poop, a hot shower, and then to the hospital.

The downstairs doorbell rang. Brandy yelped.

Vera clicked off the music and toaster oven, walked to the door, and pushed the intercom button. "Who is it?"

"Ms. Moon?" asked a scratchy female voice.

Since the murder, only tenants issued new keys could enter the building unless someone buzzed in guests. "What do you want?"

"I'm a friend of Charlie's. May I come in?"

Vera tightened the sash of her robe. The rhythmic crunch of Brandy's chewing played in the background.

"Please? It's urgent."

Vera knew better than to trust a stranger. Still, she hungered for information so she pressed the buzzer. Brandy lapped her water. The kitchen faucet dripped, each splat a counter to Brandy's slurps.

A sharp rap on the door caused Brandy to yip in response.

Vera peered through the peephole at a young woman.

Brandy's barks sharpened.

"Hush."

Her tail wagging low to the ground, she let out a muted growl.

"Is that Brandy?"

"Who are you?"

"I have important information."

Vera clicked the safety chain in place before cracking the door open as wide as the chain allowed. Bobbed dark hair framed a pale face. A black headband decorated with a bow, made her look twenty-something. Tiny crows-feet contradicted the impression.

Despite Vera's misgivings about the police, she knew they would respond if she summoned them, as she had twice in the last few weeks. Once, she heard a scraping noise on the fire escape followed by the rattle of the kitchen window. They found no sign. Last Tuesday, coming from the supermarket, she heard the heavy tread of boots behind her; she stopped. Silence. When she turned, she saw an empty stretch of sidewalk. She moved forward again and heard the same footfalls. Again, the police came quickly, surveyed the apartment building and neighborhood, and found nothing.

With her hand gripping her cellphone, Vera opened the door and let the stranger enter.

Dressed in a skirt-and-jacket-suit in what fashion magazines labeled *muted neutrals*, a purple-and-gold scarf encircled her neck. Diamond studs glistened from her earlobes. Gloved hands held a small purse. That made Vera nervous. Gloves in May?

"Charlie told me lots about you." The accent hinted at a southern past, soft and deep.

Vera took in the pumps with three-inch heels, not crime-committing shoes.

"He loved you so much," the woman said behind a half smile.

Although eager to hear whatever information the woman might share, Vera remained cautious. Everything made her jump and worry. "I am calling a friend and asking him to come by."

"That's fine." The woman exuded confidence, as if she expected people to do what she asked.

With exaggerated motions, Vera dialed Liza's number. It rang four times before the machine came on. "Paul, Vera Moon here." She swung the mouthpiece away from her face but kept the top tight against her ear. "What is your name?"

She hesitated. "Erika."

"Erika what?"

Once again, the woman paused. "Smith."

"A petite woman who says her name is Erika Smith." Vera gave Erika an exaggerated eye roll. "I doubt it is her actual name."

"I really am Erika."

"Did you hear that?" Vera asked as Liza's answering machine message sought the caller's name and phone number. "Yes, she is visiting me as we speak. She stands five foot two, a mole above her lip on the right side, weighs about... how much do you weigh?" The phone beeped in Vera's ear.

"One ten."

"One hundred and twenty pounds. I am worried. Can you drop by in the next few minutes? Yes? Great." Vera clicked the *end* button on her phone. "Please, sit. Why are you here?"

Erika remained standing, her gaze sweeping the room. "Everything's so different." Brandy, her tail wagging, came over and nuzzled Erika's hand.

Vera's insides cramped. "When were you here?" It was true. She had changed things. A piece she found at an estate sale replaced the shattered bookcase. Penny gifted her a flat screen television. Liza offered first picks before preparing for her yard sale, but Vera found little to like. The recliner came from her neighbor, Lucy. Vera bought the glass end tables and occasional chairs at a Goodwill store.

Erika's melodic voice sounded like the beginning of a familiar tune. "Twice before he..." She hesitated.

"Passed," Vera offered before Erika used a more terrible verb.

Erika's cheeks flushed. "You flew to Toronto to care for your grandchildren while Penny and Archie vacationed in Jamaica."

Vera watched the color deepen on Erika's cheeks. Real or faked?

"Another time, a friend sent you a ticket to visit her in San Francisco." Erika's gloved fingertips patted under her eyes.

"Last winter." A college chum had invited her to a retirement party and sent her a round-trip ticket. Did Charlie use those opportunities to bring lovers home? He mentioned no one named Erika. In fact, he rarely spoke about his friends. "I don't remember seeing you at the funeral."

"I intended to come, but business in Atlanta kept us away."

"Us?"

"I read the obituary in the paper. Nice."

"You missed the rally."

Erika pursed her lips.

"We walked a few weeks ago to bring attention to his case," Vera said.

"Oh."

"I advertised it in the papers."

"Hmmm." Erika stroked Brandy's fur, stopped, and examined it. With her index finger, she traced the dog's jagged scars. "They hurt her."

"Chained, slashed, and almost killed her."

Erika rubbed under Brandy's neck. "How awful."

She straightened and walked over to the mantel above the non-working fireplace. An indigo urn, small and squat, sat next to the picture of Charlie that Vera displayed at his funeral.

"Are these Charlie's ashes?" She slid her fingers along the urn's curves and ran her hand along the mantel.

Vera sprang up, grabbed the urn, and pressed it against her chest. "I am going to place it in the crypt next to my husband's." With care, she put it back. "Every day I plan to, but time slips away." Cremation was final. A dark end, leaving no traces of a well-lived life, and yet she still sensed his presence whenever she held the urn. The burial spot, a niche along a wall of other urns, meant losing Charlie again.

"I understand. My dad passed a few months back. It's difficult."

Vera nodded. Every time Erika spoke, Vera relaxed a bit more. The music of her voice, the soft almost drawl, and slow tempo. *No. Stay wary*. "What can you tell me about Charlie's murder?"

Erika's gloved hand swept along the top of an end table and then underneath in a blurring motion.

"Are you searching for something in particular?" Vera asked, eyebrows arched. "Or are you concerned about my housekeeping?"

"Nervous habit." Erika perched on the edge of one of the matching chairs, knees pressed together, toes pointed straight ahead.

Vera stared at the folded hands with a look as sharp as the tips of Erika's shoes.

"A bit chilly this morning." Erika tugged off the gloves.

With Brandy curled at her feet, Vera sat in the opposite chair. "What information do you have?" she asked again.

"How is Liza?"

Vera scowled.

"I phoned the hospital."

She made it sound like the natural act of a friend rather than something odd, something that made Vera nervous.

Chapter 10

Dani

Sunday morning brought clouds and forty-degree temperatures, another day more early spring than May. Dani lay on her back, listening to the drone of the shower. The TV's remote lay on the nightstand next to Mirko's car keys, a mix of coins, and a pack of spearmint gum. She unwrapped a stick and popped the piece in her mouth. The flat screen television set clicked on with a thumb push. Sports anchors discussed baseball. CNN, ESPN, and the Golf Channel were the stations Mirko watched. Dani searched for the local news but found stories from New York City. No mention of yesterday's crash. Surely, the local paper covered it. Barefoot, she opened the door, and scoured the hallway. *The Sunday Journal News* lay on the welcome mat of the apartment three doors down. She made a dash, retrieved it, and scampered back to Mirko's place.

The lead story featured the tough-on-crime governor seeking a third term and his rival, the wealthy venture capitalist, Hugh Lavender, who promised to return New York State to fiscal prudence and ethical standards. Not of interest. She skipped voting because she lived nowhere long enough to care.

She found it below the fold, including two pictures of the smashed Saturn and an inset photo of the woman who'd held Dani's hand, Vera Moon. A secondary story recapped the murder of her son, Charles. Dani began reading.

Mirko poked his head out of the bathroom. "Can you make coffee?"

"Sure."

Although not a coffee drinker, she made a great brew. As a kid, every morning Bogie got up, prepared a three-cup pot for their often-hungover mother, and scrambled two eggs for Dani when their mother worked or made toast and peanut butter when she didn't. On the day he left for college, he taught Dani how to do the same.

Mirko emerged from the shower. "There's plenty of hot water." He glanced down at the newspaper lying on the bed. "Where d'you get that?" He shook his head. "Don't tell me." He pointed. "Your story hit the front page." It came out like a question.

She handed him the filled mug. "I plan to put it back."

"What's it say?" He stepped into his Jockey briefs.

"Someone sliced off the guy's head."

"Ouch."

"Unsolved crime. Plus, they never found the murder weapon."

Mirko blew on the liquid before slurping several sips. "It's good."

"Expert teacher and lots of practice." Dani tried not to gawk. He was beautiful, but not girly. Damn, he gave her the shivers.

She scanned the rest of the story. "An anonymous source suggests a connection between the victim and a local gang, but they don't offer any proof."

"It's a decent paper."

"Seems like an odd coincidence."

He placed the mug on the nightstand and dragged on a pair of Dockers. "What does?" With a tug, he pulled on a golf shirt and tucked it into place. The store logo sat above his name.

"Her son gets murdered, and then she's in this terrible accident. How random is that?" One of the crowd pictures from the crash included the florid faced man. The camera caught his profile, his head ducked. Dani's index finger stabbed the photo. "That idiot tried to pull them out of the car."

Mirko took another gulp of coffee. "I gotta get to work."

Dani sensed his stare. "Okay."

"Sooo?"

"I wonder what's up with the florid faced guy."

"You're on your way to KC, right?"

She glanced up. “Oh.” Of course. He wanted her to leave. It was a help-a-friend-in-need act. Except they’d made love. “Gonna check on Vera Moon first.” Her life sounded shittier than Dani’s. “Don’t worry. I’ll hop into the shower and then bounce.” She hoped she sounded breezy. “I’ll leave the key under the mat.”

“What are you talking about? It *doesn’t* involve you.”

Dani grabbed her toiletry and make-up bags from the opened suitcase on the floor. “It does. I already explained.” Suppose the baddies could identify her. Besides, Vera had asked for Dani’s help.

“This makes me nuts. If there is no drama, you create it.”

Not fair. Crap happened to her. She decided not to argue the point. “I made two cups.” Slipping past him, she ducked into the bathroom, leaving the door open. “Last night was crazy good.”

Mirko leaned against the doorjamb. He stared at her, his expression incredulous and frustrated. She liked the way he had looked at her last night ten times better.

“Thanks for letting me stay.” She wanted to ask, “Didn’t you have fun too?” *Pathetic.*

“It was nice.”

Her face fell.

“Better than nice.” He straightened up and moved out of view.

“Yeah.” Dani closed the bathroom door and kept it closed until she heard the clank of the front door lock.

***

Eleven a.m. No matter what Mirko said, Vera needed Dani’s help. Her best shot at finding the older woman was at the hospital. Too late to drive west after that. Mirko may let her stay another night. The thought made Dani smile.

She went into the bedroom and put on a fitted white shirt. With a mirror check and tug, she covered her skull-and-crossbones tat. Then she pulled on her best pair of jeans. Taking her time, she applied lip-gloss, tied her hair in a ponytail, and inserted her favorite silver earrings. She intended to make a good second impression.

A notepad on Mirko’s nightstand would serve.

Dear Mirko,

I left my gear here while I visit the lady from the pile-up. I'll be back this evening. I plan to leave first thing in the morning. I hope that's all right with you. If not, no worries. I'm all packed.

Thanks for everything.

Should she sign the note "Love, Dani" or "Your friend Dani?" She opted for "D," clipped the note to Lefty the panda's ear, locked the door, pushed the key under the welcome mat, returned the neighbor's newspaper, and left.

Chapter 11

Vera

Erika's lyrical voice sucked Vera back in. "How bad are Liza's injuries?"

"Severed liver. The surgeon thought she ruptured her spleen, but it was far more serious."

Liza had complained of severe belly pain. Her white blood-cell-count dipped, indicating possible internal bleeding. Dr. LaSalle wheeled Liza away for exploratory surgery while Vera paced, napped, and read in the waiting room. They came for her several hours later with the diagnosis.

"I'm sorry." Erika reached out and patted Vera's leg.

"Quite unusual, they said."

"Will she be all right?"

She paused and assessed her state of mind. "I am hopeful."

"Charlie delighted in telling funny stories about his sisters – loving tales, of course."

"Which ones..." She caught herself, again lulled by the musical voice. Whenever Kinsey Millhone, one of Vera's favorite fictional sleuths, met suspects, the guilty ones tried to gain trust by sharing personal details only a friend might know. Vera jutted her chin. "You said you have information?"

"My husband was in *your* accident."

"I do not understand."

"I read the story in this morning's paper and had to meet you." She crossed and uncrossed her legs, toes once again aligned.

"Why?"

"Yesterday, my husband reserved our car service to take him to JFK Airport for a multi-day trip. Then, a few hours later, I heard a car pull into our driveway. Naturally, it frightened me."

"Naturally?"

"I watched from the front window and saw the sedan he'd hired. The driver and..." She paused. "... my husband, both got out. I listened to their raised voices but couldn't decipher actual words, only the agitated tone."

"It was hit-and-run."

"My husband appeared disheveled and sustained some kind of blow to his forehead, leaving a long gash."

"Is he the type of man who would leave the scene of an accident?"

Erika smoothed her skirt. "New driver."

"Liza almost died."

"We use this service all the time, but this driver was unfamiliar." For a second, her eyes dipped away before returning to Vera's.

"I am asking about the character of your husband."

"I almost contacted the police, but the driver climbed into the car and left."

"How did your husband explain his injury?"

"He seldom offers explanations."

For the first time, Vera heard honesty. How many times had she argued with Vincent about this? "I share on a need to know basis," he said. "I *need* to know everything," she countered.

"I still want an explanation. Why do you think my accident involved *your* husband?"

In her soothing, alto voice, Erika said, "The passenger side sported a huge dent. It met the description and time-frame I read in the paper." She circled the room. "They murder Charlie. His mother and my husband are in the same car accident." She faced Vera. "Random? Probably not."

"I require a bit more clarity."

"I met Charlie *through my husband.* They worked together on a business deal."

This sounded unlikely. "Doing what?" Erika looked like money. Car service, expensive jewelry, her suit from a high-end designer. "What does your husband do?"

"Not relevant."

"Did he hire Charlie to take photographs?" Charlie specialized in portraits, but he shot home decorating pieces, special events, weddings, and bar mitzvahs as well. The studio where he worked closed six months before his death. "Your husband has no name; *you* give me a phony one. Nothing you have told me is helpful."

"I'm trying to warn you."

"About what?" Vera's head buzzed. The man at Liza's yard sale, the accident, the telephone hang-ups, sensing someone behind her, the sounds of intruders.

"I think they were into something illegal. You knew about Charlie's side business?"

"I don't know what you are talking about." No matter what Liza, the police and this person believed, Charlie was an innocent. The buzzing became louder, like bees flitting inside her head and ears.

Her gloves back on, Erika circled the apartment, touching the family photographs that decorated most surfaces.

Vera jumped up. "Please leave." This woman shared no facts about herself, her husband, or her relationship with Charlie. "Now."

"May I ask you one more question?"

"I thought you came with information. Not to snoop."

Erika shook her head as if denying Vera's accusation.

"Let me get this straight. You think someone arranged the accident because it is too much of a coincidence. You are suggesting these unidentified people targeted your husband and me because of a sketchy business deal?"

Erika shrugged. "It's possible." Brandy, her tail swishing back and forth, took a few steps toward Erika, and then retreated to Vera's side. "I don't see any of Charlie's work around." She faced Vera.

"Who knew we'd both be at the same spot?"

"Exactly."

"Exactly what?"

"I didn't say I had answers," Erika said.

"Yes, you did." The buzzing became sharp pains at her temples. She still ached from the car crash. In her mind, she retraced her steps from the yard sale to the gas station. Someone watched them leave and followed them? She remembered a man with red pimply skin yanking on her arm after the crash. *The nosy man from the yard sale?* "Have I met your husband?"

"No." Erika sounded sure.

"What was your relationship with Charlie?"

"I told you. We loved each other."

"I doubt that." Over the years, Charlie had brought his girlfriends over to meet his mom. They all looked like Penny. Brown, tiny waist, wide hips, long legs. In fact, it became a family joke that Charlie wanted someone like his big sister. "You are a married woman."

"That smash-up was no accident."

"Tell the police. I will go with you."

"Did the murderers take anything?" Erika asked.

"What?"

"I read they trashed the apartment. Are things missing?"

"My friend Paul, the one I called before, he will be here in a few minutes." Vera pushed past Erika, opened the door wide, and stepped into the hallway. Lucy, who lived in the apartment next to Vera's, stood in the hall, keys in hand.

"Good morning," Vera said. Lucy started, then scrunched her face in a quizzical expression. What a sight Vera must be, still in her robe and slippers, her hair uncombed. "How are you?"

"I'm fine. How's Liza?"

Erika stepped into the hallway, her back to Lucy.

"Oh," Lucy said, "You have company."

"She's leaving." Vera paused for emphasis. "Now."

Erika said, "I hope things work out for you. Thank you for your time." She pulled sunglasses from her purse and slipped them on. In a low voice she added, "Be careful. These are dangerous people." She sidestepped to the top of the stairs and hurried down.

Lucy's door stood ajar. Keys in hand, Vera slammed her door shut, took three giant steps to Lucy's, pushed it in, and bolted inside. From Lucy's living room window, Vera surveyed the street below.

"What's going on?" Lucy stood next Vera. "What did that woman want?"

"Not sure."

A sedan, like the one in the accident, idled in front of the building. A white man dressed in a black suit opened the passenger door.

"I am trying to read the license plate."

Erika slid in. The driver closed the door, climbed into the driver's seat, and drove off.

"Oak Lane One," Lucy said.

Vera spun around.

"I noticed it when I came in. I'm sure — Oak Lane One."

Chapter 12

Vera

The hospital corridor hummed with muted voices. Nurses, aides, and orderlies entered and exited patients' rooms. Vera dropped off a tray of cookies she'd baked for the nurses before striding to Liza's open door. A tall white man in a knit cap and leather bomber jacket blocked the entrance.

Still rattled from Erika's visit, Vera said in a curt tone, "Excuse me."

The man turned to face her.

"Sam." Her happiness surprised her. He had been a good son-in-law, helping Vera with her taxes and household projects. They both enjoyed *Scrabble* and the card-game Hearts. "You look different." Usually, Sam Davis wore tailored navy suits, white shirts, and oxfords polished to a gleam.

"Some adjustments." He bobbed his head as if in acknowledgment of the changes she noted. "Were you hurt too?"

"A bruise here and there." The recommended brain scan seemed irrelevant now. Yes, she suffered from headaches and dizziness, but those symptoms haunted her since the murder three months earlier. "How are you?"

"Great. Busy." He scratched at his beard stubble, another recent addition. "I came as soon as I heard."

"Thanks." She meant it and hoped her relief and joy came through. "I intended to call you but wanted the doctor's news first."

"No problem. A friend saw the accident and notified me."

"Witnessed it?" Officer French's questions popped into Vera's mind. "Did he speak with the police?"

"No, not an eye-witness." Sam sounded uncomfortable. "In the area and recognized you both."

A friend was on the scene and recognized them? Of course, it could be true. She had to stop being so suspicious and jumpy.

Sam's high forehead folded into creases. "I came right away."

The room included two beds separated by a curtain, and a communal bathroom. A sign read, "Visitors, please use the bathrooms in the halls. This one is for patients only." Another sign listed the name of the attending physician and duty nurse. The room smelled like disinfectant.

Vera stepped around Sam and walked towards Liza's bed. A drainage tube in her left side oozed clotty fluids. Oxygen came from a clear tube with two prongs, one in each nostril. An IV dripped liquids into her veins. Vera took her daughter's cool, dry hand.

Sam said, "I've been here for an hour. She hasn't stirred."

"They gave her Demerol for the pain. It keeps her groggy."

"What's her prognosis?" Sam asked.

"She is quite famous among the staff."

The line etched between Sam's wild eyebrows deepened.

"I've learned that a ripped liver is something all interns need to observe."

He eased his frown. "Will she be okay?"

Vera brought the gold cross that hung around her neck to her lips. "I pray every waking minute."

"What did the doctor say about her chances?"

"The liver can regenerate. Thank God, no broken bones or other internal damage."

Sam made a sympathetic sound.

They stood in silence for several seconds. Vera needed to talk to someone smart and trustworthy before going to the police. She planned to tell them about Erika's visit, her warning, the car's license plate number and ask questions. Erika appeared to snoop and then asked outright, "*Anything missing?*" Like what? Sam might help sort things out.

An idea came to her. “I am staging another rally.”

“You tried that. It bombed.”

Determined not to sound defensive or hurt, she said, “We made the local paper.”

“Yeah, sorry. I meant nothing came of it.”

“That’s your way of apologizing?” She gave a half laugh.

Sam looked chagrined.

“This time I will contact the *Black Lives Matter* organization. They occupy a big stage.” The protests had quieted, but the multi-racial movement continued to swell. “They could use their megaphone to champion his cause.”

“The police didn’t kill Charlie and there’s no evidence his ethnicity played a role.”

“We need publicity to keep a spotlight on his death.” Vera hated to sound whinny. “The police must increase their urgency.”

“I’m sure they’re doing all they can.”

“Really? It doesn’t feel that way to me.”

As if he had read her mind, Sam said, “Everything isn’t always about race.”

“Only white people believe that, and by now, you should know better.”

The day Liza brought Sam home, they surprised Vera. All Liza’s previous boyfriends looked more like Vincent — tall, wide smile, dark-skinned, the opposite of Sam’s whiter-than-white complexion. It made no difference to Vera. She worried, however, about *his* people. Turned out they liked Liza a lot. This memory gave Vera pause. Why did the thought of Charlie with Erika upset her, but not Sam and Liza? Before the murder, she thought of herself as inclusive and unbiased. Since the murder, race loomed larger.

“I see Liza moved out of the house.”

The abrupt topic change got Vera’s guard up. Once again, Sam seemed to sense her thoughts. She would never win at poker.

He explained the subject shift. “There’s a lot of money tied up in that place. We’d agreed to sell it.”

“You decided.”

“Don’t be like that.”

"Like what?"

"Mad at me. She gets half." He paused. "Of what's left, once I pay the bank and deduct the renovation costs."

"It doesn't sound like she will receive much."

Liza stirred in her sleep. Vera brushed Liza's hair from her face. "She needs more than that. You are the one with the good job." Sam practiced law in a respected local firm. He also flipped houses on the side and owned a piece of a BMW dealership. His affluence allowed him to buy every new electronic gadget and take several vacations a year. Unfortunately, Liza had signed a prenuptial agreement.

"I've hired a handyman and painters to get it ready for sale, but they couldn't work with Liza under foot."

"Well, that is no longer a problem."

Sam raised both his hands as if surrendering.

She tipped her head in acknowledgment. "I am not myself these days."

"I understand." His voice sounded concerned.

One way to measure a life's success is by the yardstick of your children's happiness. If that were true, Vera had failed miserably.

"What's left in the house?" he asked.

His accusatory tone surprised and disturbed her. "Nothing."

"You stowed some possessions?"

"No."

"How about Charlie?"

Liza had mentioned vague "stuff" belonging to Charlie. Vera kept that to herself. "Didn't you clear out the house for the renovations? We sold or removed everything else."

"Yeah. There are only a few boxes of photos in the basement and some equipment. Did he store other things? Tucked something away?"

The man lurking around the house during the garage sale flashed in her mind. So did Erika's question about anything missing. Vera's voice rose to a higher and louder pitch. "Hid things? Like what?" The buzzing came back, a low, steady hum this time.

"Just wondering."

"Nothing I'm aware of."

Sam jammed his hands deep into his jacket pockets and shifted his weight from one foot to the other. A huff of air escaped.

Picking up on his physical cues, she asked, "What else is on your mind?"

"I'm getting married."

"Oh, no." *Poor Liza.*

"Be happy for me."

"Anyone I know?"

"Nope."

"When?"

He cleared his throat. "In a few weeks."

Vera knew she should stop asking questions since whatever she learned would hurt Liza, but she couldn't help herself. "How did you meet?"

Sam tilted his head. "She bartended at a function I attended." He looked embarrassed. "What can I say?"

Indeed.

"Please tell her." He zipped up his jacket and ran his fingers through his short hair.

"Stay and tell her yourself." She eyed him. All the gray had vanished. Definitely a young fiancé.

"I'm not the villain." He eased toward the doorway. "Give her my best."

Liza's luck stunk. Well, not all of it was luck. She caused much of the negatives. An un-Christian thought, but true. As early as ten years old, Liza bristled at the smallest slight. Nothing was good enough or her fault. Vincent's doing. He blamed others all the time. Governments, police, politicians, bosses — whoever "they" might be — were responsible for all things evil or incompetent. He wasn't always wrong. Still, taking responsibility for decisions mattered to Vera. She owned hers at great personal cost.

Sam stepped into the hall.

Vera followed him, stopping at the room entrance. "It is not my place to inform her."

"It'll go down easier from you."

"What difference does that make?"

"I gotta go."

He was entitled to a new and happier life. "I wish you luck," she said, careful to keep disappointment from her expression and tone.

"Thank you. Take care of yourself."

Vera massaged her temples with the tips of her index fingers. *When to tell Liza? Not today*. She sat on the hard chair next to the bed. Her bruised hip ached.

Now what? Who could she trust for expert advice? Charlie died months ago. If Erika was correct about the accident, why now? Maybe share her doubts with the no-nonsense Officer French? Another thought came to Vera. Erika mentioned "*they* murdered" and "*murderers*." A slip of the tongue, an assumption, or fact?

A sound in the hall made Vera start. She listened. Nothing. Grunting, she pushed herself up, walked to the doorway, and scanned the corridor. She heard the purr of distant conversations, but nothing else. What was the matter with her? They were in a public hospital. Safe. Right?

Chapter 13

Dani

Dani paced in the hallway. Tracking down Vera felt intrusive or *"rash,"* as her mother used to say, which Dani found funny since no one took crazier risks than her mom.

She rapped on the opened door.

Vera jumped. "May I help you?"

"Ms. Moon, we met yesterday at the accident." Dani tried to peer around Vera. "Is Liza okay?"

Vera examined Dani with disturbing intensity. "You know my daughter and me?"

"Sure." She needed Vera to remember her, to welcome her. "I'm Dani."

"Who let you in here?"

"A nurse." She stabbed a thumb over her shoulder in the hallway's direction. "She thinks I'm your cousin."

"Why?"

"Friends don't make the cut." Dani's voice rose making her statement a question.

"Leave before I call security."

"I helped you guys."

Without breaking eye contact, Vera backed up to the red, emergency button next to Liza's bed. "I've had quite my fill of strangers today." Her thumb hovered over the buzzer. "I am about to alert the nurse."

Dani moved closer, her hands outstretched, palms up. "You asked me if I saw the crash. You begged me to help you." She dropped her arms, making a slapping noise as palms hit thighs. "You told me to be safe." Dani's powerful desire to be useful, for somebody to want her instead of the reverse, swept through her.

Vera folded her lips.

"I was blonde."

For several beats, Vera stared at Dani. Then she blinked hard, as if clearing her vision. "You and a young man."

"Yes." *She remembered.* "My friend, Javier. We watched the whole thing from the gas station."

Staying next to the call button, Vera let her hand fall. "What happened to your hair?"

"A wig."

"You know how suspicious this sounds?"

"Testing a look before doing anything drastic." Not the full truth, but better than justifying the disguise.

"What does your mother think about that?"

Dani tilted her head to the right. "People say I look like a kid. I'm not." An image of her mother leapt into her head. Jean cutoffs, flip-flops, halter-top, her hair tied up, sitting at the kitchen table working on a word puzzle with a stubby pencil, an almost empty glass of gin nearby. "*Keeps your mind sharp. Don't be stupid. Stupid always loses.*" Neighbors often thought Bogie and Dani were their mom's siblings. She let them more times than not. "Besides, my mom is dead."

Vera's facial muscles eased. "This is a much prettier look."

"Guess I'm not the platinum type."

"What brought you to the hospital?" Another good sign. Vera's tone held less of an edge.

"My best friend's new baby." Except Dani didn't have a best friend. Javier and Mirko? Alice? She pictured a bubbly brunette who loved to listen to Dani's stories. "While I was here, I thought I'd check on your daughter. Is she gonna be okay?" She performed her perpetual-motion side-steps as she spoke.

Vera said in a shivery voice, "Cautiously optimistic."

"Oh." Dani moved forward and touched Vera's arm with her fingertips before stepping back and resuming her rock-steady dance.

A nurse hustled into the room. She gave Vera a wide smile. "Thanks for the cookies. Super tasty."

"You are welcome."

"I'm sorry, but you must leave now." She moved towards the bed. "Come back in about thirty minutes." Without waiting for a response, she pulled the privacy curtain around Liza's bed.

An awkward silence followed as Vera and Dani waited in the corridor. Vera acted okay with Dani's presence, which made her happy. But the waves of sadness rippling from the older woman tempered Dani's joy.

"You brought the nurses cookies?" Dani asked.

"It pays to be nice and I like to bake."

A loud crash. Vera jolted back and Dani yelped.

The metal tray on the tiled floor rattled to a stop, its contents, someone's dinner, splattered about. That's when Dani spotted him. Barrel-chested with flushed, pimply skin — the man from the crash. Clean-shaven this time, minus the phony mustache, but no mistake — it was him. The dietary aide stopped a janitor who slopped up the mess.

Florid Face stared at them.

Dani said, "That's the man from the accident."

He ducked into a room.

"Do you recognize him?"

"Do you?" Vera's edge came back full force.

"No. Why would I?"

"You tell me." With squinted eyes, she pressed her palm against her chest as if pledging allegiance to the flag. "You come to my daughter's room, and he shows up?"

"I wore the wig. He doesn't know who I am."

"You say."

"I made him stop hurting you. He pulled on you, and I made him go away." People often doubted Dani when she told the truth and believed almost all her lies. "Plus, he spoke to the Jeep driver who hit you."

"Really?"

"I saw them talking."

At first, Vera seemed to weigh Dani's words, then she dropped her chin to her chest and covered her face with both hands. "Please go away. Thank you, but no."

"You told me your name, and I told you mine." Bogie would be proud of her for initiating positive action. "I'm gonna help you." She made a visual sweep. No Florid Face. "Best we get out of here."

Vera lifted her head. "We?"

Two nurses chatted a few doors down. The janitor finished wiping up the spill remnants. Nothing appeared dangerous. Dani said, "We should stay in the hospital and plan our next steps."

"Why are you doing this? Tell me the truth or I will phone the police."

"I think they crashed into you on purpose." Not the complete story and not the real reason. She just knew she must help.

"Someone else said that to me today."

"See. I'm right." Evidently someone agreed with her. "Who?"

"Not a good thing. Another person I do not trust."

Ouch.

Vera watched Dani for a beat. In a less strident tone, she said, "I need caffeine."

"Me too. Let's go to the cafeteria."

"I cannot leave Liza."

"The nurse said thirty-minutes."

Vera's gaze darted about, while her hands fluttered with no place to land. "She is safer if I stand guard."

"The nurses are taking care of her." Dani twisted left, right, and left again, then gave Vera her best smile.

Vera eyed Dani again, as if weighing her options. She blew out a breath. "We will need to hurry."

Excellent.

Vera said, "My caffeine addiction is not pretty."

"Mine either," Dani said with a chuckle.

Security guards strolled by.

"Whatever Florid Face is planning, we'll still be okay if we stay in the open." It felt like being in a television cop show – *Law and Order* in Mount Kisco.

Vera took one more backward look into Liza's room. "Okay. Let's be quick."

They headed toward the elevator bank. Dani wanted to look behind her to check if Florid Face was following them or moving toward Liza, but Dani didn't want to upset Vera further. They rode down to the second floor and followed the signs to the cafeteria. People moved in both directions. Two men, each with a grim expression, walked past them.

"Hospitals are kinda scary," Dani said. The look on Vera's face made her catch herself. "I'm sure your daughter will be fine."

Vera nodded as if she agreed. "What did your friend have?"

"Huh?"

"Your best friend? Boy or a girl?"

"A boy," Dani said with ease. "Almost nine pounds by cesarean." Dani had arrived that way. *"Ripped out of me; I almost died for you."* Her mother retold the story whenever Dani got on her nerves.

Vera made a sympathetic sound.

"They're both great but it was super hairy for a while." Her mother would lift her shirt and show Dani the barely visible scar. "*You destroyed my body.*" "Emergency C-section so they couldn't do a bikini cut. She's worried her husband won't find her sexy anymore."

Vera stayed quiet for a bit. "Losing a child is the worst thing a parent can experience." She spoke in her trembling voice again. "I imagine losing a parent is the worst thing to happen to a child."

"I was ten."

Most of the time, Dani kept painful memories at bay. When they surfaced, stark images emerged. Visiting-men, sometimes two on the same day. They gave her mother money "to pay our bills." The family moved often, sometimes with a guy, sometimes to a new city. Dani recalled her mother yelling at the "boyfriends," screaming at Bogie and Dani, and the terror and confusion of the three days her mother lay dying in a city hospital ward. She blinked away the images and death-smell.

"Is your father alive?"

"No," Dani said with too much force. Anyway, he was dead to her, so not an actual lie. He never came around all those years Bogie and she needed him.

"Oh." Vera looked at Dani the way Bogie sometimes did, both sad and worried. "I am sorry."

"It's not so bad. I have my big brother." Mirko flashed through her mind. "My fiancé too."

"I wish *I* could say it is not so bad."

"Murder, I'd guess, isn't the same as dying."

Chapter 14

Dani

Families and uniformed staff packed the cafeteria. Enticing aromas from pizza, cheeseburgers, and French fries replaced the hospital smells. Against one long wall, workers with hands gloved in plastic served hot and cold food. A glass-front refrigerator filled with sodas and iced teas stood catty-corner to the salad bar. People occupied every seat surrounding the square tables for four. Dani studied each face. None resembled the barrel-chested man with the ravaged skin.

Dani said, "I held your hand, and you said, *"They can't find him."* Who did you mean?"

"Did I?"

"There." Dani nodded toward a table a couple just vacated. They hurried over.

Vera insisted on paying for Dani's Diet Coke and chocolate chip cookie.

Fake cream swirled in Vera's coffee cup. "Tell me the truth. Did you see the crash?"

The way she asked made Dani think Vera knew about her, already doubted her stories. "Yup," she said in her most sincere voice. "I'm pretty sure they hit you on purpose, like I explained before." She popped the last morsel of cookie into her mouth. "You mentioned someone else thought the same thing?"

Vera pulled out a notepad and a pen from her purse. "Tell me all you remember." She leveled her gaze on Dani. "Do not leave out a single detail."

Before Vera flipped to the next page, Dani noticed a scrawled notation on the top of the sheet — Oak Lane One. As she relayed the accident, she made a conscious effort not to embellish, which she found difficult, since she couldn't remember what she saw versus what she'd told the police and then told Mirko, her imagination filling in gaps.

"The person driving it — how old, Black, white, short, tall?"

Dani played the scene in her head. "A white guy, big, solid with buck teeth. I can't say for sure how old. The way he stared at your car instead of straight ahead made me suspect he staged the crash."

"The police questioned you?"

"Yeah. I reported what happened but not what I thought."

The older woman wrote without speaking.

Dani lowered her voice. "I told my fiancé that helping you was the right thing to do. He didn't want me to get involved."

Vera lifted her pen from her notepad. She seemed to ponder something important. Finally, as if she decided, she said, "Thank you."

Dani liked Vera from the moment their hands touched in the car. Now, as they chatted, she liked her more. She looked so much better than the day before. Yesterday, her full lips were blood caked. Today, blush lipstick almost disguised the bruises. Her mostly gray curls, swirls, and corkscrews framed a sweet face. Well into her sixties, Dani suspected, despite Vera's creamy smooth skin.

Vera asked, "What happened next?"

"Florid Face argued with the driver, and now he's here. See what I'm saying?"

"That is who we just saw."

"Yaaaa."

Vera scribbled on her pad.

"Who'd want to hurt you?" Dani asked.

"Who indeed?" She handed Dani a napkin. "Cookie crumbs."

"Oh, thanks." Dani wiped her mouth and chin. "This is bad. My brother Bogie, he's crazy smart, says if things make little sense, look for the hidden agenda."

"Should I be looking for one from you?"

***

Vera hung up after calling the nurses' station. "They are still with Liza." She massaged her neck and temples. "All is quiet."

With slight movements, Dani's gaze revolved around the room. They'd been in the cafeteria for twenty minutes. Several of the food servers chatted with each other. Two ate sandwiches. A couple got up from one of the far tables.

With a sharp poke on Vera's arm, Dani warned, "Don't look up." His body angled away from them, Florid Face stood next to a vending machine. "To your right, two o'clock."

Vera jerked her head around.

"Don't."

She snapped her head back, hand over her heart.

Dani watched him. He hovered by the vending machine, his enormous chest and thick neck added to his menacing look.

"We gotta get out of here," Dani said. She grabbed her jacket and handed Vera hers. "You can't go home." She kept her voice low.

"I must. Brandy is alone."

"You don't watch cop shows on television, do you?" Dani tried to keep Florid Face in view without being obvious. "Who's Brandy?" With her hand pressed against Vera's back, the two women edged toward the cafeteria entrance.

A small group of hospital workers, some dressed in blue scrubs, others with pink-and-white smocks, reached the cafeteria door at the same time as Dani and Vera. Dani nudged Vera through, eyes scanning the hall.

"There." Dani pointed to a single person handicap-bathroom a few steps away.

Vera hesitated.

"Come on. We don't know what he's up to." Or what he's capable of either. Totally lit, like being in a movie. "We'll go in there for a minute to plan."

The two crept into the lavatory. Dani locked the door. The restroom was large enough for a wheelchair and bars hung on either side of the toilet. Vera put the lid down and lowered herself onto the seat. "There's a Detective Monroe assigned to my son's case."

"Do you have his number?"

"No."

"Call 911."

"I liked another police officer more." Vera sifted through things in her purse. "But she's not a detective. She interviewed me the afternoon of the crash and gave me her card." Vera pulled out her phone and continued searching. "Here it is." Her hand shook. "'Officer French."

"Why did they kill your son?"

Vera's head popped up. "They?"

Dani shrugged. "I wondered. Didn't mean any disrespect."

Vera went back to her cell phone. "No signal."

Dani fished her phone from her pocket. She pressed the green button. "Shit, none here either."

"Please do not use that type of language."

Afraid for their lives, they were hiding in a bathroom, and Vera admonished Dani for cursing. She suppressed a smile. "Sorry." *Just like a real mom.* "We need to get to the lobby. Our phones will work there."

"The police will help us. At least, I hope so."

"Of course, they will."

Vera pursed her lips. "You would not understand."

"Why not?"

Vera didn't respond.

Dani said, "Let's go to hospital security."

"Liza first."

"Okay, but it seems like he's following you and not Liza."

Vera squeezed her hands together. "I hope you are correct. I pray he is not following *anyone*."

"Liza's upstairs, and he's here."

"I need to be sure he is not after her." Vera shrank into her frame with each word, lower and tighter. "Better the police. Too much to explain to the security guards." She closed her eyes and then opened them again. "I don't know what to do."

Bogie wisdom: Leaders act. "You're right. Police. We need to bounce." Dani went to the door.

"What could he do to us in a crowded place like this?"

"The question is, why is he following us?" Dani unlocked the bathroom door and slid it open a crack. Two doctors deep in conversation came into view. Once again, Dani grabbed Vera by the wrist. “Come on.”

Vera pulled back.

Dani closed the door again. “What?”

“I cannot leave Liza. We must go back upstairs.”

“Or...” Dani tried for a gentle but firm tone. “We’re leading him away from Liza and keeping her safe by ghosting.”

Vera’s worried expression deepened.

“If he follows us,” Dani said. “Then we know Liza’s safe. If he doesn’t, we circle around and head back. Okay?”

Vera nodded.

Dani opened the door. No sign of Florid Face.

They stepped into the hall and speed-walked until they caught up with the physicians.

Dani looked over her shoulder. Florid Face followed a few paces behind.

Chapter 15

Vera

Vera and Dani made it to the elevators and pushed the *close door* button before Florid Face could catch up to them. It chugged to the lobby level.

Dani stepped in front of Vera, letting the other passengers get off first. She darted a look, first left, then right. Brightly lit, the expansive lobby included a gift shop and the Lobby Café. "Come on. I don't see him."

"Maybe he took the stairs and beat us here," Vera said. She stared straight ahead at the glass entrance doors gleaming in the May sun. The parking garage, a squat structure to their right, stood a few feet away. "What does he want with me?"

"I saw him right behind us." Dani swiveled her head every other second. She bounced on the balls of her feet. "Is your car in the garage?'

"You are adding to my stress. Please stop all that twitching."

A guard, arms crossed, seemed bored as he watched people come and go. So far, no sign of the barrel-chested stalker with the damaged complexion. Vera watched the elevators.

Dani said, "The police station is close by."

With her purse clutched to her chest, Vera approached the security guard. If the man saw her talking to an official, he might leave them alone. Was Liza safe? Vera would check again the minute they reached the car. "Can you tell me when visiting hours end?"

"Eight."

She tried to think of something else to ask the unsmiling guard in case their stalker watched. "And what time may I come back tomorrow?" She pointed toward the elevator bank and then the exit sign to confuse Florid Face if he was watching.

The guard's gaze, a puzzled V between his eyes, followed.

"The start of visiting hours?" she asked again.

"Nine." The muscles in his faced eased a bit. "The nurses are pretty good about letting family who need to get to work come a bit earlier."

"Thank you." She walked backed to Dani.

"My car is easy to follow," Dani said.

"How is that?"

"Bright yellow."

"The dealership provided a loaner." She had parked it on the ground level of the three-storied garage. "I cannot remember what it looks like." She dug out the keys. "How stupid."

"You're upset." Dani patted Vera's back. "We'll wait until more people come so we can blend in. Protection in numbers."

Whatever the man wanted, Vera did not have it. She pictured her son's handsome face, eyes crinkled with laughter. *Oh, Charlie.*

The elevator doors opened, and a group of noisy visitors disembarked. They looked like a family. The fatherly member dangled car keys while the mother-person held his other hand. The younger people spanned several decades — a teenage girl, a twenty-something in a Trinity College sweatshirt, a pregnant older sister perhaps, her round belly preceding her.

Vera and Dani slipped into the group.

"Chilly," Dani said to the pregnant woman.

The woman smiled in response. "It'll be summer before we can enjoy a real spring."

Vera let Dani tug her closer.

"When is your baby due?" Dani asked.

The woman patted her swollen belly as the group moved toward the parking garage. "September."

"We were visiting my sister," Dani said.

Vera squinted as if trying to decipher fine print. *What?*

"Did you read about the awful car crash on Main Street?"

"Your sister?"

"Yup."

They reached the entrance. Vera scrutinized their surroundings. Still no sign of the awful man.

"Oh no," the pregnant woman said, her voice now full of concern. "Is she okay?"

"We are hopeful," Vera said. Sam's upcoming marriage flashed in Vera's mind. *Time enough for that*. She put it away.

The woman rubbed her belly again, as if Vera's misfortune might bring bad luck to her. "My mother-in-law has breast cancer."

"I'm so sorry," Dani said.

"Nobody's fault. Bad things happen."

"My mom died of breast cancer," Dani said. "In my arms."

"How awful."

They reached a minivan. "This is us. Nice talking to you."

Vera said, "God bless you." *And God, please bless my Liza*. Lately, Vera felt less sure of her faith. Each seed of doubt weighed her down. "That's me over there." She aimed the car keys toward a compact, its dark color hard to distinguish, and squeezed the door-open button. Its lights flashed on and it beeped.

As if Vera required reassurance, Dani said, "As soon as we get to the police station, things will be fine. They'll protect you."

Dani came across as sweet and vulnerable, childlike with a kind nature. She spirited Vera out of the hospital risking her own safety for a stranger. "You are a good girl."

A grin creased Dani's face.

Over Dani's shoulder, Vera saw Florid Face walking toward them. "Quick. Get in the car."

Dani hopped in. "Is it him?" She slammed the door and ducked down in her seat.

Vera slid down as well and used the key fob to click the door lock. They waited, listened to the whoosh and rumble of exiting and entering cars.

With caution, Vera peeked out. A couple two cars away unlocked their car. Still slouched low, Vera pressed her foot on the brake and pushed the starter.

A sharp rap on the passenger side window elicited a stifled scream from Vera and a yelp from Dani. His red face pressed against the glass. Vera leaned on the horn, blasting the afternoon air with its warning. She flipped on her flasher. The couple spun around. Vera honked the horn again. Florid Face backed up, turned, and briskly walked away.

Chapter 16

Vera

Vera's entire body trembled.

"Do you think he knew your son?" Dani asked.

Vera pulled over. "Can you drive?"

Dani jumped out, came around, and switched places. "Why try to scare you? Is he looking for something you have?"

"Or something Charlie hid." But what? Tears gathered but did not spill.

Dani drove slowly, and they both stayed quiet. In five minutes, they reached the Mount Kisco Police Department, a one-story structure on Green Street. Signs along the parking spots on the left side of the building read, "Employees only." The back of the building housed the courthouse. The lot stood empty, which wasn't surprising for a Sunday afternoon.

Vera hugged herself, trying to get her shakes under control.

"Are you okay?" Dani asked, her pale skin whiter than usual.

"Are you?"

"He scared the tuna salad out of me."

Vera recognized the line from a book about a terrible monster she used to read to her grandchildren. The memory gave her terror a momentary pause. She managed a smile. "Me too."

Coherent thoughts eluded her. The police would ask questions requiring precise answers and details. Florid Face's full description, his specific actions, and words. Should she tell them about Erika and the warning? What about Charlie's possessions in Liza's basement? She pressed her fingers against her temples.

Dani's face scrunched. "Are we going in?"

It took a second for Vera to focus. "Oh, yes, of course."

The two women clambered out of the car and hurried through the lot to the front entrance. Vera stopped. Something nagged at her. "Why did you tell the pregnant woman you were visiting your sister?" What did Vera know about Dani? Nothing of substance, not even her home address or telephone number.

Dani made a little sound at the back of her throat. "Easier." She walked ahead.

Vera stood her ground. "You told me you came to see your best friend's new baby."

Dani faced Vera. "I messed up."

"What were you doing at the hospital?"

She twisted her mouth, shifted from one foot to the next. "I wanted to help you. You asked me to."

How could all these incidents happen without being connected? Erika showed up, then Dani. The man from the garage sale and the collision came to the hospital and followed them and threatened Vera. "I do not tolerate liars."

"I really saw it. My friend Javier witnessed it too. The police questioned us."

Vera wanted to trust the girl. Her neediness rippled out in waves from hungry eyes. "Why all the fabrications?"

"Sometimes, I can't help it. They materialize from nowhere and spill out before I can stop them." She sounded as miserable as she looked, her head slung low, shoulders slumped forward. "But I'm telling you the truth now."

Vera waited several beats. "I am grateful for your help. Thank you. I can take it from here."

Dani's hands, hanging loosely at her sides, shook as if trying to speak for her. "I planned to visit my brother. I didn't go because of the accident and you held my hand and asked me to help you." She made that odd throat sound again.

"I am sorry."

"The police may want me for more questions." Dani's voice rose at the end of her sentence as if asking a question.

The girl sounded pathetic, but Vera could not take the chance. Perhaps Officer French or Detective Monroe could check out Dani. Erika, too. Besides, Vera hated doubting and worrying. Although she felt ashamed thinking it, she also wearied of grieving. She sent up a quick prayer for forgiveness. "You lied to a perfect stranger for no good reason."

"I don't mean to." Dani's chin wobbled. "I never tell lies that do harm, and I'm not lying now. I swear."

When the children were young strays filled their home — the child next door whose parents left her alone while they worked, the boys whose hearts Penny broke, Charlie's and Liza's friends who needed someone to listen. Dani reminded Vera of all of them.

"Here is a plan. Let's meet tomorrow around noon. I am visiting Liza in the morning. After that, we can enjoy lunch, and I will fill you in." By then, the police would know if Dani was a problem.

The girl appeared close to tears. "How about Gus's up on..."

"Perfect." She pulled out her cell phone. Type in your number and I will give you mine."

When they finished exchanging information, Vera said, "To be on the safe side, take a taxi to your car."

"I'm good." Dani waved her phone in the air. "I'll Uber."

Vera resurrected a tone she'd used on her children. "And never lie to me again."

***

Chairs lined one wall of the outer area of the police station, and glass partitions separated visitors from the staff. A lone officer sat at a desk typing on a computer. He glanced her way, raised a finger towards her as if to say, *one minute,* and continued working.

The officer left his desk and slid a window open. "Can I help you?"

She read his nameplate. *Sergeant Jeff Wells*. "May I speak with Officer French?"

"She's not here."

Every little set back rocked her. "Detective Monroe?"

"He's with the county. Not stationed here."

Vera wished she had not sent Dani away. She could verify things, support Vera's story. No remedy now. "I am Vera Moon," she began. "Do you know that name?"

"Yeah, sure. Tell me what this is about."

She plunged in, explained about the accident and Florid Face at the crash, hospital, and yard sale. The officer listened, occasionally asking a question. He made a few notes on a yellow scratch pad.

"The accident and this man may connect to my son's murder."

"Why?" He looked at her full on.

Dani's words popped out. "It cannot all be a coincidence, can it?"

"Did you recognize the man you allege followed you? A friend of your son's?"

"I do not allege. It happened."

"Sorry." He tipped his head forward.

"To answer your question, no. I did not recognize him."

"Did he threaten you?"

"He followed me and banged on my car window."

"I can see how that would scare you, but that's not a legal threat." He glanced down at his notes. "Could there be another explanation like an aggressive reporter trying to get a story?"

Vera mulled that possibility in her mind. He ducked and hid instead of approaching her with journalism credentials. No, not a reporter. "Three different sightings..."

The officer raised a hand, palm out. "He did nothing to you, say anything, is that right?"

"*Unfortunately,* no." She tried for a less angry tone. "I assure you, I felt in dire jeopardy."

"I understand." He took off his glasses and polished them with a square of cloth he retrieved from his desk. "There's not a lot we can do at this point."

This sounded too familiar.

"How many Black officers are on the force?"

"This has nothing to do with race. It's the law." He said this in a patient voice, the kind one might use with a child.

"You say."

"You're not hurt. I can't arrest people for knocking on a car window." The patient tone now held an edge.

"A woman came by today, two women, in fact. They both said they thought the car crash was deliberate." Vera flicked through the pages of her notepad, until she found the one she sought. She ripped it out and handed the officer the license plate number from Erika's hired car.

He took it. "What made these women suspect there's more to the accident?" He peered at the lined sheet.

"The man following me knew the Jeep's driver and the rest of the people involved fled the scene."

"Anything else?"

Vera's weariness made her entire body sag. "Please give that to Officer French."

He flapped the paper. "This is a local car service. I see them around all the time."

"I will explain when I speak with Officer French."

"Do you need a lift home?"

"Thank you, no."

"I'll ask an officer to drive by your place a couple times tonight."

"What about my daughter?"

"Why would someone want to harm your daughter? How is she connected to your son's murder?"

Impatience and frustrated filled Vera up. "She is not." Vera's car keys click-clacked in her hand. "When will Officer French be available?"

"She works three to eleven tomorrow."

"I will return then."

The sergeant nodded as if he agreed with this plan. "Contact us if he shows up again. Meanwhile, we will swing by your place, keep an eye out." He handed her his scratch pad and a pen. "Jot down your address and cell number."

"And the hospital?"

"I'll call them. Add your daughter's full name, floor, and room, and we'll watch out for you both."

"Thank you. I appreciate your help. It has been a trying few days." Months, in fact, of stress and pain.

Vera trudged back to her car. She looked around before climbing and sagging into the driver's seat. Florid Face had acted so brazenly. Weariness gripped her neck, shoulders, and every limb. All the grief and worry took a greater toll than she cared to admit. The crash left her physically and mentally banged up.

Dani popped into her mind. So much energy, that one. *Was she in danger too? Who would keep watch for her?*

Vera hit her left hand against the steering wheel. She'd forgotten to ask the police to investigate Erika and Dani.

Chapter 17

Erika

Erika watched the fucking thug Bigelow wriggle his waistband as if trying to get more comfortable. The movement exposed a gun in a shoulder holster under his sports jacket. Clearly his intention, and one more bit to terrify her.

Moments before, Bigelow banged on Erika and Griff's bedroom door. "Out. Now." Griff lay on the bed, inert, his breathing shallow. She shook him awake. "Your *friends* demand our presence." Her Georgia accent thickened when she dropped her public voice.

With persistent shoves, Bigelow herded them into Erika's expertly decorated great room. Fifty-feet long, and twenty-feet wide, the space centered the house. Area rugs covered the polished hardwood floors. A glass tabletop with seating for twelve balanced on three marble columns dominated the dining portion of the space. In the middle of the room, the sectional couch formed a U with a cabinet that housed a huge flat screen television at its opening. Glass shelves holding collected artifacts lined either side of the breakfront. At the far end, two doublewide armchairs sat angled in front of the fireplace. Recessed lighting gave the room a warm glow. Outside the floor-to-ceiling, wall-to-wall window, the after-light of sunset layered mauves and grays along the horizon.

Erika channeled her inner Angelina Jolie, cool, confident, and dangerous, despite feeling the opposite. "Let's all take a seat." *Fucking assholes*.

Cappy watched her with narrowed eyes. Still dressed in his shiny suit, hands jammed in his pockets, he continued to stand. No matter. He wasn't the real problem.

Tiny spittle-beads foamed at both corners of Bigelow's smirking mouth. Bucked teeth protruded. Was he the shit-heel in charge? There could be a higher-up, an invisible general barking orders into captive ears. To what end? Still playing her role, but with no hope of support, she glanced at her husband.

Griff's eyelids drooped. She suspected he'd doubled up on his anti-depressants and pain pills, or he used something else to escape their situation. Long silver locks framed his face. The gash on his forehead glowed under the recessed lights. He lifted his clouded gaze and studied her with a puzzled expression, as if not recognizing her or understanding the situation.

"The crash shook and battered Griff." Of course, miscreant Bigelow knew that since he caused it in some way Erika had yet to figure out. "He needs to go back to bed."

Bigelow shook his massive head. "He stays."

"He'll be more helpful after he rests." Erika sat down next to Griff. The pencil skirt rose, exposing more of her thighs than she intended. She tugged and smoothed. "I told you. I found nothing in Charlie's apartment." With her right hand, she squeezed Griff's left hand, more to comfort herself than to communicate anything to Griff. "The old woman replaced everything. Besides, if your people couldn't find it when..." She stopped. The thought of Charlie's naked, decapitated body sent spasms across her shoulder blades. "I don't believe the mother knows anything." She spoke in her slow, deliberate manner — her public voice, tinged with her musical Georgia roots and devoid of foul language.

"He hid it somewhere." With his right thumb on one side and his right index finger on the other, Bigelow wiped the saliva from his lips.

"Perhaps." What a fucking dunderhead. Brandishing his gun, threatening Griff, and almost killing him. Worse, having the idiot Cappy with his opaque eyes move in with them. How could any of this help find the photographs or whatever the hell they were after? A digital card packed with demeaning pictures? What was worth killing for? *Damn Griff and damn Charlie Moon.*

Erika rose. "Is our business concluded?"

Bigelow's jacket stretched across his gut. With his index finger jabbing the air, he hissed his demand. "Go back. Get her trust. Find it."

"You couldn't locate it or scare her with that ridiculous car crash. What makes you..."

"Shut up." His face colored.

She'd hit a nerve. *Good.* "Whose idea was that stupid move?"

"I said, shut the fuck up."

"Whatever." She lifted her hands, dismissing the issue. Not her problem. "If you're quite finished." She walked to the archway separating the great room from the wide entryway. "I'm sure Cappy will keep you apprised."

"I leave when I want to." Bigelow said, his expression and tone flat. With a deliberate stride, he walked toward her. Floral aftershave, cheap, almost girlish, twitched her nose. He stopped, his face inches away. Erika's composure crumbled.

"Don't come back without it." His left hand shot up and grabbed her right breast. Fat fingers closed on her nipple, and he twisted. Hard.

Erika cried out.

Griff screamed across the expanse of the great room. "Leave her." He rose on wobbly legs and staggered over to Erika and Bigelow.

"Go hide in your hole." Bigelow took a threatening step toward Griff. "Shoot up or whatever it is you do and leave this to the grown-ups."

Erika, her breast still aching, her humiliation complete, dug deep for strength. *They can't win.* "We get it, okay. Leave us." She didn't know Bigelow's full capacity for violence, but Griff couldn't take the thug on in his current state.

Griff stumbled forward. "You touch my wife again and I'll kill..."

In one swift, smooth move, Bigelow reached under his jacket, pulled out his weapon, and smashed the butt against Griff's skull.

***

An owl hooted. Minutes went by. It called again. In between the owl's solo cries, Griff snored, creating a musical interlude. The clock read 1:00 a.m. On the nightstand, Erika's iPhone vibrated each time a new email or text arrived alerting her to some news event. The outside temperature dipped below forty, forcing her to turn on the heat. Air moved through the vents, pumping out warmth. Neither the hoots, snores, nor heat comforted her. Bigelow's stench lingered in her nostrils. The lowlife fucking bastard. She felt his fingers wrenching her nipple and heard the crack of the gun against Griff's skull.

She shifted so she could see Griff, his head swollen and bandaged, the cut on top of a bump from the car crash still black, blue, and orange. Cappy had helped her half-drag, half-carry Griff to their bedroom. With undisguised threats, Bigelow kept her from getting Griff help, so she used what she could find in the medicine cabinet to clean the wound. *What if he suffered a concussion?* How stupid of Griff to come to her rescue. She kissed his cheek — foolish but gallant. She swung her legs over the side, climbed out of bed, put on her robe over her negligee, and padded into the kitchen.

She needed a plan to free them both.

The yellow lined pad by the phone listed scratched out to-dos over half the top page. The round glass table in the breakfast nook served as her unofficial office. She enjoyed looking out the bay window into the garden that cost so much to keep up. She started a fresh sheet.

Griff owes a lot of money to fuckers. Nothing new. His gambling and other destructive habits kept them in debt. What made this time different, more perilous?

Charlie and Griff cooked up a scheme together. Something goes wrong. Someone murders Charlie. The killers or their minions smash into the car with Cappy behind the wheel and Griff in the backseat. Were they trying to kill Griff and Vera or scare them? Who thought up that the stupid idea? Bigelow by the look on his face when she spoke of it. But who is in charge? She pressed the pen against her lips.

Bigelow wants the digital card last seen in Charlie's possession. Photographs of what? Something illegal? Pictures of damaging or insider documents? Why kill Charlie before snagging the card?

Cappy. Hired help. What about Bigelow?

She put down her pen. Questions continued to circle in her mind. What purpose did bringing Erika and Griff into their drama serve? Why not intimidate Vera Moon, rather than send Erika to snoop? Why stage a car crash rather than point the gun and demand what they wanted?

Erika sank her fingers into her hair and held her head. Critical pieces of the puzzle eluded her.

"Can't sleep?"

She started.

Cappy, dressed in boxers and a T-shirt, approached her. His flip-flops slapped against the soles of his feet. "What time are we leaving tomorrow?"

Good question. "Early is better." Vera would probably visit her daughter at the hospital first thing. "Eight."

"Fine by me." He looked around. "Any coffee?"

Coffee sounded like a good idea. "I'll make some." She overturned the pad, shoved it under a small stack of magazines, pushed back from the table, and walked over to the coffee machine. "Decaf okay?" Anything stronger and she'd never get to sleep.

"Why bother?"

"Regular. No problem." She measured out the coffee grounds and water. "Is Bigelow your boss?"

Cappy took his time responding. "Fellow soldier."

"Why did he kill Charlie?"

"Who said he did?"

The coffee machine gurgled. "I'm trying to understand what's going on." She gave him the warmest smile she could pull off. "So, I can be the most useful."

Cappy snuffled, scratched his flat, hairy belly.

Disgusting lowlife bastard.

"Surely, you're privy and can share a scrap." She let her bathrobe open for a flash, as if a careless error, and then pulled it closed. "I won't tell anyone."

"Seems like you skipped asking questions when your druggy husband got you all this." He waved his hand, taking in the large kitchen, Sub-Zero refrigerator, and double oven that added to the image of Erika as a gourmet cook. But that wasn't true. Similarly, the wine rack against the south wall stood filled with pricey reds and whites. When alone, Griff and Erika drank beer.

"Griff worked hard for *this*."

Sort of. His Uncle Al leant then nineteen-year-old Griff $100,000 to start his first business. A Princeton dropout, Griff used the money to buy recording equipment that he set up in his parents' garage. Wannabe singers and musicians paid him to record their demos. A couple of his clients landed contracts. Five years and many lucrative deals later, he sold the recording business to a mega-company for a nice sum.

Cappy's laugh came out like a snarl. "Owning a car service is hard work?"

"His third successful enterprise."

"From what I can see, he slides on other people's grease."

Defending Griff to this fucking idiot wasted precious time. The machine pinged its completion. She poured them both a cup, offered sugar and cream. They drank in silence for a few minutes. Time to change tactics.

"How did you and Bigelow get together?"

"Mutual acquaintances."

She waited for more information, but he slurped his coffee without another word. She asked her real question. "Is Bigelow capable of murder?"

Cappy wiped his mouth with the napkin she handed him. "Never seen him do it. Then again, why carry a gun if you ain't prepared to use it."

Chapter 18

Erika

Erika pretended to search her bag for keys. Moments before, Cappy dropped her off in front of Vera's apartment building. If Erika rang the bell, Vera wouldn't let her in, so she waited. A brown-skinned man with a goatee approached the front door, keys already in his hand. With what looked like a practiced sidelong glance, the kind men learned right after puberty, he checked her out. She shook her handbag and made a distressed sound.

The man unlocked the door and held it open for her.

"Thanks so much." Most men liked to look at her, no matter their age. It often helped.

"Elevator's been acting up." He pressed the button.

"Awful."

It arrived. They stepped inside and he pressed number two. "What floor?"

Erika said, "Three, please." Cover her tracks.

Two pings bleeped as the elevator reached the second floor. The man stepped into the hallway. She pushed four.

Buzzed and scared, operating on less than four hours sleep, she sucked in a steadying breath, wrapped on the door, and spoke in a loud, clear voice. "Good morning, Ms. Moon. It's Erika Smith from the other day."

Brandy barked.

"I have additional information."

Vera cracked the door but left the chain in place. "This time I *am* calling the police."

Erika leaned in, trying to make eye contact through the narrow opening. Good thing Cappy stayed with the car. "They threatened me too. I'm frightened for my life and yours." She paused. Vera said nothing. "Liza is in danger as well."

Vera released the chain. Dressed in loose fitting slacks and a roomy top, her bleary hazel eyes greeted Erika. It occurred to her that Vera might be a stealth drinker.

"Two men came to my home and threatened my husband and me." Brandy stuck her nose out the door. Erika petted her. "I'm certain we're all in danger."

Funny thing about the truth — sometimes it could be an ally. For hours, Erika had tried to figure out a way to elicit Vera's help in finding the digital card. It was the best way to get Creepy-Cappy and Bastard-Bigelow out of their lives. She decided to bring in Vera. Not all the way, of course, but deep enough to gain her trust.

"I can spare forty-five minutes," Vera said. "I have to visit Liza."

"I'll be succinct." Something smelled wonderful, rich, and sweet.

Vera stepped back and let Erika in.

"What is that amazing aroma?"

"I made banana bread this morning. Would you like some?"

With a reluctant shake of her head, Erika declined.

"I'm waiting."

"One of the goons threatened me with a gun."

Vera pulled back. Her right hand flew to her throat.

"He said if I didn't find something of Charlie's, he'd harm my husband and me. He hit my husband over the head with the butt of his weapon and physically hurt me." She kept the nipple-twisting to herself. Too humiliating.

Vera's lips parted. "Is your husband okay?"

Erika had left Griff sitting at the kitchen table with a fresh pot of coffee and two slices of buttered toast. "Groggy, but stable." She paused for effect. "For now."

"What could Charlie possess that they want? Is that why they murdered him?"

"A digital card from one of his cameras."

"Photos?"

"I've been up all night trying to figure this out." With her index finger, Erika pointed to a chair. "May I sit?"

"Of course." Vera sank into the matching upholstered chair. Facing Vera, Erika perched on the other one.

"Charlie and my husband owed money to the wrong people. Still does, as far as I can tell." She shrugged. "Can you think of anything Charlie said that might shed light on this?"

"On what?" Vera bounced up. Brandy raised her head with a low growl. "I don't understand what is happening. What are you asking me?"

"I'm sorry to upset you." Erika folded her hands. "Not my intention."

"Sweet Jesus. A man coming to your home, hurting you and beating up your husband." Vera paced. "What did he do to you?"

Stay with the strategy? "He assaulted me. Grabbed my breast and twisted my nipple." The embarrassment and pain flooded back. Unexpected tears sprang. Erika dabbed at her eyes.

"That is horrible."

"These fuckers are brutal people." *Shit. A slip.* Her public voice lost for a second.

"Language."

Vera said this like a kindergarten schoolteacher chastising a student. Erika suppressed a chuckle.

"I am going to the police station this afternoon. I'll tell them everything." She reached out and touched Erika's arm. "Come with me."

Not good. "Let's look for the card first and bring in the police if we need to." She hoped her argument sounded reasonable.

"A pistol whipping does not constitute *needing to*? Besides, yesterday a man threatened me too."

"Who? What happened?"

"A white man with a barrel chest and bad complexion came to the hospital. He followed me to my car. Do you know him? Is he at your home?"

Not Bigelow or Cappy. "No." *Another "soldier?" What did scaring Vera accomplish? Perhaps they think if Vera is distraught, she'll let me help her.*

Vera stepped forward. "Something is bothering me." Her tone changed, not wary or worried, something different.

"What's that?"

"Yesterday, you asked if the murderers took anything." Vera leveled her gaze on Erika. "Why did you use the plural?"

"Did I? A slip of the tongue." Vera was not as naïve as she appeared. In the future, Erika must be more careful. "I don't know who killed Charlie, but I plan to find out."

The frown on Vera's face deepened. She tucked her lips under.

"With your help, we can solve this," Erika said.

"I am planning another march, like the one we held last month, to get more attention on Charlie's case. Poor turnout and no traction in the media." She gave Erika a frank look. "Do you want to help?"

Oh, no. "Sounds like a lot of work." *Public scrutiny would not be good.* "That's not the best way to solve Charlie's murder."

"I have to do *something*."

"Help me find the digital card."

Vera glanced at her watch. "I am going to be late for Liza."

"This is the best and safest way."

"I am meeting Officer French at three o'clock. She is quite competent."

Erika made note of the name. "*What* will you tell her?"

"I am not sure." She paused and looked up at the urn on the mantle. "Everything."

Erika rose, walked towards Vera's front door. "These people are cruel and ruthless. Don't organize a rally. Tell the police nothing. This is for your protection. Liza's too."

Vera didn't look convinced.

"Look what happened to Charlie."

Chapter 19

Dani

Dani sat on the edge of the bed. The large-faced clock read 8:00 a.m. She'd spent the evening waiting, watching *Blue Bloods* reruns, and worrying. By 2:00, Dani gave up and went to sleep hugging her pillow. She dreamt about killers with blood-caked knives. She woke up thinking about Vera.

What would Mirko say when he came home and found her still here? He despised her lies and drama. Vera said the same thing. Why did Dani draw trouble like a magnet or a bad news sinkhole?

Her stomach growled, so she dragged herself into the kitchen. In case he came home soon, she brewed a small pot of coffee. She thought about her last conversation with Bogie. Even he sounded down on her. The phone call yesterday to explain her change of plans wasn't the best. *"Why do you care so much about a stranger? You're letting a good job go."* How could she tell him she had lied about the job?

Feeling sorry for yourself never fixed things. In fact, it made it harder to find a path out. Dani learned this not from Bogie but from experience. Instead of boo-hooing, she needed to take stock and face facts.

Okay, so chances were, Mirko had moved on from Dani. He probably met someone. The sex the other night meant nothing to him. Whatever the explanation for not coming home, he didn't want her back in his life.

Her stomach rumbled again. Still deep in thought, she opened the refrigerator. Half a dozen eggs, a carton of milk, wheat bread, butter, jam, and a container of orange juice. She pressed the sides of the milk carton's opening and sniffed. Questionable. She put it back.

There was another way to look at things. He'd been sweet to her. And concerned. There were no signs of another woman in the apartment. Not that Dani snooped, but she didn't see a toothbrush or girl stuff in the bathroom. Maybe he crashed with some friends so as not to drive home after a few beers, or he tried to phone her while she slept. She reached for her mobile, checked messages and missed calls. She found a text from Javier sent thirty minutes earlier. *"U okay?"* With quick thumbs, she reassured him and ended with *"R U?"*

Pots and pans nested together in a cabinet under the stove. Dani chose a small frying pan, poured a drip of olive oil, and cracked two eggs. She resumed her mental checklist. She stood on shaky ground with Vera. At least she had agreed to meet Dani this afternoon at the diner. Then what?

Her phone vibrated. Another text from Javier. "Need to talk."

She punched in, "Okay, what's the lowdown?"

He responded, "Later."

Hmmm. Javier kept his worries to himself. "Catch you this afternoon." She signed off and slid her phone back into her back pocket.

She returned to pondering her situation as she ate her breakfast straight out of the pan. A staged crash, for sure. The police case stalled. Perhaps Vera' s visit last night persuaded them to renew their efforts.

She washed the dishes, trying not to worry about Javier. After cleaning up the kitchen, she went into the bathroom. A hot shower made planning easier. It also helped her look at the toughest part of her checklist. She pulled the shower curtain closed and let the water run across and down her body. Steam filled the small space. She breathed in the warm dampness.

Each time she used her looking-at-the-facts technique, it always came down to one truth that trumped all the others. At thirteen, she'd run away again. Bogie drove from college, searched everywhere until he found her sleeping in the local multiplex, a favorite haven, moving from one theater to the other until closing. An all-night diner served until dawn, and the staff let her stay sipping a soda. When Bogie found her this time, her empty stomach ached, and she stank.

He sat her down. “Time for a reality check.” They huddled in his dorm room, a cluttered space with two beds, two desks, two chairs, and posters pinned-to-the-wall of shapely girls in bathing suits and NBA stars dunking. “You're a kid; you gotta go to school.” True enough, but she could go to school anywhere. Their mother moved them at least once a year and always enrolled them. “You pissed off Dad. If you keep doing this, you'll end up in some juvie hell hole.” Her father might let that happen. Then the trump card surfaced. “You can't stay here, you have no money, and you're a minor. It's live with Dad or on the streets.” *Boom*. Dead mother, no money, no rights, no place else to go except with her father, who barely cared about her, and the miserable Missy who cared less. Swept into the system? Not an option. Their mother warned against this. *“They treat you like shit. You'll get raped or murdered.”* Probably not true, but it scared the crap out of her. Honest assessment. Bogie drove Dani home.

Time, once again, to examine the bottom line. Mirko left her and Vera didn't trust her. Moving in with Bogie would never work for more than a few weeks. No job and no place to live. Reality.

Spending so much time in trouble, however, had taught Dani. She knew how to overcome negatives and transform them into something good. It was her super-power. Time to use it.

***

The front door opened. Mirko, dressed in his uniform from the golf store, stared at her. Dani took a deep breath. The apartment smelled like fresh-brewed coffee, dish soap, and Lysol.

“Morning.” Good thing she'd showered and dressed in clean jeans and a purple T-shirt. Mirko once said purple made her eyes glitter.

“You're still here.” He dropped his keys on the table by the door next to Lefty with the unread note still pinned to his stuffed ear. “What happened?”

No job, no place to go. Stick with the plan. “Vera and I need your help.”

"You found her."

Dani followed him into the galley kitchen. "So did the killer." Probably true, so not an actual lie.

"Whoa."

"He tracked her to the hospital. We escaped and went to the cops."

"Escaped?"

Dani told him about Florid Face.

"You think this man killed her son?"

Dani rocked her body, shifting from one foot to the other. "Ms. Moon, Vera, kept trembling from fear. I consoled her." She gnawed her bottom lip. "After a while, she composed herself and managed things well. She's quite brave."

Not for sure, but Mirko seemed a little impressed. He opened the refrigerator and took out the remaining eggs. "What'd the police say?"

For a nanosecond, Dani thought about telling him the truth — Vera sent Dani packing and went to the cops alone. But then she'd have to explain. Plus, she had a plan. "They told me not to leave town." *Bogie wisdom: Good things happen if you help them.* She decided another white lie might get her an invitation to stay with him. "They offered to put me up."

He beat the eggs in a bowl and shoved two slices of bread into the toaster. "And you said?"

"I'd consider it." She rummaged through a cabinet for a clean mug.

He dumped the stirred eggs into the frying pan Dani had cleaned an hour before. "The Holiday Inn?"

"I wish." She poured. "No, some no-tell-motel outside of town." Was there a crummy motel in this upscale county? Dumb thing to say. She watched his expression, trying to anticipate his response. *Lying again. Where? Give me the address. Who are you kidding?*

Mirko kept his head down as he worked on his breakfast. "How are they protecting you two?"

"Check-ins." That sounded plausible, at least for Vera. "While they investigate."

He peered at her. Long, thick eyelashes made it hard to read his expression. She waited and considered her options if Mirko kicked her out. Javier might take her in and let her sleep on his floor, clean and cook for her keep. Sleeping in her car was another possibility. She couldn't leave town.

The toast popped up. Mirko snagged the slices and put them on a plate. He scraped his eggs onto the bread and sat down at the table, barely big enough for two.

Dani joined him. She focused on her physical reactions. Smile. Be upbeat no matter what he said. Don't cry if the news is bad. And under no circumstances, beg.

"Do the police have any clues?" He shook ketchup out of a plastic jar. Flipped one slice of bread on top of the eggs and hefted his sandwich.

"Not so far."

After several bites he said in a soft voice, "You can stay here if you wanna."

It took all her self-control not to jump up and down and holler. "If that's okay."

Used to Mirko's long stretches without a response, Dani let the silence sit.

Finally, he said, "It's hard for me to never know if you're telling the truth."

Dani tried not to look or sound pathetic. "I understand." She watched his Adam's apple slide up and down as he swallowed.

"Promise not to lie."

Dani made that commitment to Vera. Could she keep it to both? Why not start now? "I'm not sure I can, but I swear to try my hardest."

"Growing up, my parents never told me anything. They put a painted face on all their problems." He kept his gaze fixed on his plate.

Dani waited. Seconds ticked by. She asked, "What did they hide from you?"

"I'm telling you this because lies make me nuts. They hurt."

"Something bad happened?"

"Promise me."

Dani bobbed her head with vigor. "Absolutely." Questions swirled in her mind, but she sensed Mirko's reluctance to share more, so she refrained. His mom lived nearby. He never mentioned his father or invited Dani to meet his mother.

Mirko looked straight at her. Several more seconds went by. "You said Vera wants my help?"

Telling the truth was both complicated and simple. "Vera doesn't *know* she needs you... yet." Dani fidgeted. "Mostly though, I do, to help me figure things out."

Another long pause. Dani gnawed on her thumb.

"Tell me everything, and then we'll see."

Excellent.

Chapter 20

Dani

Dani and Mirko planned to begin by going online and researching the murder of Charlie Moon. Mirko took his second cup of coffee to the computer and booted it up. Dani grabbed a folding chair and scooted next to him.

They found dozens of articles reporting much the same information. Charles Moon, a freelance photographer, brutally murdered in his home. Some stories played up the beheading. The scandal-prone-media suggested a shady lifestyle and possible mob connections. Fringe bloggers saw conspiracies since another murder, somewhat similar, occurred in nearby Connecticut the year before. A serial killer on the loose?

"Look at this one. There's Vera leading a rally."

"Not much of one. How many people in that photo?"

Poor Vera. "This is exactly why we have to help her. She can't do this alone."

"I see nothing here that's useful."

"The list of possible perps is long."

He gave her a look and then put his hands on his keyboard. "Go."

"Safari hat. Fat and his teeth stuck out. Before the crash, he had an argument with Florid Face. I'll get to him in a minute. The hat guy stared at Vera's car as he slammed into the sedan ahead. Then the Jeep vanished, and so did he. He saw me..." Should she tell him about the wig and glasses? How to justify that?

"And?"

Dani ignored the question and plowed on. "Then there's Florid Face, like I said. He's the one who scares me the most. On the day of the accident, he wore a fake mustache and a scruffy beard. Shaved a day later. Big chest, no neck. He tried to pull Vera and her daughter from the car and then stalked Vera to and in the hospital. He cornered us in the parking lot."

Mirko stopped typing. "This sounds bad."

"Yaaaa, that's what I've been saying."

"Vera tell the cops this?"

"They said it's all speculation, no proof."

"Okay. Any more potential..." He paused. "... Perps?"

With a balled fist, she play-punched his arm. "Another possible *doe*r is the silver-haired dude in the sedan. He acted dazed or injured. Disappeared as well."

"Really? Come on, Dani. Stick to the facts."

"I am. The driver, a thin guy with an evil glare, dragged silver-hair from the scene. By the time the police started their canvass, no sedan, no Jeep."

"What does Vera have to add?"

Good question. "She said a woman came to her house asking questions. We're supposed to get together this afternoon at the diner. Once she meets you and sees how smart you are, she'll want us both to help her."

Mirko's brow creased. He shook his head and almost grinned, a twitch around the corners of his mouth. So that must be good. Things were on the upswing.

Then his doorbell rang.

***

She looked older than Mirko, too old, but Dani had to admit, hated to in fact, kinda attractive. Dark curls hung down to her shoulders, full lips, dewy-brown skin, and round honey-brown eyes fringed with thick-mascaraed-lashes. Okay, attractive. She also seemed familiar.

"Sorry to crash in on you like this," she said.

Mirko leaned in and pecked her cheek. "Not a problem."

With her arm extended towards Dani, she walked deeper into the apartment. A French manicure adorned graceful fingers. "I'm Stephanie Mack."

"Dani." They shook hands.

Stephanie dropped a huge leather tote onto the scatter rug. "Save me. I'm going to flunk out if you don't."

To Dani, Stephanie didn't sound as upset as her words suggested.

Mirko said, "Sure," sounding all goofy-like.

Stephanie plopped onto the love seat, put her feet up on the ottoman. "This computer class is kicking my butt." She laughed. "I have a test in three hours and wondered if you'd walk me through the most important points. I'm such an idiot with technology."

He explained to Dani, "Stephanie works for Channel Twelve News."

Ah. One of the field reporters with a microphone in front of a local fire or dipping a ruler into two feet of snow, telling the viewers information they already knew.

Stephanie said, "Trying to graduate. Can't make it without this genius." She jerked her thumb in Mirko's direction.

When she smiled, Dani saw perfect white teeth, even, and well-spaced. Caps for sure.

"I gotta do this," Mirko said to Dani. "We can talk more later, okay?"

"I have to meet Vera."

"That's right." He thumped his forehead. "I forgot."

Forgot? Really?

"I'll catch up with you at the diner." He offered a shrug like an apology.

"She's in danger."

In a tone changed from flirty to professional, Stephanie asked, "Who is?"

"Long story," Mirko said.

"I like sagas."

"Dani witnessed that big pile-up on Main Street."

"Lots of mystery around that one — hit and run, I heard."

"And the women involved..."

"The Moon family."

"Yeah. Dani's friends with the mother."

Throughout this exchange, Stephanie's gaze stayed focused on Dani. "Is there a relationship between the accident and the murder?"

Stephanie might help them. Reporters enjoyed connections to the right people and had access to special research resources. But Dani didn't desire Stephanie's assistance. Totally the opposite. She wanted Stephanie out of Mirko's life.

Dani lifted her shoulders and hands, palms up. "Anyway, I gotta run." She forced a breezy tone. "So, I can leave my suitcase, backpack, and cooler here?"

Stephanie sent a questioning look toward Mirko that appeared part interested, and part amused.

"Dani's squatting here for a few days."

Squatting?

The almost pout reemerged. "Don't mean to intrude."

Ha.

To Dani, Stephanie said, "Here's my card. Let me know if you uncover anything interesting. The press can be a friend." Without waiting for a reply, Stephanie returned her attention to Mirko. "Got anything to drink?"

"Diet Coke?"

My Cokes? That's why he kept a stash? Argh. She snatched up her bag. "Okay, see ya. Nice meeting you."

No response, not even a wave from either of them.

Chapter 21

Vera

Vera pulled into the circular driveway. She planned to go to the hospital this morning, meet Dani at lunchtime, and to the police station at three when Officer French came on duty. Finding Charlie's digital memory card, however, eclipsed everything. After a call to the hospital, and a chat with Liza, Vera drove to Sam's.

The two-story colonial, including an acre of land, sat on a cul-de-sac. To the right, a wooded lot abutted the plot. On the left, another home's green side lawn edged Sam and Liza's less healthy grass.

Workers dressed in paint-and-dirt splattered overalls emptied their truck of ladders, buckets, and tools. How much did all these renovations cost? Seemed like an excessive amount of work just to sell the place. She counted five people moving across the lawn. Odd, since Sam and Liza completed a major renovation a few years ago. He could afford it, of course. Real estate in the area, stable for years, began appreciating faster over the last eighteen months. The pandemic sent millennials out of the city to the suburbs, buying first time homes and city dwellers in search of less congestion. At least Sam and Liza would get a good price for it, which would help perpetually broke Liza. Thinking about her youngest daughter caused Vera's spirits to sag.

She caught herself. She had work to do. Composing her expression, she straightened up.

A tall, fit man spoke to the workers, gesturing with his hands, his sleeveless vest accentuating tight forearms and biceps. Vera climbed out of her rental and thought about her excuse for entering the house.

"Good morning."

The man swung around, all grace and rhythm, as muscles flexed and rippled under his skin. "May I help you?"

She put out her hand with a straight arm. "Vera Moon, Sam Davis' mother-in-law."

He shook her hand with a firm single shake. "Benny Lopez. What can I do for you?"

Vera acted as if she belonged. "I assumed Sam told you I would be by."

"No." He sounded more wary than hostile.

In a breezy tone she said, "Picking up a few things."

"Mr. Davis never said."

"Have you started the work?"

"First full day."

"Sam speaks highly of you." Vera gave him her most self-assured smile. "I will be less than five minutes."

"I guess it's okay." He still sounded unsure.

She handed him her driver's license. "Contact Sam. He will explain."

With a quick glance, he examined her license before returning it. "Five minutes?"

"Promise."

***

The basement smelled of wet paint. The oily scent of turpentine drifted down from the floors above. Vera coughed. The string to the bare bulb swayed from her pull. Dust particles filtered down from the light shaft like a miniature blizzard.

A photographer's black umbrella and two white ones, opened as if waiting for subjects, stood in one corner. A tripod lay on the concrete floor. Charlie's equipment, for sure. No cameras in view.

Up against the adjoining wall, a work sink stained with yellow, green, and blue splotches sat under a half-window high up the wall. Diffuse morning light seeped through the panes. Where would Charlie stash something both small and important? Erika described it as a digital card from a camera. Vera walked to the water heater and boiler in the far corner; her cushioned soles made no sound.

Nothing suggested a hiding spot. She poked her head around the two fat cylinders. Only grunge. Coming back to the umbrellas and tripod, she ran her hand along their edges. Dust coated her fingers. How she missed her sweet boy. On Sundays, he bought her flowers because Vincent used to — tiger lilies, orchids, and irises in the spring and summer, red berries, and holly at Christmas. Why kill him? And why were men trying to hurt her? If only Vincent were alive. He would sip his coffee and she her tea and together find answers.

Benny called from above. "You find what you're searching for?"

"Oh."

"Thought I heard you talking to someone." Long legs in paint-stained boots clambered down. "Need help moving things?"

Vera covered her mouth and swallowed. *Was I speaking aloud?* Tears gathered.

"You okay?"

She pressed her fingers on either side of the bridge of her nose. "Memories." She sniffed. "My son... he died."

"I heard about that. The killing a few months back." Benny shuffled his feet. "Sorry for your loss."

"Thank you." Everyone expressed sympathy, but no one was helping her find his murderer. Dani entered her mind, and then Erika intruded. Whom to trust?

"We made a quick sweep. Only saw that old photo equipment." He pointed to the pile. "Is that what you're looking for?"

"Yes, and a few other things."

"Take your time." He thundered back up the steps.

Vera blew her nose and straightened her spine and shoulders. She reminded herself that three months wasn't a long time. Of course, the pain was still close to the surface. With a slow step, she walked over to a tarp and lifted a corner. Under it she spied a clear plastic carton. She tugged the tarp, clicked the carton cover off and flipped through the dozens of folders, reading the labels as she searched. *Allan family shoot, Holiday Inn Christmas, Hudson Valley Crafts, Max Tannenbaum's Hanukkah Celebration*. She grabbed a stack of files and sifted through them. Tucked into a thick folder labeled Mansion article, another folder seemed misplaced among pictures of houses. *Griff and Erika Noble*. She stopped.

Erika Smith, Erika Noble — the same? Vera slipped the papers out of the manila sleeve and shuffled through them. Invoices and work orders dated back several years. She spilled the contents onto the concrete floor. Three, four-by-six, black and white photos of Erika spread out in an arc. In one, she smiled over her right shoulder. The strapless dress and diamond stud earrings suggested a formal ball. A man with long silver hair showed up in several. The pictures of Erika, however, outnumbered those of the man, and some were intimate poses. One in a bikini, close-up, full lips parted. So, Erika told the truth. Charlie and Erika knew each other. He had taken the last from a distance. Erika held a half-empty glass of red wine, her head bent forward and down. The silver-haired man stood next to her, peering over her head toward something or someone beyond the camera's lens. Vera turned it over. No notations. She put the papers and photos back into the folder and slid it into the plastic container. Deep in thought, Vera checked the rest of the tabs. She ran her fingers along the inside of each file. Nothing else of interest emerged.

She sat back on her haunches. Erika lied about her last name, but not her first. Was she in danger as she claimed? Almost absently, Vera retrieved three photographs and slid them into her bag. She swung her head from side-to-side. What was she looking for exactly? Footsteps clomped across the floor above her, making her look up.

That's when she spotted it.

A strong box lay squirreled high up and to the left of the top step on a shelf almost hidden from view unless your sight line landed just so. She climbed the steps, held onto the bannister, and stretched her arm. Leaning as far over the railing as possible, she extended her fingers. First one, then two, then three touched the box. She inched it out of its concealed spot and grasped the handle.

Muffled voices, sharp-toned, intruded from upstairs. Vera shook the heavy box. The contents rattled and clunked. With a hard pull, she tried to open the container. Locked.

Benny's voice, this time clear, cut into the fetid air.

"You can't be here. I have to call Mr. Davis."

The visitor's response was too low for Vera to hear. Her heart rate sped up. Had someone followed her? Beads of sweat popped out on her forehead. She was being paranoid again. The visitor could be anyone.

Benny's voice again. "You gotta leave, sir." He sounded distressed.

What if the person came because of her? She needed help. Officer French? Detective Monroe? Suppose the contents incriminated Charlie? Erika failed to tell Vera the complete story. Vera sensed it. Dani? She was resourceful, and so far, the only person who helped Vera without an obvious agenda.

Vera decided. Find Dani and ask for her help. First, she had to sneak the box out of the house undetected. She shrugged out of her windbreaker, wrapped it around the box and pressed it into the crook of her arm. Then she slung her purse over her shoulder and pushed open the basement door. "Benny?"

Sweet Jesus, the other voice came from Florid Face, now standing toe-to-toe with Benny.

Vera prayed the jacket looked natural. Her hands shook. "Thanks, Benny." It came out like a squawk. Vera cleared her throat. "I will send someone around to pick up the equipment. It's too much for me to carry alone." She didn't look at the intruder. "I will let Mr. Davis know how helpful you were." Determined to leave, she kept moving. Florid Face's glare followed her. She stopped and swung around on wobbly legs to face Benny. "Do you mind walking me to my car? I am a bit unsteady."

"Sure."

Vera worked to keep her expression unruffled. *What was Florid Face doing here?* "Going up to sixty-degrees today." She hoped that explained the windbreaker still bulked between her left arm and chest.

Benny cupped his hand under her elbow. "Okay?"

"Yes, thank you very much."

Turning toward Florid Face, Benny extended his right arm. "After you."

They all walked to the front door. Several workers passed by them, their eyes sliding over the threesome. *Good. Witnesses.*

Florid Face said, "Charlie Moon borrowed something from me. I need it back."

It sounded like a threat. "I have no idea what you are talking about." Her voice cracked like a pubescent boy.

Benny stepped in. "This is news to me." He met Vera's distressed gaze. "I want to hear it from Mr. Davis. Meanwhile, you gotta go. This is private property."

Pointing his finger at Vera, Florid Face said to Benny, "She knows me." He twisted toward Vera. "You better give me my stuff." The threat was now clear.

Chapter 22

Erika

Erika felt a damn sight better. After making a strong case for gaining intelligence, Cappy let her out of the cage for three fleeting hours and Erika intended to enjoy each one.

A server walked by with a tray of filled champagne flutes. Erika lifted one, breathed in the bouquet, and took a sip. Kate Lavender hosted the best fundraisers, the best parties. Who else could get a crowd like this on a Monday afternoon? Of course, it helped that her husband, Hugh, twenty-years her senior and a Wall Street wolf, was running for governor.

Kate's opulence dazzled. The ballroom overflowed with towering vases filled with cascading floral arrangements. A beveled mirror reflected the light from a hanging crystal chandelier. The canapés, passed by wait staff, included caviar, bite-sized quiches, shrimp, skewered roast beef, chicken, and pork. A buffet of exotic cheeses, breads, dips, and fruit ringed the room. A temporary dais, erected for the event, stood against the far wall. Two staffed and well-stocked bars occupied opposite corners of the room. Woody Wells, planted in front of one of them, beckoned Erika with a wag of his finger.

Asshole. If anyone witnessed that, Erika would scream. So common. He signaled again, this time moving the finger with urgency. She took her time.

Woody was a past mistake. Griff had disappeared again into one of his drug-fogs. Woody made the local charity circuit without his wife in tow. Not handsome, or particularly cultured, but accomplished, smart, and fit. Those were his best qualities. Loud, controlling, and just an okay lover erased the appeal. After two months, she broke it off. Then Charlie swept into her life.

She made her way over to Woody's spot.

"You're looking good," he said. The tan suit, bronze tie, and pale-yellow shirt hung elegantly on his six-foot, 180-pound frame. "Been a minute."

Erika wanted to say, *lower your fucking voice*. "Thanks. You too."

"I said it's been awhile."

A server, balancing a tray of cut-crystal glasses, half of them filled with Chardonnay and the other half with Shiraz, came up to them. Erika placed her empty Champagne flute on the tray and lifted a glass of the red wine. "I heard you." She took a sip.

"Ouch."

She lowered her glass. "Something in particular?"

He loosened his tie knot and stretched his neck. "Yeah, as a matter of fact."

She waited. An acquaintance waved to her from across the room. Erika tipped her head in the woman's direction.

"I'm keeping you?" he asked, the sarcasm clear.

"Please tell me what is so urgent that you'd flag me over, not come to me like a gentleman, and then not get to it."

"That's why you're mad? I *flagged* you?"

Erika gave him her condescending, no-teeth smile.

"I heard your name."

"And?" Erika attended the luncheon to unwind, get away from her fucking minders, and breathe in the distinctive scents of wealth and sophistication. Woody's presence clouded her pleasure. Plus, time was zipping by. Bigelow expected her to garner helpful info. He doubted her but let her come anyway. Time to get to it. "What made hearing my name so important?"

Woody leaned forward. She smelled the Chardonnay on his breath and hoped hers was not equally unpleasant.

"I miss you."

"So, you're lying. No one mentioned me." None of her affairs ended well. She needed to take more care.

"I got here early, me and the caterers. I wandered around checking out the place. I mean, this is a fucking palace."

"I've seen it." She kept her tone ice cold. "Many times."

"Yeah, well, I ran into our host during an intense argument with a man. Lavender kept finger stabbing the guy's fat gut."

Erika arched her eyebrows.

"Lavender said, *you fucked up*. Called the guy incompetent."

"What does that have to do with me?"

"I'm getting to that."

Erika shot him a look.

"I thought I should move on before he spotted me, but then he said *that scammer Charlie Moon* — the guy who got murdered a few months back."

"Charlie?"

"You knew him?"

"You're still not telling me how my name came into the conversation." Erika touched the base of her throat and dabbed at the moisture coating her skin.

"I started to walk away, but then I heard your name. You still affect me." He winked. "Griff's too. Erika and Griff, Lavender said."

"Can you be a bit more specific? Our names regarding what?" She faked casual interest, but inside her worry gnawed.

"He said, *If Erika and Griff fail* or something like that. The guy with the gut looked up and caught my eye. I beat it."

Who fucked up and why would Hugh Lavender be in a heated conversation about Charlie, Erika, and Griff? If we fail? Does Lavender have something to do with the missing digital card? "Did you recognize the other man?"

"You sleeping with Lavender?"

"Of course not." Woody was a mistake that kept coming back, like a rotten meal. "Is Hugh like that?"

"He's a man, and you're hot."

Erika smoothed her new suit along her thighs, its lightweight wool silky to her touch. She'd bought it a month ago in anticipation of this event. One always showed up at a Lavender fundraiser in a new outfit.

She repeated her question. "Did you catch the name of the other man in the argument?"

"Not an argument. Lavender reamed him and the guy just stood there."

Erika, ever conscious of her public persona, sucked in her breath in disapproval.

"Sorry. Schooled. Is that better?"

"Can you describe him?"

"Big fella. Enormous head with bad buck teeth."

Bigelow. The physical memory of the fucking-ape wrenching her nipple was palpable.

"You okay? This info means something to you?"

"Great seeing you again. Please give my best to your *wife*."

"You can be one cruel..."

Erika left before he finished his sentence. Bigelow and Hugh talking about Charlie, Erika, and Griff. Erika spotted Kate Lavender speaking with a small circle of women across the room. Without thinking it all out, she walked over and joined the group.

"Lovely to see you," Kate Lavender said.

She looked stunning. Ash-blonde hair in a perfect French twist, diamond earrings, purple Shantung silk two-piece dress that skimmed her curves.

"You remember Mildred and Loretta."

With a nod of recognition, Erika smiled at the other two guests.

The four chatted about nothing for a few minutes. "Kate, may I speak with you?"

Kate appeared a bit startled, but she recovered quickly. "Please excuse us."

The two women stepped away.

"Is everything all right? How is Griff doing?"

Her tone made Erika cringe. Everyone seemed aware of Griff's fucking drug habit. Was she an object of pity or ridicule? "He's great. Thanks for asking."

Kate, rather than focusing on Erika, peered over Erika's shoulder with darting eyes.

Erika understood. The hostess checked out the crowd, probably looking for a more important guest to greet. "It's a small thing, really," Erika said, keeping judgement from her tone. "Can you tell me about Hugh's relationship with a man named Bigelow?"

Kate made eye contact. "I don't understand."

"Does Hugh know him well?"

"Of course."

With no idea where to go next, Erika waited, hoping Kate might volunteer more.

"Nate Bigelow works for Hugh."

"How so?"

Kate's face scrunched. "Hugh owns Oak Lane car service. Is there a problem?"

"No. Not at all. I'm sorry to trouble you. Someone seeking a reference asked me about him." Erika heard herself babbling. "I thought I'd ask Hugh."

"And not Griff?"

Thinking fast, Erika said, "A second opinion."

"I can't say that I like Nate, but the car service seems to do well."

This new information swirled in Erika's mind. Griff met Bigelow and Lavender through the car service, the business she believed Griff owned out right. She shifted her strategy. "Such a wonderful event."

Kate's facial muscles relaxed, and her eyes widened. "We've raised $650,000 already, and the auction hasn't started yet."

"Bravo."

"It's all for the children."

"Congrats."

Kate's normally tight smile spread into a grin.

Erika pivoted. "May I ask one last question?"

Kate's mouth collapsed into its practiced pose. "Yes?"

"Did you and Hugh know Charlie Moon?"

A local news celebrity climbed the three short steps to the dais and grabbed the mike. "Good afternoon, everyone."

Kate said, "I have to go. The program is starting."

"Yes, of course."

Kate patted her hair.

"Perfect." With strained self-control, Erika quieted her hands and kept her smile in place.

"Charlie took terrific photographs. Such a tragedy." She slipped out a compact, flipped it open, and grinned into its mirror, obviously checking her teeth for food or lipstick. "He took all of our family portraits."

The celebrity host said, "May I introduce our incredible and generous hosts, Kate and Hugh Lavender."

Kate marched to the dais leaving Erika behind. The Lavenders mounted the three riser steps to the podium. Hugh beamed at the audience. His Roman nose, wide-set blue eyes, and firm chin made an appealing, if not handsome, face. Dark suit, American flag lapel pin, white shirt, and politician red-and-white striped tie added to his image of a confident and successful executive. A man to trust.

Erika turned to go. For as long as she knew him, what he projected seemed consistent with his character. Now she realized there was more to his story.

***

Erika dreaded going home. She'd left Griff napping, *again*. Cappy wouldn't look for her for another hour. They expected her to come back with intelligence about the location of the digital card from one of Charlie's cameras, information she didn't have. She gained new, disturbing facts. Their meaning, however, still eluded her.

"Can I get your vehicle for you, miss?" A lanky young man in an orange-and-white uniform extended his hand toward her. "Got your ticket?"

She pulled out a blue stub and handed it to him.

"Just be a few minutes." He took off at a trot.

Bigelow worked for Hugh. Was Hugh the one in charge, demanding Erika find the digital card via Bigelow, or was Hugh an innocent in all of this? He said Bigelow fucked up. How? Something with Oak Lane? But why mention Erika? The crash? He called Charlie a scammer. None of it made sense. Yet.

She surveyed her surroundings. Cultivated trees and flowers lined the driveway on either side. Although the luncheon guests numbered at least one hundred, no vehicles marred the vista. Erika had no idea where the Lavenders hid fifty or more cars. To possess that kind of money, not pretend money, up-to-your-fucking-ears in debt money like Erika and Griff. Never be hungry, cold, or afraid. Why would someone with Hugh's assets and stature in the community risk it all by being involved with shit-eating, reprobates?

Then another thought pushed forward. A thought that chilled her. What might he do to her if she uncovered his reasons? As Erika said to Vera, look what happened to Charlie.

Chapter 23

Hugh

Perspiration ran down Hugh Lavender's face, stinging his eyes. He'd forgotten his sweatband. The NYU T-shirt clung to him. He grabbed the small towel draped over the dashboard of the elliptical-machine and wiped his face.

Forty-five minutes down, fifteen to go.

He tried not to watch the clock, but his anxiety and impatience soared. The charity luncheon had gone well. Monday events had no competition, and lots of folks sought to curry favor with the governor-to-be. Unfortunately, it started poorly with Nate Bigelow showing up minutes before the first guests. Hugh's anger surged again, his face flush from both the workout and the memory of the bumbling Bigelow. The car accident was an ill-conceived plan. Hugh expected Bigelow to confront Vera, get her to stop her stupid rallies, and get out of town. Why would anyone stay in that apartment? He pulled the towel from around his neck and wiped his face. How could an accident accomplish that? *Put it behind you. There are more pressing matters requiring action.*

Most days, Hugh exercised at home first thing in the morning. Kate set up a well-equipped gym, including a ballet barre and wall mirror, punching bag, spin bike, and sound system. Two treadmills and two elliptical machines along with a dozen free weights gave both enough options. This afternoon, however, Hugh worked-out in the Sawmill Club — a large facility near the Holiday Inn in Mount Kisco. He kept a membership for exactly this purpose — a meeting under the radar.

Anna Vernon waved as she walked past him. She usually dressed in fitted suits and heels, so Hugh almost missed her in her sweats and sneakers, or *trainers,* as she and her fellow Brits called them. Cinnamon-colored skin, mahogany eyes, and curly, sandy-brown hair tied back. She strode across the floor. Anna, one of the smartest political operatives he knew, surprised him since she didn't grow up in American politics. Born and raised in London, the daughter of Jamaican physicians, Anna immigrated to the United States to attend college and never went back. They met at NYU Law, and they'd been friendly colleagues ever since. Having an intelligent Black woman on his team helped him understand that part of his constituency and look inclusive to the liberal down-state voters. Of course, among his biggest supporters, he kept her role as invisible as possible. Some people in his circle would not like it — tricky balancing act.

The campaign's conscience, as Hugh thought about her, she exhibited a strong moral core, asked the tough questions, and kept them from going too far astray. Tom "Rake" Ratchette came off less savvy but able to roll in the mud when necessary. Between them, they recommended strategy, messaging, and solved problems. Today, Hugh needed them both.

On cue, Rake arrived. Like Anna, he'd dressed for a fake workout. He joined Anna at the free weights, grabbed two ten-pound dumbbells, and executed a few lateral lifts for show. Rake stood almost as tall as Hugh; slim and wiry with perceptive, coffee-brown eyes.

Mopping his face and head, Hugh finished and walked over to them. He watched his reflection grow in the mirrored wall, red-faced and glistening. "We've got a problem."

"Hello to you too." The tinge of reprimand in her tone countered Anna's smile.

Few people felt brave enough to tease Hugh. He'd made his bones in high-stakes venture capital. Known for his temper, he also earned a reputation for swift and terrible revenge whenever crossed. New to politics when he decided to run, he called Anna first. After practicing law for years, she'd pivoted and helped elect several mayors and a senator. When Hugh reached out, she dove in; cleaned up his image and chiseled down his sharp edges.

Rake asked, "What's the deal?" He eased the barbells back onto their stand.

Hugh debated how much to tell them. Enough to get their advice and help him out of the corner he'd painted himself into but not so much that they'd learn the reasons for the blackmail.

"I made a mistake and brought lowlifes into my sphere. Now they're crapping over everything and putting the campaign at risk." When Hugh first declared his candidacy, his interest was more an idea than a real quest. As time went by, winning the office became a passion.

Anna's forehead puckered. "How low and how bad?"

"Nate Bigelow is an ex-felon. He runs my limo service."

"And?"

"He's been taking care of a personal problem for me, a less-than-clean one."

Rake said, "Not doing a good job of it?"

"Exactly."

With all ten fingers, Rake scratched the stubble on both his cheeks. "What do you need from us?"

"If things hit the press, a fast turnaround to spin it. I gotta distance myself from Nate and his posse." He paced and weighed his options. "Should I sell Oak Lane? Make a big deal about not knowing Nate's history?"

"Let me look into that," Rake said. "See how quickly we can dump it."

"I got a lot of money tied up there."

Anna raised an eyebrow.

"More than the obvious." No reason to share the amount of cash he funneled through the car service; money that gave him leverage rather than raise red flags with the government.

"Will getting rid of it spook this Nate person? Sounds a bit dodgy to me," Anna said.

"I got this." Rake sounded offended.

Anna said to Hugh, "Can't you give us more details? We're flying without our instrument panel."

Once again, Hugh considered how much to share. "There's more than being associated with the car service." Better to plunge in rather than ease a toe at a time. "I'm being blackmailed."

"Shit," Rake said. "About what?"

"Can't tell you."

Anna pursed her lips. "Hugh, how can we help you if you..."

He cut her off. "Dump Oak Lane and contain Nate Bigelow. Be ready for blow back."

Neither her tone nor her expression suggested offense. "I can work on a story. You gave this guy a break. You believe in redemption." Anna paused before sharing the punchline. "He betrayed you."

"Like it." Hugh nodded.

Rake picked up the narrative. "You're stunned by his accusations, which aren't true."

That was the snag. If the damn thing got out, then no spin would help him. He had to get the video at all costs and pay off Nate and his crew. Could he silence Griff with more money and scare Erika enough to make her run? The Moon woman represented a loose end and potential threat. Less so if Nate found the pictures before she did. Hugh worried when she held a big rally about her son's murder. The walk fizzled. But her next idea, whatever that was, might work. Nate's bungled attempts to scare her away were not working.

"Get the ball rolling on the sale and make sure Bigelow doesn't get wind of it. Plant a few seeds about his instability from unidentified sources." Hugh's confidence bounced back. He hated not having a workable plan. He turned to Anna. "Let's get a story out about my support of rehabilitation programs and the importance of not seeing prison as a revolving door. More apt punishment stippled with hope."

***

Shaved and showered, Hugh headed back to the house for a light dinner with Kate. Nate had better wrap things up, fast. Ever since Charlie's murder, Hugh stayed on edge, waiting for the other shoe to drop. No, not shoe, *shoes,* a wall of them.

He trusted few people, Griff Noble least of all. Half the time he appeared harmless and drug addled. Other times, he seemed crafty, with a secret agenda. Threatening Erika provided the best way to press him. From what Hugh saw, and Bigelow concurred, Griff loved her.

Hopefully, he loved her enough.

That brought the Moon woman to mind. He'd have to up the ante there too. Offer a carrot. But if that flopped, she'd suffer his mighty stick.

Chapter 24

Dani

The Malibu's idling engine rumbled. Mirko's goofy act around Stephanie could mean anything. With the heels of her palms, Dani banged the steering wheel and then bumped her forehead on its edge. *Bogie wisdom*: *Suck it up or suck it down. Don't let it ferment.*

Her phone vibrated. Taking in a deep breath, she glanced at the screen. "Hi, Vera." She hoped she sounded upbeat.

"Are you using that caller ID thing? I have to get that."

"And a twenty-first-century phone too?"

"You sound better now than when you first picked-up."

Dani gave a genuine laugh, small and quick. "You all right?"

"We need to talk." Her tone became agitated. "I found something."

"A clue?"

"I'm not sure."

"Where?"

"Where did I find it?"

"Okay." Dani strung out each syllable.

"At my daughter's house."

"*Where* do you want to meet?" Dani clarified.

"You mentioned a diner."

"Gus's on Route 117. Do you know it?"

"Ten minutes?" Vera asked.

"Deal."

Lifting one butt cheek, Dani slipped her phone into her pocket. A taxi rattled by. A guy on a bike, his body angled right, took the corner.

Think positive, act with purpose. Things might work out with Mirko. One more glance at Mirko's window, the blinds slanted open, but she couldn't see anything. *Like what? Them getting naked?* She stuck the key into the ignition. No fermenting here.

***

The diner stood back from the road. Parking spaces lined the front and right side. Several vehicles filled the spots closest to the door. Dani locked the car, jogged up the three steps, and entered the short, narrow lobby. Bacon, eggs, hash browns, and syrup-soaked pancake aromas hung in the air. Large plastic covered menus flopped forward out of a too-small holder fastened to the wall on her right. She stepped into the diner proper. Straight ahead stood a long counter with twelve stools, several occupied with eating, newspaper-reading men, their hunched backs to Dani.

Larry, a lanky male in his mid-forties, approached her. "Welcome back. Been a while."

When things were good, Mirko and Dani met there regularly. "How've you been?"

"Can't complain. Who'd listen?" He chuckled at the oft-told joke and grabbed a menu. "One, or are you expecting another?"

"Meeting a friend."

"No one's asked for you, yet." Larry lifted a second menu, examined it, and scraped an unrecognizable substance off with his thumbnail. "Want to wait at the counter?"

The door opened behind her. Dani swung around. "Vera."

Disheveled, her curly hair matted on one side, she had a bulky jacket slung over her right arm. "Let's find a quiet corner."

"No problemo," said Larry. "This way, ladies."

He led them to the left, away from the few customers in the main dining area and offered the last booth in a row. They thanked him and ordered tea and a Diet Coke.

"Anything else?" Larry asked. "Apple pie just came out the oven."

The two women gave each other a knowing nod, and both smiled. "With vanilla ice cream?" Dani asked.

"You got it."

Larry took their menus and sauntered towards the kitchen, just behind the counter. He pushed open the swinging doors with his right shoulder. They swished back and forth behind him.

Vera unwrapped her jacket and placed a rectangular metal box on the table. "I found this hidden at Liza's house where Charlie kept a few of his things." She ran her right hand over the top — smooth skin taut over swollen fingers and knuckle joints. "The stalker from the hospital showed up and tried to get it, but I got away."

"For real?"

Vera's left hand trembled. She placed the right one over it. "They are after something related to Charlie's murder."

Dani leaned forward. "Did you open it?"

"No. Not yet."

"We're safe here," Dani said. Vera's caramel skin looked ashen. "I promise."

Larry approached their booth again, this time carrying flatware, napkins, tea, soda, and two apple pies a la mode.

Vera draped her jacket over the box. She slipped it off the table and onto the space next to her.

After arranging the food and drinks on the tabletop, Larry said, "Anything else I can do for you?"

Dani said, "We're working on a super sensitive project that requires absolute privacy."

"No worries. I'll fill tables as far from you as possible." He laughed. "Not that we've got a line or anything."

Dani gave him a broad smile. "You're the best."

She scooped up a forkful of pie. "Let's see what Charlie hid." She slid an ice-cream-covered bite into her mouth. The pie tasted just sweet enough. "You need to try this."

Vera placed the box back on the table.

Dani eyed the three-digit lock with rotating discs. "We need the combination."

"We both use the same code for our phones and passwords so maybe..." Vera twirled each disc. "Not the safest practice." It clicked open. She lifted the lid of the box and peeked in. With one hand over her mouth, she slammed it shut with the other.

"What's wrong?" Dani dropped her fork, leapt up and scooted around to Vera's side of the booth. "Let me see."

It lay on its side in a battered leather holster, its ribbed brown handle visible.

Dani's gaze darted about the diner. She pulled the box between them on the seat, unhooked the holster and slid the gun out, keeping it low in the container and out of view of anyone passing by. "It's heavy." She read *Glock* engraved on the barrel. A battered cardboard box, its edges crumpled, held twelve bullets. "Did you know Charlie owned this?"

"Of course not." The tremor in Vera's voice matched the vibrations of her hands.

Dani held herself still.

Finally, Vera said, "A woman came to see me." She told Dani about Erika. "She claimed Charlie and her husband had illegal dealings, which cannot be so. Plus, men she described as thugs were holding her hostage, which might be true."

"I told you someone staged the accident."

"How could they be sure I would be there at that moment? Why now and not right after the murder?"

Dani twisted her mouth right and left and then right again. "Anything happen out of the ordinary on the day of the crash?" Her right leg executed a rapid-fire pump.

"We held a yard sale. I helped my daughter move out of her home."

Dani angled her body toward Vera. "The house where you found this box, right?"

Vera nodded.

"That might be the trigger."

"Liza complained about a creepy man hanging around." Vera's face collapsed. "I saw him. Malevolent eyes."

"Florid Face?"

"Now that you mention it, it is possible."

"Maybe he started following you then, or alerted someone."

"Why hurt me?"

Dani contemplated the gun and bullets. "Puzzling, for sure." She slid the gun back into its holster and snapped it closed.

"Do you think they were trying to harm Liza?"

Dani bit into her right thumb. "Was Liza in the know about Charlie's other life?"

"He did *not* have another life."

"Sorry. Anyway, at the hospital, Florid Face seemed only interested in you, not Liza." Dani brightened. *Bogie wisdom: Walk away from the problem and give it space. Answers will come faster when you don't press the questions.* "What else is in there?"

Vera shoved her plate aside, melted vanilla ice cream pooled around the pie wedge. Using two fingers, she withdrew the rest of the box's contents. She spread five photographs across the table.

"That's Erika. These are racier than the others I found." Bare-breasted, close-ups of swollen pink nipples, another of Erika on her stomach, her naked bottom the obvious object of the shot.

Dani stared at the photos. "Wow. She's sexy."

"Disgusting is more like it." Once again Vera's voice trembled like earthquake aftershocks.

"Blackmail pictures?"

"No."

"How come?"

"They were lovers."

***

Vera told Dani the rest of Erika's story. She went into detail about finding the first set of photographs, discovering the box, and finally Florid Face's threat.

"I did not want to believe Charlie and this married... woman..." Her voice trailed off again. She dug her fingers into her temples and rubbed.

Dani wrapped her right arm around Vera. "This is good news."

She lifted her face and swiveled her neck in Dani's direction. "Nothing about this is cause for celebration."

"We're getting closer to the truth. Erika's the key, and now we have these pictures..." Dani poked at the photos. "... to take to her and demand more information. This is great."

"And the pistol?"

"Can you shoot?"

"Yes. My husband owned a gun and taught me."

"Then keep it. We may need it."

Chapter 25

Dani

At the sound of laughter, Dani glanced up. True to his word, Larry sent the new arrivals to the other side. Dani sorted through the photographs again. She paused over a close-up of Charlie and Erika, heads together, grinning into the lens. "A selfie?"

"What is a selfie?"

"Really?"

"Don't make fun of me."

"When people take photos of themselves, holding the camera in front of them."

"I knew that." Vera cracked a smile. "Charlie had a timer. He set up the shot, put it on delay, and then ran in front to get into the frame." Her grin grew wider. "See, selfies are not anything new." She took the photo from Dani's hand. "They seem happy."

"Did he love her?"

Vera slid her index finger over Charlie's face. "No."

"Why not?"

"You would not understand."

"You keep saying that. Try me."

"He always dated Black women. I shouldn't care. Liza's husband is a white man, and I like him."

"You like me."

"No, I mean yes, of course. I do. It's not about friendships..." Her voice trailed off.

"You can like anyone but not marry them?"

"When you put it like that." She heaved her shoulders. "But a white married woman?"

"You can't always choose who you love." She thought about Mirko. "And people don't have to love you back."

"You are right. Blessed by forty-five years of marriage when my husband died." Vera picked up all the pictures and put them back in the box. "Loved him from thirteen years old."

"Get out." Dani had met no one who'd stayed married for that long. She found it hard to imagine. "How'd he die?"

"He got colon cancer, and it metastasized."

"Huh?"

"Spread to other organs. We were sure he would die from it. Instead, one day after chemo, he did not come home." She fished out a tissue from her bag, dabbed at her eyes, blew her nose.

Dani's mother used to ghost them. Bogie never reached out to anyone. Who would he call? Not drifter boyfriends. The family never got to know their neighbors because they didn't stay anywhere long enough. Plus, their mother hated nosey people asking questions. Teachers might report them to social services, the ultimate bad guys, according to Dani's mom. *"They'll take you away from me, spilt you up. You'll never see each other again."* Instead, Bogie prepared dinner for Dani using whatever he found in the refrigerator, or he'd scrounge money from the coin jar and take Dani to McDonald's for a burger and fries. Together they worked on her homework. Later, they watched TV shows Dani liked. When she begged him to let her sleep in his bed, he complained she hogged the sheets, but he always relented.

Vera said, "The police found him slumped over the steering wheel of our car. Heart-attack."

"I'm sorry."

"My fault. I usually went with him to the hospital. Drove him home. This time my church's annual women's convocation was that afternoon, with me responsible for a thousand details." Tears dribbled out of the corners of her eyes. She blinked them away and raised her face. "Our partnership had its missteps and bruises, but far more good days than bad. Every day I miss him. Each night I pray for him and tell him I'm sorry."

"Is that why you lived with your son?"

"I couldn't pay the mortgage, so the bank foreclosed, and I lost our house. Charlie took me in."

"Your son sounds like a good guy."

"Sweet and kind. Helped us around the house, called to check on us when it snowed or stormed. Shared whatever he had when times became rocky."

"My brother's like that."

"It looks bad, but he is innocent."

Dani bit her lower lip.

"An affair with a married woman is wrong. It does not, however, make him a crook."

The two women sat quietly for a few minutes. The buzz of voices, clank of dishes, and sixties music played in the background.

Vera lifted the cover of the box. It hovered in the air for a second.

"Wait." Dani shot out her hand. "Look." She pointed to a small key taped to the inside of the lid.

Vera peeled it loose.

"To unlock what?"

Vera mulled it over. "A safe-deposit-box?"

"Where'd he bank?"

"The same place I do."

***

Dani's Chevy stayed close behind Vera's navy-blue loaner. *Holy moly*. Scary as heck, but also exciting times. She asked Siri to call Vera's cell.

"Do you remember my friend Javier?"

Red light. Vera's car slowed and then stopped.

"Let's go by there first and leave the box with him."

"I trust people I know."

The light turned green. Vera didn't move.

"He's a great guy."

Someone behind Dani honked at them. Vera pulled ahead.

"He is a stranger to me."

"We need to put the box in a safe place." Dani tried to think of an alternative. Mirko, but Stephanie might still be there. "How about with your son-in-law?"

"No." The answer came quick and sharp. "I do not want to get him involved. How about Officer French?"

"She'll keep the gun."

"What will I do with a gun?"

"We're private detectives now, on a case." They were a block away. "Let's just leave it with Javier until we get back from the bank."

"You are giving me a headache."

They passed the quick lube place and funeral home. Dani saw Javier, just ahead, filling up a taxi's tank.

"I will consider it, after I meet him." Vera put on her right blinker and Dani did the same. She pulled into the gas station with Dani behind. They parked side-by-side and climbed out.

Vera made a strangled noise.

"What?"

"That car."

A gleaming black sedan idled in a spot on the opposite side and away from the pumps. Dani read the license plate.

Oak Lane Three.

Chapter 26

Erika

Erika sat on their deck, a glass of unsweetened iced tea sweating in her hand. Bigelow, Hugh Lavender, and Cappy, all in business together? Hugh must be the big dog. The contents of the camera's memory card probably hurt Hugh or Kate unless Bigelow had something going on the side without the Lavenders' knowledge. She had to find out the truth. If she knew what the card contained, she could dig them both out of this cluster-fuck. Erika sipped. Tangy and cool, a metaphor for the situation's requirements.

"Hey."

She jumped.

"Didn't mean to scare you." Griff pulled up a mesh patio chair and sat. A round table, big enough for eight, centered the upper level of the deck. An ancient oak off to the left provided shade. Three steps led to a lower level furnished with lounge chairs, end tables, and large market umbrellas. A stone path down a grassy slope led to the in-ground pool.

Griff appeared clear-eyed and sober. "Nice outfit. Where've you been?"

"At the Lavenders."

"Oh yeah. I forgot. How'd it go?"

Erika took another sip. "Where are our jailers?"

"Bigelow's out. Cappy's watching golf if you can picture that."

She made an amused sound. "They raised over $600,000 and still had hours to go."

Griff narrowed his gaze. "Everything they touch becomes platinum." He sounded bitter.

"Fuck yeah. Anyway, it's for charity." She didn't have to use her public voice with Griff. Besides swearing freely, her Georgia drawl became more pronounced.

"And political contributors lining up favors for when he's governor," Griff said.

"Their philanthropy seems real to me."

"Don't trust him," Griff warned.

No worries there, not anymore. "Will he win?"

"Polls are strong but it's early."

The election, six months away, might give Lavender enough time to heal from a brutal primary fight. Hugh's detractors accused him of being in bed with Wall Street and big business, not caring about the middle class, much less the poor. Minorities were wary, but the polls had him gaining ground, block-by-block. Going against an incumbent added to the uphill climb. The current governor, on the other hand, had troubles of his own, especially with upstate and more conservative constituents.

"Why is he running? All the scrutiny and shitty-vitriol."

Griff leaned forward. "Power. Hugh craves and loves to wield it."

"Hubris," she said with disdain.

"Like you don't hunger after it." He laughed. "And wield it in your own special way."

"True enough."

This conversation reminded Erika of the old days. Griff sounded like the man she'd fallen in love with and married, confident, funny, attentive. He looked good too. White open-collared shirt, tan slacks, and deck shoes without socks. His silver hair swept back from his face. Patrician nose, thin lips. They'd met through a professional matchmaker. Erika viewed it as an experiment, something just for laughs. Griff had just sold his start-up music company. Flush with cash with no time to find dates, he signed up with the same woman. Handsome, a hint of danger, and loaded — a winning combination.

"Did you know Bigelow works for Hugh?" she asked.

Griff jerked his head back, face muscles scrunched. "Yeah. So?"

"Is Hugh the one who's messing with us?"

The screen door slid open. Cappy leaned out. Small eyes lingered on Erika's crossed legs. "What d'you find out?"

She tucked her legs under her chair. "Nothing."

"He's not gonna like that."

Griff made a growling sound under his breath. "Fuck off. We're having a husband-wife conversation."

"Your funeral." The door scraped closed.

"What'd they ask you to do at the Lavenders'?"

"Spy."

"No additional information, like you told Cappy?"

Instead of answering, she inquired again. "Is Hugh our master incarcerator? I thought your gambling debts caused this imprisonment."

He chuckled. "You've obviously never been in jail."

Erika joined in his joke with a smile. She liked hyperbole staked in truth. Still, he dodged the question again.

Dogged, she tried one more time. "How do the Lavenders fit in?"

Griff stretched out his legs, leaned back, and laced his fingers behind his head. "Did you plan to leave me for Charlie?"

His tone and manner suggested causal interest. Erika knew better. She drew in her breath.

"You think you hid that from me?"

She regained her composure. "Nothing to know." She said it with conviction. "He liked snapping portraits of me."

Griff dropped his arms. "You're telling me you weren't doing him? All my imagination?"

"The man is dead. This isn't productive."

"I saw the way you looked at him."

She lowered her shoulders, folded her hands on her lap. "We're in a fucking mess, and we have to get out of it." She paused. "Together."

"I remember when you used to look at *me* like that."

"Tell me what Hugh has to do with our situation."

Griff's eyes dug into hers. "Charlie scammed everyone."

She didn't blink.

Finally, he said, "Including blackmailing Hugh Lavender."

Erika's mobile rang. She glanced down at the screen. "Gotta take this, but we're not finished."

"I'm getting a Stella." He stood up. "Want one?"

She shook her head and pressed answer on her cell. "Hello, Vera."

"Does everyone have caller ID?"

Despite the tension, Erika laughed. "Who doesn't?"

"Point taken." Vera sounded as stressed as Erika felt.

"What happened with the police today?" Erika stood up and paced along the edge of the upper deck. Vera had promised not to speak to the cops about Erika. A breeze moved through the oak, sending a few dead leaves afloat. Erika waited.

"I kept my word."

A momentary reprieve or permanent? "Smart."

"We have to meet."

The hairs on the nape of Erika's neck rose. "What's this about?" She glanced through the glass doors into the living room. Griff's thumbs flew over the keyboard of his phone. *Texting who?*

"I found something important."

Shit. Didn't sound like the memory card. She kept her tone as mild as possible. "Sure. Where and when?" She strode to and opened the sliding door. "Wait. I need paper and a pen." She walked into the breakfast nook and retrieved the yellow notepad. "Okay, shoot."

Vera gave her an address. "In fifteen minutes."

Erika stared at the pad. "What is this place?"

"A friend's house. It is safe."

She doubted that.

Chapter 27

Erika

Erika pulled into the driveway. Yellowed grass, dandelions, and brown patches of dirt marred the spacious lawn. Cans of paint stacked alongside the front steps stood catty-corner to a ladder laying on its side. Parked at various angles, Erika saw a Ford pickup, maroon Nissan, and yellow Chevy Malibu. *Who knew it was a fucking party?*

Griff had helped her escape by bringing Cappy a beer and joining him for the golf tournament. She waited until the men fell deep into analysis before walking off the deck, around the pool to the driveway. She opened the attached garage, slid behind the wheel of her electric-blue convertible, and punched into her GPS the address Vera had given her.

Sober, Griff could hold his own, especially with Cappy. Bigelow represented another pot of shit, but fortunately, he'd gone out. She'd have to hurry to get back before or soon after Bigelow. By then she might have the information that ousted Bigelow and Cappy from their lives.

She hurried toward the house entrance. A tall, muscular man greeted her. "I'm Benny." He stuck out his hand.

"Erika." They shook.

"Ms. Moon is expecting you."

What the hell? Erika followed the shirtless man. She watched his muscles flex as he walked. *Damn, he looks sexy. Was he part of this drama?* "Is this your place?"

Benny opened the door. "Nah." He ushered Erika in. Vera and a teen-aged girl with dark hair and violet eyes sat on a couch covered with a drop cloth. The glistening walls smelled freshly painted. Vera popped up and waved Erika over.

"This is my friend Dani."

On closer inspection, Dani wasn't a kid. "How do you do?"

"Great." Dani shook Erika's hand. "Thanks for coming."

Vera said, "We brought bottled water."

Erika sniffed wine on Vera's breath. She peered into Vera's eyes. A bit red, but otherwise clear. "I'm fine. What's this about?" She half-expected to hear police sirens. "Who lives here?"

"Liza," Vera said. "Used to. Now it's vacant."

"Sam."

"You know all about us..." Vera sounded accusatory. "But you have told us nothing about you."

"Charlie liked Sam a lot. They talked politics." Erika had met Sam only once. Charlie had promised her a romantic dinner along the Hudson River. On the way, he made a stop at Sam's office on Smith. It sat among rows of wood-frame houses converted into professional offices. His law firm rented space on the first and second floors of a three-story building. The men left her in the waiting room. A receptionist served as her watchdog while they talked behind a closed door. She'd asked Charlie about the meeting and remembered his answer came out smooth and sure. "Sam's my brother-in-law. He's helping me with a legal problem. No biggie."

"That is until now, *Mrs. Noble*," Vera continued.

Erika struggled to sound and appear unruffled. Of course, Vera uncovered Erika's actual name. "I don't suppose there's a beer in the cooler." A six-pack container stood in one corner of the room on top of a plastic tarp covering beige carpeting. "I'll take the water you offered."

Dani hopped up and snagged a bottle. "No glasses." She proffered the *Poland Spring*.

"Thanks." She unscrewed the cap and took a swig. "Are you a member of the family?"

"Never mind who she is," Vera said. She lifted a metal box the size of a shoebox and handed it to Erika. "Look inside."

"I have news and questions too." She let the container rest on her pressed together knees. From beneath lowered lids, she scanned the room. The potent smell of turpentine overwhelmed the new paint scents. "Is Sam selling this place?"

Vera said, "Open the box."

Erika placed the water bottle on the floor. She eased off the cover of the metal container. Pictures of her taken by Charlie lay lined up across the bottom, each one overlapping the next, the last one in Provincetown, Cape Cod. She'd told Griff she was going on a spa retreat for a week of dieting, yoga, hikes, meditation, and massages. Instead, she'd met Charlie at a condo resort on the bay side of the peninsula. He caught blue fish off the shore and grilled them on the beach. They swam every day, slept-in most mornings, made love in the afternoons, and went dancing in the evenings. A community theater in Truro, just south of them, performed *As You Like It*. That week, she seriously thought about leaving Griff and marrying Charlie.

Charlie shared all, no secrets. No lies between them. *Ha*. He'd lied to her too. Bigelow, Cappy, Hugh, Griff, and Charlie, intertwined lives, and fabrications.

"Proof I told you the truth. We loved each other."

Vera pursed her lips. "Are you worried about these pictures landing on your husband's doorstep?"

She lifted a photo. It stirred memories of the first time they made love. She'd hired him to take racy pictures for Griff, or at least she told herself that. Until then, Charlie and Erika flirted with each other, but nothing else. Griff left town on business and her affair with her latest lover, Woody, ended several months before. Charlie came by with a bouquet of wildflowers and a chilled bottle of Champaign.

"These pictures offer no threat." Griff's question on the deck came back to her. *Were you doing Charlie?*

"My husband and I have an understanding." The hairs on her neck lifted again. She picked up another picture. "Charlie made all his subjects beautiful, no matter how unattractive. He had a gift."

"Did you know about these?" Dani asked.

Erika had seen the photos before. She'd asked Charlie to destroy them. Griff could not see them. Ever. "Who are you again?"

"A friend."

Vera asked, "I found them stashed in the basement in an obscure place."

"What else?"

To Erika, Vera looked caught, as if she there was more to this story.

Dani said, "Your actual name for one and more revealing pictures of you."

This conversation required redirection. "Charlie blackmailed Hugh Lavender."

"The man running for governor?" Vera asked.

Dani swiveled her head back and forth between the two of them. "About what?"

"Let's locate the memory card and find out." Erika waited. Neither Vera nor Dani offered anything.

Finally, Vera said, "Charlie would not do that."

"I'm not positive it's true."

"From whom did you get this libelous information?"

Erika hesitated for a beat. "My husband." She remembered Griff's accusation. "But I guess he has reasons to lie to me."

Chapter 28

Vera

Vera heard them before she saw them. First Benny clattered into the room. Sam followed. The man who stalked them at the hospital and here earlier, the one Dani named Florid Face, entered seconds behind.

She tried to process the scene before her. Sweat trickled from under her armpits.

Dressed in khaki's and a lightweight beige sweater, Sam spoke first, his steady gaze trained on his ex-mother-in-law. "What's going on here?"

Benny seemed embarrassed. "I let her in boss. She said you knew."

"This is not Benny's fault." Vera tried for confident strength. She strode over to Sam. "Who is this man?" she demanded, but heard the crack in her voice.

Sam twisted around and stared at Florid Face, then faced Vera again with a deep frown. "He works for me."

That could not be true.

"Tell me why you're trespassing."

"Trespassing?"

Sam's features softened. "Liza doesn't live here anymore." He hiked a shoulder, his expression conciliatory, as if offering an apology.

Vera tried to put the pieces together. Since the murder, she had become paranoid, looking for trouble and hidden agendas. After Dani and Vera spotted the sedan at Javier's gas station, they left. Were the murderers spying on Javier, waiting for Dani and Vera to show up? She checked the rear-view mirror every few seconds in case the car followed them until she reached the hospital's parking garage. Dani pulled alongside and rolled down her window. They hid the gun in Vera's locked glove compartment. The safe-deposit key went into her coin purse. Now she was glad they had only brought the pictures with them to Sam's.

Vera tried to get a hold of her emotions. "This man frightened and threatened me." Her head throbbed.

Sam turned back to Florid Face. "Zeek? What's she talking about?" Sam's query sounded genuine to Vera's ears.

Zeek appeared less menacing. He'd combed his hair with a part on the left, shaved clean, his pimples irritated and raw.

"I came to make sure everything was okay," Zeek said. "Saw Ms. Moon stashing something under her arm. Asked about it." He curved his lips up into what might be a smile, but came off as a sneer. "Protecting your interests, boss."

With a stamp of her right foot, Vera said, "Benny heard him threaten me."

Scarlet blotches popped out on Benny's neck. "Ms. Moon acted scared for sure."

"And you can verify that this degenerate claimed Charlie possessed something belonging to Zeek."

Benny didn't meet her gaze. "Not sure about that part."

"I am," she said. "Dani witnessed this awful man..." She pointed at Zeek. "... threaten me at the hospital."

Dani said, "And he was at Vera and Liza's collision. *And* he knows the guy who plowed into them. I saw them talking."

"Who the hell are you?" Sam asked.

"Vera's friend, Dani, and witness to everything Vera said."

Sam confronted Zeek. "You told me you just happened by. Why were you at the accident?"

Zeek shrugged. "I can see how the ladies might have misunderstood."

Sam crossed his arms. "Okay?" He stretched out the O, making him sound skeptical but open to being convinced.

"Chance encounter, like I said." Zeek's hands and fingers moved as he spoke, creating tiny pictures of sincerity. "In the neighborhood, tried to help."

Vera said, "You poked around at our yard sale first."

Dani added, "You hurt Vera at the accident. I made you stop."

Zeek ignored everyone in the room except Sam. "I went to the hospital to inquire about your ex, pay my respects." He tugged on his tie, rubbed his talking hands along his pants' legs. "Came here for an update on the renovations, like you asked." He stretched his neck and lifted his head toward Vera. "She took stuff that didn't belong to her."

The air in the room weighed on Vera, making it tough to breathe.

Sam spoke in a kinder tone that rang false. "What did you take?"

"Liza told me Charlie stored a few of his things and they needed to go in order for you to sell the house." She hoped she came across as confident but, indignant.

Sam's eyes narrowed.

"I dropped by to assess the effort it is going to take to remove them." She sucked in a breath thick with the paint smells and coughed. In a choked voice she said, "Everything is still here, just as I found it."

"Nothing is missing?"

"Asked and answered." Vera glared at Sam. "Did you hire this man to follow and frighten me?"

"You know better."

"I thought so, but now I am not sure." She had to get out of here before she fainted. Her knees buckled.

Dani hurried to Vera's side. "Come, sit." She hooked her arm through Vera's. "Are you all right?"

"I'm having trouble breathing."

Benny opened two of the closed windows, and cool air swept in.

Dani rubbed Vera's back. "Try putting your head between your legs. My mom said that keeps people from fainting or upchucking."

Until now, Erika had remained silent and motionless. Now she rose. "I can see this is a family matter. I'll excuse myself." She smiled at Vera. "Let's reconnect as soon as you're free." The metal container no longer visible. "We can continue our conversation."

Vera said, "Call me when you get home, so I know you are safe."

"How sweet." She faced Sam. "Nice to see you again."

"We've met?"

She slipped on her sunglasses. "Once, a while back." She glided past Zeek.

Vera's shoulders sagged. Six months ago, her life had been hard but sane. Three-months ago, it turned upside down, and now she had no idea what to do, or whom to trust.

"You have to check on your daughter and Brandy probably needs a walk." Dani pulled Vera up and propelled her toward the door. "Nice meeting you, Sam. Wish I could say the same about you, Zeek."

That lifted Vera's spirits. Dani possessed grit. Well, Vera could be brave too. "Leave us alone, Zeek. Do not come near me or my daughter again." Her glare met Sam's. "You should reconsider your allegiances. Benny is a good person. Zeek is not." They reached the front door.

Sam spoke to their backs. "What did you take from my house?"

Without a second's hesitation, Vera said, "I already told you. Nothing."

Chapter 29

Vera

Vera surveyed the lobby. The line for personal attention from the two tellers looped around stanchions strung together with colored cord. The safe-deposit key might belong to any bank. Charlie, however, was a man of habits. They both banked at Chase for years. His checking and savings accounts resided here, so surely the safe-deposit box did as well.

A woman with an iPad approached her. "May I help you?"

Vera explained her business. Within minutes the greeter ushered Vera into a small, glass-enclosed office. The woman behind the desk introduced herself as Maureen Snow.

"Do you have the death certificate?" Jammed into a brown pants suit, fat bulged in layered rings along the banker's sides. "And documentation naming you as your son's executor?"

Vera produced both documents. For a second, the setting and papers took her back to Vincent's death. Except back then, there was nothing left, nothing to claim. The landlord for her flower shop shut her down within a month. Vincent departed this world broke, leaving Vera in a financial mess.

"I'm sorry for your loss," Maureen Snow said. "I need to see your driver's license or passport." She scrutinized all the documents. Apparently satisfied, she asked, "Do you have the key?"

Vera dug into her bag and retrieved her coin purse, unzipped it, and plucked out the key. Did it hold answers to all her questions?

The two walked into the safe-deposit vault. Number 1090 stood in the middle of stacks of slim drawers. Ms. Snow inserted her key and Vera did the same. She pulled out the drawer and placed it on a narrow wooden table.

"Take your time. I'll be right outside."

Vera studied the box. Flatter and longer than the metal container she found hidden in Sam's basement, she lifted its lid. *Oh, my goodness*. Inside lay stacks of bills — hundreds and fifties on top. With trembling fingers, she shuffled through them. Twenties and tens on the bottom. She pulled them all out and counted. When she reached ten thousand, she stopped to catch her breath. She kept going. Twenty thousand total. She thought about their scrimping on food and clothing, trips to the movies only on Tuesday afternoons for the cheapest tickets, the last time she had a manicure. But he pre-paid the rent, and now this. Erika's belief about shady dealings might be true.

Remembering how she discovered the hidden key, Vera examined the box. There it was. Taped to the cover with clear cellophane, she spied a tiny square. A camera's memory card. She peeled back the tape with her fingernail and placed the disc in the palm of her trembling hand. Relief flooded every pore. The end of the road. The proof they sought.

Sadness swept over her like a cold fog. Murder, threats, all for this. The police would examine it, understand the significance, and solve the crime. She had done it. Dani, too. They had cracked the case together. Vera thought about Erika. Okay, all three of them.

With care, she placed the digital card in her coin purse. She returned the bills, stacking them with care. Later, she would retrieve the money, after she figured out how Charlie had earned it. She could not keep funds obtained illegally. Twenty thousand dollars. That plus the insurance — enough to transform her life. She closed the lid with shaky hands. Her entire body trembled. Silent tears flowed down her cheeks, slid along the side of her nose, and rolled off her chin.

It was over. Almost.

***

Liza's room smelled like a bedpan in need of changing. Her head lolled. Dried spittle clung to the corners of her mouth. The colors around her eyes, now a faded yellow, no longer looked like someone had punched her in the face. Even her bruised cheek and forehead appeared less damaged.

Vera went into the bathroom, emptied the bedpan and, after washing her hands, rinsed a white cloth with cool water. "Lots of progress on the house renovations." She wiped Liza's face. "You should get a respectable price for the place." Money mattered a great deal to Liza, and Vera could not think of what else to talk about. Not the drama at Sam's and especially not the safe-deposit box. She smoothed lotion onto Liza's chafed skin.

"Did they find..." Liza stopped, swallowed hard. "Did they find who hurt us?"

"We are very close."

Liza opened her eyes a bit wider. "We?" Her voice croaked.

"The police seem quite busy with other investigations."

"Mom." She sounded like the old quarrelsome Liza. A good sign of recovery.

"I'm going to speak with Dr. LaSalle at three o'clock. Find out when you can come home."

"I don't have a home." Liza's throaty words came out bitter.

True enough. Vera and Liza had not finished moving Liza's belongings into the new apartment. They had sold the old bedroom set and planned to buy one. *Get rid of the memories and start fresh.* And, at least for a while, Liza might require around the clock care.

"I can't be alone." Tears leaked. Vera wiped them away with the still moist cloth. "I could stay with you."

Not possible. Vera's apartment had two bedrooms, one shut tight, door locked. Her spine concaved. *Almost over.*

Liza coughed. Vera grabbed a cup of water from the tray alongside the bed. The straw bent, making it easier to drink. Liza took a sip.

Fifty thousand dollars from the insurance. After paying pressing bills, Vera planned to put money into a college fund for Penny's children. For Vera's sanity, she must vacate the apartment. She had enough for a down payment on a condo. Another twenty thousand sat in a safe-deposit box at Chase Bank. Ill-gotten gains? How much would a home health aide cost for Liza?

"Mom?"

"Not to worry. We will work something out."

Liza pushed herself up on her elbows. "Do you love me?"

"What kind of question is that? Of course, I love you." Vera stroked Liza's face. "I'm sorry. I'm sorry you have to ask."

Chapter 30

Dani

Facing Main Street, Dani and Javier sat side-by-side on the wooden bench in front of the gas station office. To their right, a mechanic drove a Buick into one of two garage bays. The day had warmed to sixty-eight-degrees, but a stiff breeze made it feel cooler. The late-afternoon sun shimmered above the skyline. Trucks, cars, and vans moved along Main Street, most obeying the thirty-five-mile-per-hour speed limit. Across the street, Mr. Kim swept in front of his shop.

"You seem kinda down," Javier said. His uniform had his first named stitched in white across the breast pocket, under it his title, "Owner." A Met's baseball cap covered his spikey-straight hair.

"I'm fine."

But she wasn't. Vera went to the bank alone. Even though she explained it nicely, she still didn't trust Dani. Not one hundred percent. She should. Dani hadn't lied to her in a while, not since her promise. Plus, Vera was in danger and she needed Dani to protect her. And Dani had called Mirko on his cell. No answer. Twice. She texted him, twice. No response.

Javier asked, "What's up with you?"

"Nothing."

"Something."

"How's by you?"

Javier swung his head side-to-side. "Trouble."

"Oh, no. Is your wife okay? The baby?"

"They're fine, but I lost my best guy today and the other one..." He shifted his head in the direction of the garage bay. "... got scared."

"Of what?"

"I.C.E. came around asking for papers."

"He's illegal?"

"No. I don't do that, but it doesn't matter to these immigration guys. They intimidate everyone. One of my men could have an illegal relative or friend so they go underground."

"Are you in danger?"

"Wife and me, we're good, but a lot of the landscapers, at least some of them... I'm not sure. Could cut into business if they see immigration here."

"Will they come back?"

"Said so."

Dani twisted her mouth this way and that. "Lots of coincidences. Makes me wonder."

He shot her a quizzical look.

"Did you see that sedan with the license plate Oak Lane Three parked by the fence?"

"When?" Javier unscrewed the cap of a Half-and-Half Snapple and took a swig.

"A couple of hours ago."

"They're headquartered about a mile from here."

"Really?"

"Yeah. They own a fleet," Javier explained. "After the crash, I searched Better Business. Nothing. Googled them. Clean enough, mostly."

"What does that mean?"

"A few bad reviews."

"Like?"

Javier drained his Snapple and tossed the bottle in the recycle bin that stood next to the trash can. "One customer wrote the car never showed up. Another claimed the driver made rude comments. The only one that might be significant stated the driver threatened her."

"Like how?"

"You better give me a five-star review."

"Hmmm."

"Anyway, they were from last year, not recent. A company rep responded, apologized, and said they held customer service classes as a result."

Dani mulled over Javier's news. "Not really helpful."

"Anything on your end?" he asked.

"Not yet. Are they regulars?"

"Nope."

"With at least four gas stations within a five-block radius, why fill-up here?"

"Because we're the best." He chuckled. In a more serious tone, he added, "Another coincidence?"

"Did you see the driver?"

"I wish. Had my hands full. Happens like that. Crazy busy followed by nothing, like now."

That's how Dani felt. Everything was moving fast, the diner rendezvous with Vera, finding the pictures and the gun, going to Sam's, confronting Zeek, and seeing the sedan identical to the one in the accident. Then slam. Vera and Mirko shut her down.

"I'm not sure what to do next," Dani said.

"About the crash and the old lady?"

"About everything."

The two friends sat watching the traffic hum by.

"Hear from Bogie?"

"Yeah." She heard the lie and modified her answer. "Not exactly."

"No comprendo." He angled his body and stared at her full on.

"I messed up. With everyone. Bogie, Vera, Mirko. I'm a trouble sink hole."

"Whoa. Come on. You're one of the best people I know."

"I got fired."

"From the new job?" Javier's accent thickened under stress. "Because you're late getting there?"

"From the party place." She peered at him from the corners of her eyes, too ashamed to do more. "They let me go."

Three deep lines creased his forehead. "So, it embarrassed you. I get it."

"There's more."

"Like?" His tone held a note of wariness.

"Like, I don't have a new job. Mirko dumped me, and I skipped out on my rent." She wanted to explain how it all happened, but she opted not to. *Bogie wisdom: Excuses negate apologies*. "My brother thinks I'm visiting for only two weeks."

"Why are you telling me this?"

"I lie. About lots of things. I'm trying to stop."

He clamped his hands over his ears. A truck loaded with bags of soil pulled up to a pump, followed by a taxi. A SUV packed with kids and a harried-looking male driver rumbled in front of a third pump. Javier rose slowly. "Let's drop it." He walked toward the first car, stopped, and turned around. "Is Bogie's wife even sick?"

Miserable, no longer trusting her voice, Dani shook her head.

Chapter 31

Dani

Dani thought confessing, being a better person and not lying, would make her feel good. It didn't. From her car, she peered up at Mirko's windows. Although the apartment appeared dark, Mirko could still be home. Should she go in? What if he was canoodling with Stephanie? That would make this day perfect. Icing on the misery cake. Javier used to be her fall back. He helped her out of tons of slumps. They hung out. Once he took her to a salsa party with his wife and cousin. Never going to happen again. She saw it in his eyes and heard it in his voice. Liar.

She let everyone down. All the time. Loser, just like her mother, just like her father. No Bogie wisdom to make that untrue.

In Dani's earliest memory, she stood in her crib, diaper full, smelly, and itchy. "Want Mama," two-year-old Dani said.

Ten-year-old, Bogie came to her. Rail thin, dimpled chin with sandy hair streaked gold from the sun. Maybe she'd colored the flashback with images from other, more recent times. His voice came back to her, clear and strong, weighed down with gloom. "Mama's gone."

"I yucky," she said.

"No more diapers." Did he mean she was too big to wear them? Both Mama and Bogie tried to get her to use the pink potty decorated with butterflies.

"I hungry."

"Nothing to eat."

Dani fell back in her crib, threw herself face down on the damp mattress, and wailed. Was it possible to remember an event so clearly and completely from that far back? Bogie might have told her the story. No matter. Whenever she thought about it, a blanket of sadness wrapped around her. You had to be darn unlovable for your mother to leave you without food or diapers.

She trudged up the steps to Mirko's apartment to retrieve her belongings. No key under the mat. Either he was home, or he'd locked her out. She rapped on the door.

"Who?"

"Dani."

"Door's open."

The glow from his computer screen and back-lit keyboard provided the only light. The blinds stood open as if the setting sun surprised him at his work. An empty pizza box stained with tomato sauce, clumps of cheese, and lines of oil sat on a snack table.

"Hey." She watched him tap away on the keyboard, noticed the hair stubble almost as pale as his skin covering his dome and cheeks. She loved looking at him. "Working on an article?"

Mirko kept his head down. "Stephanie gave me an idea. I don't want to lose it."

Perfect.

He tapped on the keys with two fingers, moving as fast as any trained touch typist. Dani stayed put. Finally, Mirko focused on her. He stood. "You okay?"

"No."

Mirko's long legs carried him to her in three strides. "Babe, what's wrong?"

He hadn't called her babe in months, not since even before the breakup. She buried her face on his chest. Mirko slipped his arms around her, stroked her hair, and rubbed her back. She pressed into him. His hands slid up and down. With strong fingers, he massaged.

Dani said, "I miss you so much." His hardened dick pulse against her left thigh. She lifted her face. He kissed her, tongue circling, darting. He tasted like spearmint gum.

"I miss you too."

Like characters in an old-fashioned movie, he scooped her up and carried her into the bedroom. When Mirko set her down beside his bed, they tugged off each other's clothes, kissing and laughing, until they were both naked.

He said he missed me. She scrambled onto the bed and under the covers. Mirko stood looking down; his swollen penis glistened. She kicked the sheet and comforter off, so he could see her.

"You're beautiful." He climbed into the bed next to her.

Beautiful. Goosebumps rose on her arms.

They kissed for a long time. Mirko licked and sucked each of her nipples. She moaned joyful noises.

From the nightstand, he dug out a bottle of baby oil, held it up with his head cocked.

"Hmmm."

Liquid oozed out. With gentle fingers, he massaged her clit.

"Ooh, ooh, ooh." Dani arched her pelvis. The electricity was so intense, she eased his hand away.

"My turn." He splashed oil onto her palms then lay on his back, lips curled in a smile of bliss as she rubbed the length of his cock.

When he entered her, he gasped. He took time to suck her swollen nipples again, kiss her neck and mouth before the urgency took over and they moved together in rapid rhythm until they both came. For a long time afterward, he lay on top of her, the only sound their ragged breaths.

I love you. She thought it so loud, he surely heard it.

He rolled onto his back. "Wow."

What a ridiculous moment to think about Vera and Javier. She'd promised both no more lies. Vera aloud and Javier in her head and heart. She had to tell Mirko the truth. How could he love her if he couldn't trust her?

"That was awesome," he said.

Confessing would ruin everything. Lose if she did, lose if she didn't.

They hadn't bothered to switch on any lights, but now Mirko stretched his torso to the right, arm extended, and switched on the nightstand lamp. "Did I do something wrong?"

Lies were hard to unravel. Do you start at the beginning or at the end and move backward? When would he stop listening?

"No." *Do you love me, even a little?* "Better than good."

"Then what's the matter?"

Traffic noise seeped through the cracked-open window. A siren wailed in the distance. *Beginning or end, all or a little?*

"Nothing." *Will you ever forgive me?* "I'm great." She said this with enthusiasm, so he'd know he'd made her happy.

It worked. He smiled down on her, ran his index finger along her skull and cross bones tat just below her collarbone. "You never told me the story behind these."

"Stories." *Best not to tell him the truth today. Another time.* "I was mad at my dad. Cross-bones is my revenge tat."

"Did he get it?"

"Nope. Didn't notice."

His finger moved down to the tiny heart above her right breast and along her nipple.

"That one is in honor of my oldest niece. Bogie and Sally named her Danielle." Lies were hard to undo. "Sally's sister has the same name." She shrugged.

"They named her for both of you."

Where to begin?

"And the dragon?" He kissed her stomach.

Gertie had big eyes and a wide wingspan. She flew beneath Dani's navel. "When I was little, Bogie told me stories about Gertie the dragon. She breathed fire when the older kids bullied me. Plus, he said, she suffered from terrible halitosis — double whammy."

Laughing, Mirko said, "Your breath is sweet. I love kissing you."

They kissed again. When they stopped, Mirko asked, "What else can Gertie do?"

"Whenever she sensed danger, she swooped down, lifted me onto her back and we flew away. We also rescued others who needed us or just went for a ride for fun." Night after night, Bogie lay down next to Dani, wiped away her tears, and wove tales of Gertie and Dani's adventures until Dani was too old. On her eighteenth birthday, an artist first sketched the dragon and then inked her onto Dani's belly. "Gertie is fierce and brave."

"Like you."

"I'm brave?"

"You are. Look how you're helping Vera. That takes grit."

Fierce and brave. "I lied to you."

"About Gertie?"

"No. Other things."

For several seconds he searched her face. Then, with a low wounded-animal groan, he sank back on the pillow and closed his eyes.

Chapter 32

Erika

Erika tried without success to distinguish the words that accompanied angry tones. Bigelow shoved Cappy. With fists balled, he stumbled back. The two men faced-off on the deck, eight empty beer cans lined up on the glass tabletop. One of Erika's china dessert plates overflowed with cigarette butts and ashes.

She let herself in through the front entranceway. No use pretending that she hadn't sneaked out, but whatever the cause for their fight, it gave her momentary cover. She moved through the house, looking for Griff and going over in her mind all she'd learned. What were the smartest next moves? If he were still sober, he could help her. Almost at the endgame. Vera would find the digital memory card soon, and she was too nice to use the photographs against Erika. Interesting about Sam, Vera's son-in-law, and who the devil was Zeek? Vera had a partner, Dani, someone else requiring investigation.

As Erika searched, the muffled hum of the central heating and cooling fan from the overhead and wall vents accompanied her. The southern view from her ceiling-to-floor window stopped her for a second. Low clouds on the hills and streaks of color from the setting sun. How she loved this house. She could not let Bigelow and Hugh Lavender take it away. She slipped into the master suite, closed, and locked the door without a sound, and sat on the edge of the king-sized bed. A cold Brooklyn Lager would help, but what if she ran into the two stooges?

With the balls of her feet, she eased off her pumps. Three-inch heels made her legs look great. They also hurt by hour three. She bent over and massaged her left instep, lay back on the bed and stared at the ceiling. *Hugh, Bigelow, and Charlie. A hidden box in Charlie's house. Sam and Zeek. Dani. Did Benny the construction guy have a part in this play? What was on that memory card?*

The banging on the bedroom door made Erika start.

"Open the fucking door."

Bigelow. "I'm not dressed. Give me a minute."

"I don't mind." He sniggered.

Malignant creep. Erika got up, grabbed her cotton robe, and wrapped it over her street clothes. She searched around for something to protect herself. Griff used to own a Smith and Wesson, but she made him give it up. Too dangerous. Since the invasion, she regretted not having it.

Bigelow thumped on the door again. "Open up." Another bang. "I'll kick it in."

A forgotten paperweight, swag from a charity event, sat on a corner of her nightstand. Italicized "Friends" floated in the semi-circular glass. She grabbed it. With the paperweight now in her bathrobe pocket, she said, "I'm coming."

Deep breath. Steady. She opened the door.

"Took you long enough." Bigelow's neck and face shone bright red. Bucked teeth cut into his lower lip. His eyes swept the room. "Where you been?"

"Investigating." She clutched the robe's collar against her throat.

"Oh, yeah?" He stepped deeper into the room, his head swiveling right and left. "What d'you come up with, Sherlock?"

Erika fingered the paperweight's smooth glass dome. *Swing up and hit his chin and then crack it over his head*. "Vera knows where the memory card is. I'll have it by tomorrow." She needed time. "Evening."

With irritatingly slow scrutiny, Bigelow looked her up and down. "Get it now."

She smelled cigarettes and beer on his breath. "What were you and Cappy fighting about?"

"Who says we were?'

"I saw you."

"None of your business."

During one of Griff's violent periods, she'd taken a self-defense course, but she could barely remember anything she learned. Besides, Griff only hit walls and smashed furniture, dishes, and glasses. He never laid a hand on her. Images came back. Knee to the groin. Stiff fingers into his sockets. "I like my jailers to get along."

"Go in the morning and get it. I'm tired of hanging out here." His fists balled. "You got that?"

"Hugh Lavender doesn't punish you?"

Bigelow stared at her, unblinking. "Wadda you talking about?"

It didn't sound like a question. More like a threat. "You work for him. No worries. It doesn't matter to me." She turned away, hoping she appeared casual and unhurried. "Kate Lavender and I are friends." Erika edged along the bed toward the windows. The master bath to her right. "I heard you pissed him off. You, screaming at Cappy; Hugh, yelling at you." She faced him again, but now several steps away, giving her more room to react.

"Listen to me, bitch. Get that card first thing, or don't come home. You feel me? Run. Cause your life won't be worth a damn if you fail." His eyes narrowed to slits. "Ask your asshole husband what happens when people cross me."

He swung his body around and walked out.

Erika re-locked the door and dragged a chair over to block or at least slow down Bigelow. Not enough. The dresser wouldn't budge. With effort, she pulled the nightstand over and added it to the barricade. A sampling of her favorite books lined a wooden table under the window. She grabbed several and piled them on the chair and nightstand and went back for the rest. The barricade completed, she sank back onto the bed and snatched her bag from the floor, dug out her phone, and dialed Griff's number. The ringtone came from the master bath. She followed the sound.

Griff lay on the tile floor naked, a rubber tourniquet and syringe next to his bruised arm. His head lolled. The cellphone vibrated on the closed toilet seat.

Erika lifted Griff's eyelids. Unseeing, pinprick pupils greeted her. She cradled his head on her lap. *Cretins. This was Bigelow's doing.* He'd all but confessed.

Labored breaths huffed from Griff's mouth.

Bigelow said Griff crossed him. How? Why now? With her right middle finger, she felt for a pulse. Weak, thready. She reached for the purple-and-white striped towel on the rack, dragged it down, and eased it under his head.

Banging shook the door. "Open up." Bigelow again, bellowing.

"I'm calling 911."

"You'll get us all arrested."

"He could die."

Another heavy thud against the door. The flimsy lock gave way. The furniture moved, and the door opened a crack. Bigelow put his face up against the opening. "You don't want to explain crap to the cops."

She punched in the numbers.

"What's your emergency?" a female voice queried.

Bigelow again. "You hear me?"

Erika ignored him. "My husband is on the floor, he's barely conscious."

"Is he breathing?"

"Not easily."

"Give me your name and address."

Next, the operator asked Griff's age and weight.

"I think he overdosed on drugs."

"We're on our way."

Mount Kisco was a small town and response times were quick.

Bigelow said, "I'm leaving, and you're going to Riker's."

The thought of the infamous jail gave her a jolt.

Cappy's voice cut in. "Pigs won't hassle her. Good Samaritan state."

Erika didn't know what that meant, but she pushed the question and worry about jail aside. She had to get Griff warm. Not trusting her legs, she crawled to the bathroom door and retrieved Griff's cotton robe from a hook. She stood, wobbled her way to the dresser, found a pair of boxers, staggered back to Griff's side, and tugged on the underwear. Next, she lifted and maneuvered his inert body and put on the robe, testing both her strength and ingenuity.

The front doorbell rang. Once again, unable to catch the words, she heard Cappy's voice and a woman's in response.

"In here." She swept the books off the chair and nightstand and tugged the furniture aside. "In here, please." She opened the door.

The EMTs, a tall man with a bushy mustache and a woman with visible biceps, hurried in with a rolling stretcher and medical duffle bag.

"What did he take?" The woman asked.

Erika swung around to Bigelow, still standing in the doorway. "Tell her."

"Not sure." The gun bulge that usually protruded from under Bigelow's jacket had disappeared.

"Tell her," she repeated, this time screaming so loud the effort scraped her throat raw.

"Okay. Heroin."

The male EMT pulled out a small device and stabbed it into Griff's leg."

Griff sputtered awake.

"Oh, thank God." She grabbed his hand. "They're taking you to the hospital. I'll be right there."

He stared hollow-eyed and said nothing.

The same EMT slipped an oxygen mask over Griff's face. Together, the two professionals heaved Griff onto the stretcher and covered him with a blanket. They put the syringe in a plastic bag.

The woman had a firm voice and spoke in clipped phrases. "Keep one of these around at all times." She handed Erika another of the devices she'd used to wake up Griff. "Narcan."

They rolled him out past two officers waiting on the front porch. Erika followed.

"May I ask you a few questions?" The name on the officer's badge read, *French*. Angular cheekbones in a heart-shaped face softened the severe appearance given by her tawny hair tucked under her police cap.

"I have to follow my husband."

The unsmiling Officer French nodded. "We'll meet you there."

Chapter 33

Erika

To Erika's relief, Cappy was right. New York State had passed a Good Samaritan law. No prosecutions for overdose victims or their 911 callers if the police only recovered drug paraphernalia and not a stash for sale. Officer French explained this to Erika in the emergency waiting room.

"Who were the two other men in your house?" Officer French stood about five feet one or two inches, the same as Erika. Even in her unflattering uniform, Erika noticed the small waist and large bosom for someone so petite.

"Business associates of my husband."

An elderly couple sat on two of the orange and yellow chairs that lined the walls. Wolf Blitzer on CNN reported the evening news from the mounted television. A doctor made notes on a clipboard before approaching the pair.

"Nate Bigelow and Francis Capparella. Do I have that right?"

Erika glanced at the now-weeping couple, the woman's head on the man's shoulder. She had to be cautious and avoid potential traps.

"Can you tell me what happened?"

"I wasn't there."

The officer lifted her head. "Where were you?"

It wouldn't be smart to mention Vera. "At a charity event."

Officer French stayed quiet.

"At the Lavenders'."

"Who are they?"

Really? "He's running for governor."

"Ah." She jotted a note in her pad. "What time did you get home?"

The old couple's sobbing grew louder. The doctor made sympathetic murmurs.

Erika sat down, pressed her knees together, and folded her hands on her thighs. "Around 3:00 p.m. I found him on the bathroom floor. Dialed 911." She leveled her gaze to meet the officer's. "Do I need to contact my lawyer?"

The cop closed her notebook and stood up. "May I ask one more question?" Wisps of hair escaped her bun.

Erika waited.

"What's your husband's relationship with Nate Bigelow?"

"I told you, business acquaintances. How is that relevant?"

A few more strands fell across her face. She tucked them back into place. "Curious. Something unrelated."

Was this an opportunity to get Bigelow out of her house for good? "Can you give me a few details? Maybe I can help."

"Can't say."

Another officer approached them. "French, we gotta roll."

"Thanks for your time." She handed a business card to Erika. "Let me know if anything else comes to you."

Perspiration beaded on Erika's nose and upper lip. *Why the interest in Bigelow?* How might Erika find out and use the information to get him out of their lives?

"Erika?"

Erika moved her head toward the familiar voice. "Ms. Moon, I didn't expect to see you here."

Dark smudges edged Vera's eyes. Her entire body slumped forward.

"I'm worried about my daughter and came to check on her."

"Sit next to me." Erika patted the orange chair next to her yellow one. "We parted so abruptly at Sam's place."

Vera sagged into the seat. Was that booze Erika smelled again? Erika's mind raced. Vera walked right into Erika's arms. She'd get the memory card from her tonight and not tomorrow, look at its contents, and then decide on next steps without informing Bigelow.

A man rushed into the ER carrying a small boy. "Someone help us."

A nurse scooped the child out of the man's arms and peppered him with questions.

Erika dragged her eyes away. "Can I get you anything? You look done in."

"Because I am."

"Water? A soda? A snack?"

"Very kind of you, but no thank you."

Definitely alcohol on Vera's breath. An opportunity? The second the thought entered Erika's mind, she felt bad. *Fuck, who wouldn't drink with all this shit slamming them?*

The child-emergency disappeared down a hall. Once again, the waiting room grew quiet.

"Are the doctors with her now, is that why you're down here?" She had to wend the conversation around to the digital card, step-by-step.

"She's asleep. They are going to run more tests tomorrow."

Erika tried to keep her tone empathetic and calm. "My husband is here too. Tests as well. I'm sure that's a good thing, but hard on us."

"Oh. Here I am wrapped up in my own worries."

"No. Perfectly understandable." *Shift gears. Now*. She reached out her right hand and patted Vera's left. "A lot going on today. All that drama at Sam's."

"So, upsetting."

"What do you know about the man with him, not Benny, the other guy?"

Vera's words, tinged with suspicion, slurred a bit. "*You* did not recognize him?"

"No." Erika tried to sound offended to counter Vera's doubts. "Is he a friend of Sam's, a colleague, an employee?"

"He's dangerous."

Too many moving parts and players, but she had to concentrate on the prize. "Did you find the digital card?"

A ripple moved across Vera's features.

Too abrupt. So much for wending. Down shift. "Once you secure it, all this commotion will be behind you and you can put your energy into helping Liza recover."

"I am taking it to the police."

Crap. "Good thinking." *She found it, but the cops would not do.* "May I ask where it was?"

"In Sam's basement."

Didn't the idiot fuckups check that? "This is excellent news. It brings an end to our troubles."

"I will deliver it in the morning. I am too tired to do it tonight."

Too drunk, you mean. Erika swallowed hard, took a few quick breaths. "Did you look to see what was on it?"

"No."

"Perhaps we should do that first. There might be things on it that will hurt Charlie."

"We?"

"Yes, we." She dropped her voice an octave, leaned in closer to Vera's right ear. "Let me help us both."

"No harm can come to Charlie."

For fuck's sake, give me the damn card. "Yes, it can. His reputation at the least. If there is incriminating information and Charlie blackmailed Hugh Lavender, you could be in trouble with the law too."

Vera tilted her head and crossed her arms. Her bleary gaze tracked Erika.

"Where's the harm in looking at it first? None. But the other way around..." She lifted both hands, palms up.

Vera stayed quiet for a long time. Her shoulders caved forward even more. Finally, in a defeated voice she said, "I will examine it and call you."

"No."

Vera twitched.

"I mean, I'd like to be there. I have as much at stake as you do. More. They molested my husband. It's their fault he is in the hospital now. They threatened me with a gun. I'm terrified for our lives."

"I am sorry to sound callous, but I do not see how that is a reason for me to trust your character."

I'm losing her. Erika used all her self-control to keep from screaming. "I'm not asking you to trust me. You'll always have the device in your control. We'll look at it together, that's all. I won't touch it."

Vera covered her face with her hands again.

"Are you driving?" Erika asked.

"Why?"

"You seem a bit wobbly. Probably should get a taxi."

Vera appeared to weigh Erika's words. "I will call Dani for a lift."

"Good idea."

"She'll want to be with us when we look tomorrow."

Thank goodness. Point won. Now she had to figure out how to win the fucking game. "Why? Who the hell is she to you? What stake does she have in this?" Erika's tone came out too sharp, plus she cursed. Did *hell* count as a swear word? "The fewer people involved the better."

"I have asked you to watch your language around me. It is quite unbecoming."

Guess so. Erika watched Vera straighten her back and lift her chin.

"I trust Dani, not you." Her full lips, folded under, became a straight line. With her arms crossed again, she said, "Dani comes. You decide if you do too."

Chapter 34

Vera

Vera sat in what she now thought of as "their booth" at Gus's diner. The Tuesday breakfast crowd, older folks, and families with young children, paid their bills and left in staggered intervals. Most booths and tables stood empty. Staff bused the soiled dishes, wiped the tabletops. Vera chose this setting since they could not meet at Erika's because of the evil men Erika referred to as Cappy and Bigelow. Vera's apartment was not secure either. Zeek had followed her from before the accident. When Vera asked about Dani's place, Dani scotched the idea, with an excuse about her fiancé studying for an exam. Here, Vera felt safe. Relatively.

Dani and Vera sat side-by-side, waiting for Erika.

"You okay?" Dani sounded unsure of herself.

"This is all quite stressful." Vera folded her trembling hands in her lap. "I am fine."

"Last night, when I picked you up..."

"I appreciated your help."

"My mom drank a lot." Dani's mouth turned down. "She started early, lacing her coffee."

"I do not drink all day. Things have been hard. I am not like your mother."

"We'd be hungry, and she'd be drunk." Dani's eyes darted about without landing. "Bogie, my big brother, worked after school on and off, but he had me to look after plus housework and homework, so not enough paid hours to feed us."

Vera rubbed her forehead. "You deserved better."

Dani closed her eyes.

"I'm sorry." She thought about her own pain. *Alone. No Vincent, no Charlie, Liza in the hospital and Penny far away.* Vera hated self-pity. A waste of time and energy. Yet, she wallowed.

Dani lifted her head. "She smelled like flowers and booze. When people came, she used Listerine, hoping it masked the alcohol."

Startled, Vera jerked back. "Do I smell?" *What a horrific thought.* She only drank a little in the evening to help her sleep.

"You couldn't drive yourself home last night."

"Someone murdered my boy."

"You slurred your words."

"What?" Her precise speech defined her. Her parents drilled it into her. "White folks judge you by your diction," her father declared at least once per day. A decade before the sixties civil rights revolution, Vera practiced speaking like her father. Now she slurred her words?

"Remember when you asked me to stop lying?"

"Of course." She straightened her shoulders, tried to sound, and look motherly. *Ha. More like grandmotherly.* "I'm proud of you." She dabbed at her tears.

"You didn't give me a pass, even though I had a shitty life."

"Language," she said halfheartedly.

Dani tilted her head in acknowledgment.

Vera recognized the truth. Her hands trembled all the time. Despite her denials, she could not get through the day, not just the night, without several glasses of wine. The buzz made the pain hazier, Charlie's death less real for a few hours. Still, she should not drive like that. Suppose she hurt someone? Or the police stopped her?

"Promise me you'll stop drinking, like I promised you I'd stop lying."

"Sorry I'm late." Erika hustled over to their booth. "Awful traffic."

Dani touched Vera's hand. "Promise me."

Erika asked, "What's going on with you two?"

Vera said to Dani, "I promise."

Dani smiled an ear-to-ear grin.

"Fine, keep your secrets," Erika said with an edge in her voice. After several shifts, she settled into her seat.

With effort, Vera tried to keep her fear in check. Small talk might help them all. Vera asked Erika, "Is your husband doing better?"

Erika looked a bit startled.

"Is he out of the hospital?"

"Oh, yes, thank you." She pushed her mouth into a sort of smile. "I take it you got home all right."

Vera flushed. "Thanks to Dani."

Dani's grin came back full force.

"Let's get to it," Erika said.

Vera shot a glance over her right shoulder but didn't see anyone acting suspicious or even interested. "Here is what we are going to do." Her notebook lay opened beside her. "Together, we will examine the device contents." Her voice caught. She cleared her throat. "Then we will discuss it. Each one shares her opinion and recommendation for how to proceed." Vera paused. "But the decision is mine. My son, my digital memory card." She looked both women in the eye before continuing. "Agreed?"

Dani said, "Yes," with vigor. She pulled her computer onto the tabletop and flipped it open. Her left leg pumped in rapid rhythm.

"Erika?"

"Of course. Understood."

Dani angled the laptop toward Vera. "Good?"

With one more sweep of the diner, Vera reassured herself that it was safe. She placed her hand over her heart and tried to steady her breathing.

"Can you see my screen?"

"Yes. Thank you," Vera said.

Dani offered her right hand, palm up. "Let's see what we got."

Vera dug into her bag, grabbed the coin purse, unzipped it, and shook out the tiny card. She passed it to Dani, who slipped it into a narrow slot on the side of her computer. Erika slid back in her seat, angled her body sideways, and focused on Dani's screen. Dani pressed the icon to open the files on the card.

The first picture appeared almost comical, like a Halloween parody in poor taste. A close-up of the man, broad forehead, a long nose, and thin lips, his face covered with black paint or make-up.

"Oh no," Vera said.

Erika made a gasping noise.

Dani said to Erika. "You recognize him?"

"What else is on there?" Erika's eyes squinted at the screen.

Dani tapped, and the next image emerged of the man in blackface, standing in the foreground, naked, his penis partially erect. In the background was a naked woman, hands bound above her head.

Bile rose in Vera's throat. Her tongue felt thick.

Dani clicked again. This time a movie began. Along with the first man, three other men, all in blackface, all naked, making monkey gestures, danced around the woman. Now they saw the woman's hands tied to a bar fastened to the ceiling. The camera panned the space, moving in a jerky motion. Blank screen for a second.

"Charlie couldn't have taken these," Erika said in a low voice. "He wouldn't. So, who did? And how did Charlie get them?"

"That is your question?" Vera's voice shook with rage and disgust. "Not what are these racist, misogynistic, vile men doing?"

The movie started again. Now the woman was bent over a table, her buttocks the focus of the shot. The man spanked her with a switch. Red welts rose on her white skin. The man, his penis fully erect, approached her. The screen went blank again.

"They're going to rape her," Dani said, her voice filled with both horror and anguish.

"Charlie would never, ever be part of something like this. Blackface, men acting like apes, raping a woman. No. Never." Vera turned to Erika. "Who are they?"

Erika didn't respond.

Vera said, "I recognize one of them. I mean, he looks familiar."

Erika sat motionless, back straight, head high, with the slightest quaver around her mouth.

Chapter 35

Vera

"Who are those dudes?" Dani asked Erika, the disgust still in her tone. "Are they friends of yours?"

Erika kept her gaze on her folded hands.

In a flash of recognition, Vera said, "That is the man running for governor."

Dani said, "You're right. I saw him in the paper on the day of the accident."

"Hugh Lavender," Erika said, the quiver around her mouth spreading to her voice. "I'm friends with his wife."

Dani asked, "You're friends with the wife of a racist rapist?"

"I never heard him say anything like that. Nothing against women or Black people." She pushed out her lips, her fists banging at the air. "Fuck, fuck, fuck."

Vera was about to admonish Erika for her foul language, but she caught herself. She had witnessed something despicable. *Who cares about a foul mouth amid this horror?* She sagged against the back of the booth. For *this* he murdered Charlie, for these horrible pictures, this unforgiveable behavior?

Dani asked, "If he's such a big shot, how does this stay a secret?"

"I do not believe it," Vera said.

"That the video is real?" Dani asked.

"No one would murder for..." Vera waved her fingers in the computer's direction. "This is not a reason."

Erika said, "If it got out, he'd never be governor."

"Politicians weather a lot worse. Seek office and win. Unfortunately, people tolerate all kinds of racist, misogynistic, homophobic behavior."

"His business might take a hit," Erika said. "Plus, if they raped her, he's looking at prison."

Vera thought about the woman in the video. Poor thing. Was she a prisoner or a part of an act, or someone who enjoyed what was happening? "Surely, she would report gang rape."

Dani said, "Not everyone reports stuff," her voice low and soft. "Bad things happen all the time that women don't tell the cops."

"Rape and mocking Black people." Erika paused. "This is New York. He'd be toast socially and politically, if not financially."

"That justifies killing someone?"

"No, of course not," Erika said. "Just talking about motive."

There had to be more to it. Lavender murdered Charlie, tried to kill or harm Vera, Liza, and Erika's husband for this? "He is a man of means and paid..." She stopped. Twenty-thousand dollars plus twelve months' rent paid in advance. Did he give Charlie money to shut him up? Then why kill him? Besides, Charlie would not look the other way, not from blackface mockery or a gang rape. No.

"I have to go home." Vera paused. "No, not home, to the police." *No more thinking and planning. Time to act.* "Demand they arrest him. Expose him." Despite the horror and seriousness, she gave a mirthless chuckle. "So to speak."

"Wait," Erika said. "You said we'd discuss next steps."

Vera said, "Dani, please give the card to me."

With practiced ease, Dani ejected it and held it out to Vera.

Erika moved swiftly. With one hand on her purse, she snatched the memory card and bolted from the booth.

"What are you doing?" At first stunned, then barely a second later, furious, Vera jumped up and ran after the fleeing Erika. She heard Dani's footfalls behind her. "Stop."

Erika neared the diner's front door. A family of four entered. Erika elbowed them out of the way, pushing a small boy to the side. Vera collided with Larry, stumbled, righted herself, and swung open the glass door.

The two women pounded down the steps to the asphalt parking lot. No sign of Erika. "Let's split up. You go left, and I will go right. She has to be near, perhaps hiding in her car." Huffing, the thudding of her heart scared her. Vera had not run like that in years.

"Anything?" she asked Dani as they circled back to the front door.

"No."

Hugh Lavender murdered Charlie because the photos and movie would end his career in politics and hurt his business. If they raped the woman, he faced years of prison. When did this happen? *Was there a statute of limitations on rape? A man who had all the money and power in the world killed my Charlie.*

She had to get justice.

***

Vera climbed the stairs to her apartment, the elevator once again on the fritz. The images from the memory card flooded her mind. Then a different picture emerged. Seventy-thousand dollars total, counting the insurance. She could move into a better building, get out of debt, and still have enough left over for Penny and Liza. Did it matter how Charlie received the cash or why it landed in the safe-deposit box? Shame swept up from her gut.

Fourth floor. One more flight to go.

"Hey." Dani sat on the top step outside Vera's apartment.

"How do you know where I live?"

"Internet."

Of course. Silly question. "Shrewd Erika planned that little maneuver. How could I be so gullible?"

Dani's thick hair hid most of her face. "We both let our guard down."

"I should have expected it and positioned us differently in the diner."

"It's okay," Dani said. "It doesn't matter."

"Just when I started to like her." Vera's tiredness ran deeper than needing sleep or rest. She felt this same way right after the murder, her mind cloudy and unable to process information. She thought if she solved the crime, it would bring a measure of peace. Foolish hope. "Join me? I will make you a cup of tea." Vera longed for a drink, but she had given her word to Dani and promised herself. "I have some banana bread left."

"No thanks. Wanted to make sure you're all right."

Vera plopped down on the step next to Dani. "How about you?" Dani's right leg pumped. "Is there something else?"

"Did you ever do the right thing, and it all went wrong?"

"What happened?"

"You told me to stop lying." Moisture filled Dani's eyes. She sniffed.

"And you did."

"Yes, but I still lost everything."

"Repenting shouldn't be too easy."

Dani twisted her mouth. Her fingers plucked at her clothes. She shifted her weight, almost rocking. "Nothing in my life is ever easy."

"Self-pity is a thankless indulgence. Trust me. I learned from grievous experience." The bits and pieces Dani shared of her childhood pained Vera. "We cannot let our past dictate our future." Vera needed to heed her own advice.

Dani almost smiled. "My brother Bogie says things like that. I call it Bogie wisdom."

"Worth paying attention to."

"I'm trying."

She pressed down on Dani's jack-hammer leg.

"Anyway, like I said, the info is safe."

"What do you mean?"

"The photos are still on my computer."

"How did you manage that?"

The bounce returned to Dani's voice. She popped up, shifted from one foot to the next. "Each time we moved to another image, I saved the last one we'd seen."

"Clever girl."

"Not so much."

"Good job."

"Thanks."

"We will give them to Officer French," Vera said. "Get justice for Charlie."

"Bad for Erika."

"She should have thought about that before she stole from me."

"The pictures won't be enough. They'll hurt his campaign for sure, but they don't prove he killed Charlie." Dani paced on the stairwell landing. "We gotta find out the how of it, get proof positive."

"I do not understand. The awful video condemns him."

"Motive but not the means. He might have an ironclad alibi. Dudes like him hire other people to do their dirt."

"Sit. You are hurting my head looking up at you." Vera massaged her shoulders and neck.

Dani flopped back down.

"Probably right." Vera thought a minute. "We will speak with the officers *and* the media."

"If we go to the media too soon, we're tipping him off that we're on to him."

"Where do you get these ideas?"

Dani made a face.

"I am not sure how we can find proof beyond motive. The police have to take it from here."

Dani leapt back up and walked in a tight circle, her hands gesturing as she spoke. "Maybe one of Erika's thugs, that Bigelow guy, did the deed for him."

Vera pulled herself up by the bannister and stood next to Dani. "I am exhausted. Tomorrow this evidence goes to the police and ..." Would newspaper coverage be best or television or social media, which she knew almost nothing about? "We need to find someone responsible to run the story along with the photos."

"Gotta nail down proof first. He came after you once already."

"You are sure you do not want to come in?"

"Give me a day. I'm working on a plan. Plus, I met a reporter and I'll introduce you."

"Who?"

"Stephanie Mack. A friend of my boyfriend. I mean, of the guy I used to date."

"Used to? Before your fiancé?"

Dani's eyes dropped. She wrung her hands. "We broke up."

The complexity of duplicity. Poor girl. So young. Years younger than Liza and Penny. "Let's meet tomorrow and figure out what to take to the media." They were probably all in danger. "I better check on Liza. You go home and stay there. Come by for breakfast tomorrow and accompany me to see Liza before tracking down Officer French and your reporter friend."

Dani's perpetual motion slowed to a stop. "I can't lie to you. I'm not going home. I'm gonna find proof." She started moving again, shifting and fidgeting. "I have to."

Chapter 36

Erika

Cars sped past Erika, going at least eighty or ninety miles per hour. She pulled onto the shoulder of I684, Westchester's Autobahn, and switched off the engine. She'd been to Germany once with Griff for a business convention in Hannover. First, they'd flown into Amsterdam for a long weekend. They hooked up with an ethnically mixed crowd of partiers, smoking weed and drinking dark ales. This was long before Griff turned to serious drugs. Dancing, laughing, they fell off the bed and made love on the rug. The next morning, a little stiff from sleeping on the floor and a bit hung-over but happy, they rented a car and drove across the northern German border. They joined the other speeders zipping along the famous five-lane highway. Young and in love. *What happened to them?*

She closed her eyes and caressed the digital memory card with her thumb and forefinger. For years, she'd worked on her brand, demonstrating sophistication and discretion. Through strategic networking and doing favors for the right folks, she had gained connections to people of affluence and influence. She hired the same decorators the Lavenders used. Joined the right nonprofit boards. Attended the best parties and charity events. Hosted some. Griff's betting ate up money faster than he could make it, and the insatiable addiction-beast swallowed the rest. For a while she wallowed in despair. A string of lovers provided temporary relief. They took her to the theater, ballet, opera, and the best restaurants in New York City, far enough away from knowing eyes. They bought her necklaces, earrings, and diamond bracelets. If Griff noticed, she pretended she treated herself.

Relief? Not really.

Just as her crumbling life hit bottom, she'd grabbed a lifeline. Charlie Moon. Sweet, sensitive Charlie. He didn't have money or connections, but he loved her completely and unabashedly.

Studying the miniature card in the palm of her right hand, she snuffled and wiped her wet cheeks with the back of her left. Their ticket out of the hellhole Griff created. She was clinging to the edges. Soon, if she didn't save herself, the dirt and debris would bury her. The pictures and video provided her with a shovel. Erika grabbed tissues from a box on the car seat. Charlie died. But she was alive and still young enough, pretty enough, to reclaim her spot on the society-success-ladder or find a new one to climb in a new town. She blew her nose. With care, she repaired her makeup using the car's visor mirror and the contents of her bag.

She'd sneaked out of the house early, before anyone was up. She had to find a safe place to make a copy. Then get the money from Lavender and hand it over. Would Lavender trust that creepy-crawler-bastard Bigelow to close the deal?

Griff used to talk about life in Brazil. He lived there for a time. A magical place, he said. The music, food, beaches, nightlife. How much to start over? Can't be greedy. One million from Lavender. Next, put the house on the market. They'd get at least another million. Pay off the mortgage and net two-hundred thousand. One-point-two-fuck-you-world-million. Erika also kept a small stash of getaway money she'd saved when she thought Charlie and she might make it work. She could sell her jewelry. Things could still workout okay.

First, she had to deal with Vera. She grabbed her cell and punched in Vera's number. It rang four times before voicemail answered. "You've reached the home of Vera..." A male voice added, "and Charlie Moon. Leave a message and a callback number and..." Vera's voice again, "one of us will return your call."

Hearing Charlie's voice sent a shudder through Erika. Clearly, Vera hadn't gotten around to changing the message yet. Erika hung up and dialed again, listening to Charlie's baritone.

"Vera, it's me, Erika. Pick up."

"What do you want?" Vera sounded angry, tired, and a little sad. "Was that you phoning me a few seconds ago?"

Embarrassed, Erika ignored the question. "I'm sorry for taking the digital card, but Bigelow and Cappy are armed and vicious."

Silence.

"I'll make copies and get them to you. You'll have your proof."

Vera's ragged breathing came through the phone.

"Don't pull the cops into this yet. Give me a day. I'm begging you."

Erika pictured Vera with arms crossed tightly across her chest, not buying one word of her pitch. She tried one more ploy. "They know who you are. Liza and Dani too."

A breath sucked in.

"I'll give the thugs the card. I'll lie, swear to them I didn't access it. We'll all be safer. I promise."

"I am going to the press."

Fuck no. "Wait. Please wait. Give me until tomorrow."

"And to the police."

"How did Charlie get the photos and video? Doesn't that suggest there's another copy? I'll dig. Find out. I just need a bit more time."

Another long silence.

"It's almost over," Erika said.

"Dani has a plan to find proof he murdered Charlie. She says the video is not enough."

A lifeline. "She's right. Dani will work her lane and I'll work mine. You figure out what you want to tell the media, who you'll tell. Then we can all meet tomorrow evening to compare notes and make a final plan."

The quiet on the other end sounded like a loud no. Finally, Vera spoke again. "Lavender has to pay for killing Charlie."

"I agree. Give me one more day so we can wrap this up the right way." She had to keep Vera from the police and press until Lavender came through. Top priority. But she also owed Vera, for Charlie's sake. Erika didn't believe in an afterlife or in ghosts, even though she often sensed Charlie close by. No. There was only the here and now. Still, Charlie would want her to be kind to Vera. "Once they're out of my house, I'll call you. The three of us can share all the info we've gathered, take it to the cops, the media. Anything you want. We'll celebrate."

"We'll see."

"I understand your skepticism, but..."

"Do you? You lied to me. You swore you only wanted to watch, and then you swiped it and ran."

"They're armed. What part of that don't you get?" She took control of her emotions by breathing in and out. Spoke more quietly. "I'll make it up to you, to Charlie. I can't do that if I'm dead."

"Oh."

"Yeah. Dead. He killed Charlie. What will keep him from murdering me? I can do this. Tomorrow I get out from under them, then we meet." She waited. Brandy yipped in the background.

"Be careful."

Words to live by. "Yes. You too."

"Do not let me down."

The line disconnected.

Her breathing, heavy like an out-of-shape-jogger, slowed. People always let Erika down. Despite that, she intended to do right by Vera. If the video and the photos solved the murder, then Vera's nightmare ended as well. She'd witnessed enough karma to trust it. She smiled, imagining Charlie's sweet face. "Okay," she said aloud to him. "I'm going to do the best I can. Make it all come out for everyone. Promise."

Erika started her engine, pressed down the left-turn signal, and pulled out into the whizzing traffic. Lavender's headquarters owned dozens of computers, and the manager acted a bit smitten with her. She glanced at her watch. It was early, but perhaps not too.

***

The campaign office on Moger appeared deserted. Erika gave the front door a push. It swooshed open.

A deep, familiar voice said, "We're closed. Come back in an hour."

Erika bustled in, big smile, wide eyes. "Jim, it's me, Erika Noble."

In front of her, a dozen cluttered desks filled the office. Empty mesh waste baskets stood next to them as if waiting for the day's debris. No other workers, and therefore, no prying eyes. She heard a scraping noise; the kind metal chairs make on tile floors. Jim Bayer emerged from a room in the back and approached her.

"Hello." She extended her hand, leaned in, and gave him a quick peck on his bristly cheek. "How've you been?"

"Great." He tipped his head forward, shoved his hands into his pockets and then immediately pulled them out.

The first time Erika walked into the campaign office, she'd been with Kate Lavender. They'd brought sandwiches and doughnuts for the volunteers. Jim's eyes tracked Erika. Whenever she looked his way, she caught him staring at her. "Have we met?" she'd asked, her smile softening the sarcasm. "Yes. No." Jim stumbled over his words. "You probably don't remember. We were at the Lavenders' house last year." She didn't remember, but nodded her head anyway. "Of course." He'd thanked them for the food, offered both women coffees, and continued to make hungry eyes at Erika. Since then, she'd made three or four visits with Kate. Each time, he tripped over his feet to get to her.

Now, looking a bit rumpled, his face held a quizzical expression. "What can I do for you?"

"It's silly."

Jim towered over her. "Let's sit. I'll do what I can."

"I promised Kate I'd help her with the party she's throwing on Saturday."

"Boys and Girls Club?"

"My computer is on the fritz." Good thing she'd taken the time to fix herself up. "May I use one of yours? I can email the documents to her and a backup copy for me."

"Sure." He stood, offered her his hand to help her up.

"Thank you so much."

Jim showed her to one of the many workstations. Lists with red check marks covered the top of the desk. "Dialing for dollars." He flipped the papers over, bent forward, woke the computer, and typed in a password. "Here you go."

Fingers poised over the keys, she waited. He took the hint and left her alone.

In seconds, the pictures and video downloaded. She emailed them to her personal account and exited the page. "Have to run. Thanks again." She grabbed her tote and rushed out the door. The drive home took less than ten minutes. She pulled into the garage and pressed the *enter* button to close it.

No sounds from the house. Could everyone still be asleep? Too good to be true.

"Where've you been?"

Shit. Cappy. The smell of stale cigarettes poisoned the air. How many times had she asked them not to smoke in her home? *Apes. Neanderthals.* "None of your business." *Fucking mongrel.*

A second voice, the dark menacing tones of Bigelow, said, "Damn straight it is. Answer the question. Where you been?"

The two men sat on her couch, egg-smeared plates, and the ends of toast between them on a snack tray.

There was something in their manner, in the air. "Where's Griff?"

Bigelow growled under his breath.

"I demand to speak to him right now."

Bigelow rose. "You think he can help you? Stop me?"

He stepped closer to her, his eyes piercing her composure, the gun-bulge prominent.

"I've got it. I have the memory card."

Chapter 37

Dani

Dani had found a quiet street, parked, locked all four doors, lowered the front seat to as flat a position as possible, put Lefty under her head for a pillow, and closed her eyes. Sleeping fitfully, the conversation with Mirko the night before looped in her head. She'd confessed it all. Every white lie. At least, all the ones she remembered. He'd stayed quiet throughout her miserable tale. When she'd finished, she lay still and waited. Would he yell, kick her out of bed, stomp into the living room? Instead, he'd rolled over onto his side, away from her, and slept.

She cried quietly, her face pressed into the pillow. She must have dozed off. The last time she'd checked, the clock read 4:00 a.m. A sound woke her up. Eyes still closed, she reached for Mirko, swept the space next to her, and pondered the noise. It came to her. The front door slamming shut.

A lot transpired since then. The photos and the truth about Hugh Lavender. Erika's deception. Dani's commitment to find proof of the murder.

Reclined in her Chevy, listening to the muffled rumble of cars in the distance, Dani tried to puzzle through how she could get into Lavender's house and search for evidence to prove his guilt. By the time the sunlight slanted across her face, she had firmed up her plan.

The spacious Holiday Inn lobby smelled like fresh lemons. Bowls of the fruit decorated various counter tops including the registration desk. The ladies' room stood just off to the left. Dani scrubbed her face, washed under her arms, and brushed her teeth. Her crammed suitcase lay on the tile floor, its top unzipped and flopped open. She dug out clean underwear and her best work outfit. Black skirt, white no-iron shirt, and ballet-style flats. She smoothed the wrinkles and changed her clothes in the stall. She wished she had washed her hair that last morning at Mirko's. The pounding in her head and the weight of her misery was so heavy that shampooing her hair didn't make the cut. No sense worrying about it now. She brushed and patted.

The mirror over the sinks showed a presentable reflection. One of her mom's sayings was, "Make yourself presentable." That meant child welfare or a school representative coming to check on them. Her mother sober, Dani and Bogie's teeth brushed, clothes clean, and eggs for breakfast. "No one is taking my kids from me." Dani clung to Bogie. "Don't worry. I won't let anything happen to you." They ended up in foster care only twice, and not for long. Both times her mother got them back. Dani had to give her that; no matter what, she kept them together.

***

Dani Googled Hugh Lavender's Westchester County headquarters. She located it in a storefront on Moger. Two American flags, each hanging from a pole on either side of the entrance, greeted passersby and visitors. Dani pushed into the brightly lit space. A dozen desks piled with posters and papers, phones scattered around the room, overflowing wire trash containers abutted the desks. People bustled about. A box of doughnuts, their frosted heads gleaming under the lights, reminded Dani she'd not eaten in a long time. A stomach grumble loud enough for others to hear underscored her situation.

"Can I help you?" Thinning dark hair with gray fringe around the temples framed tired amber eyes.

"I've come to volunteer." Dani flapped the local paper, found the ad seeking college students to serve as interns, and pointed to it. "Erika Noble, Mrs. Lavender's friend, told me to come by." Dani stopped lying to her friends, but that didn't mean she couldn't lie to strangers.

At the mention of Erika's name, the man straightened up and pushed his glasses from the tip of his nose to the bridge. "She dropped by last night but didn't mention you were coming."

What was Erika doing here? "Oh, she called me early this morning. Must have occurred to her after seeing you." She gave him her most sincere smile.

He lifted his chin to the right. "Okay, fill out an application over there."

Westchester Community College seemed like a solid choice for a school. English major. She loved reading novels about powerful women who saved the day and family sagas with great parents who sacrificed for their kids. Her pen hovered over the spot. No. Political Science. Much better. She scribbled the information on the form. Vera's address (in care of) and Dani's cell phone number, Social Security ID, and driver's license. If asked, she'd explain the lack of address alignment with a recent move. For references, she put down Kate Lavender and Erika Noble. Hopefully, they wouldn't bother Mrs. Lavender. Worth the risk.

She looked up their addresses and phone numbers. Easy-peasy. At the bottom, the form sought her motivation for volunteering. *Mr. Lavender's ideals and vision for our state inspire me. I'm determined to make a difference*. Considering what she already knew about him, writing this made her feel bad, but it was a worthy lie. She signed her name.

Staring at her signature she remembered the IOU she'd left Alice and Pete, her former landlords. She must make that right as well. Just not today.

The man in charge came over. "Finished?"

"Yes." She thrust the application forward.

"Political science at WCS. Frank Bass still teaching American Politics and Policies?"

Dani shrugged. "Haven't taken that course yet."

"You'll like him." He offered his hand. "Jim Bayer."

Dani shook it. "Dani Gerrity."

"Okay, Dani Gerrity, let's put you to work. We'll check your references but we're kind of shorthanded now. I assume you drive."

"Sure do."

"Any speeding tickets, things like that?" He perused her application again. She'd checked all the *no* boxes for outstanding warrants, or felonies. He handed her a scrap of paper. "Know where Staples is?"

"Uh-huh"

"Supplies are low. We keep an account there."

"I'll be fast."

He gave her a once over as if visually assessing her competency. "You do that. When you get back, Marcus will show you the ropes."

Marcus, short and skinny with mocha skin and eyes, appeared at Bayer's side.

"Welcome to the madness."

"Thanks, back in a few."

Dani bustled along the aisles at Staples, filling her cart with printer paper, ink cartridges, pens, lined writing pads, highlighters, cellophane tape, and Post-Its.

Using the campaign's account, she checked out at the cashier with a scribbled signature, loaded her packages in the car, and drove to the office.

"I stored all the supplies."

Jim Bayer peered at her over his glasses. "I like you."

"Thanks." Most people liked Dani until they found out about her. "What else can I do?"

First goal — get into the Lavender's house. On crime shows, the detective asks for a glass of water and then snoops around while the person gets it.

Goal number two — find proof that Charlie blackmailed Lavender and take the evidence to the cops. *Would Lavender leave threatening letters around?* Most computers required a password, and she knew squat about uncovering codes.

Goal number three — connect him directly to the murder. The vile video on the memory card might hurt his chances for the governorship but not convict him of the actual crime. Once in the house, she'd dig, find proof. Her plan felt a bit shaky. Never mind. A positive attitude made things happen. Bogie taught her that.

No one asked Dani to go to the Lavenders' house. Marcus explained how they researched stories about the opposition, what made something worthy of keeping, and showed her how to flag and file the info. The boss sent her for coffee at Starbucks a few doors down. Pizza delivery arrived for lunch. Twenty people filled the storefront. Everyone except Dani and Marcus seemed to be on the phones asking for money. Another trip to Starbucks.

Dani said to Marcus, "I don't have a computer to finish the research you asked me to do. During my last coffee run, I lost my seat and use of a laptop."

With his face scrunched in concern, he looked around. "I guess you can use Mr. Lavender's. It's the office next to Jim's." A computer sat on a clean desk.

Even though her butt hurt from sitting and her shoulders ached from hunching over the keyboard, Dani's heart rate picked up. This could be a lucky break. "Are you sure it'll be okay? I promise not to snoop or anything." *Stupid remark.* She'd put the worry in his mind.

Marcus shook his head. "Nothing to see. He barely uses it."

She followed him into the office and watched as he logged on. WINNING, he typed in the spot for the password.

"Here you go."

People often used the same password for many things. If so, *when* they sent her to Lavender's house, she might find and access his home computer. She dove in and stayed on task.

Finishing the requested research, but making no progress on her real agenda, by 4:00 p.m. her frustration level hit red alert. Not to mention the two nights of little sleep catching up with her. She gulped down a cup of tepid coffee, something she almost never drank. *Ugh. No wonder.*

"Can you make another trip for us?" Jim Bayer, his tie shed, rolled up his shirtsleeves above his elbows. Mixed gray hair covered his arms. "This has to get to the Lavenders' place before five."

Her heart rate rocketed. "Sure."

"Ring the bell. Drop it off." He handed her a cardboard box about the size of a book. "Then get back here. A local TV reporter is coming by — Stephanie Mack."

Mirko's Stephanie.

"Be good training for you. You'll see how I keep the jackals from trapping me into stupid."

"Cool." Finally, her shot at nailing Lavender. Time enough to worry about Stephanie.

"Not that this one is that bad. Seems more balanced than most."

Great. Beautiful, competent, and fair. Dani gave herself a mental shake. *Stay focused.* She pictured the house from newspaper stories. "You ever been there?"

"Sure, lots of times."

"Must be big."

"Twelve thousand square feet. They entertain in the east wing." He chuckled under his breath. "The west wing is all about business. I'm guessing he has bigger plans than being governor."

Dani nodded, not sure she got the joke or inference. "Like being president?"

"Hmmm." He shifted to a serious tone. "About six months back they ran a big spread on the house in *Westchester Magazine*. There's a stack of newspapers and magazines around here somewhere."

Dani spied the pile on the other side of the room. No time to look for the issue now. "Who should I ask for?"

"I'll call ahead and inform them you're coming." Jim dug his phone out of his pants pocket. "Ms. Lavender might be home and invite you in."

Hopefully not since Ms. Lavender never met Dani. "I can thank her. I love this. Great first day." She beamed at him.

"How do you know Erika?"

"She's good friends with a friend of mine, Vera Moon." Dani waited. He appeared to want more. "She's beautiful and kind. Offered to help me."

Ear-to-ear grin. "You're a good kid. Hope you're sticking with us. Lots going on."

"For sure."

Dani pulled out her iPhone to tap in the Lavenders' address into the Maps app. A missed call from Vera. Dani clicked on her voicemail.

"Thought we were having breakfast together. Are you okay? Heard from Erika last night. She asked for time to get the thugs out of her house. Then we are going to meet, compare notes, and make a plan."

Are you kidding me? Erika wriggled herself back onto Vera's good side? Dani typed a quick text. Her hands sweated. "No way. She's a liar & a thief. Got an angle. Will be in touch as soon as I can."

Chapter 38

Vera

Liza looked better, stronger. She was sitting up. Pale, bruised smudges still created a semi-circle under her eyes, but her skin no longer appeared ashen.

"I can't wait to get out of this miserable place. It smells so bad, and the noise and lights kept me awake most of last night."

She was also back to her complaining ways, a clear sign of healing.

"They want to be sure you are well enough." Vera sat on the edge of the bed. "Hungry? I brought you tomato-and-basil soup." She pulled the container from her thermal bag. "And a bit of chocolate."

"I'm okay." Liza closed her eyes. After a few minutes, her breathing slowed.

Vera stood. In her bag, the thumb drive Dani gave her containing the copied evidence of Lavender's racism and possible rape sat tucked in a zippered change purse. She tried to assess their position. Dani required time to find more incriminating information. And what was Erika up to? How long would it take her to evict the thugs once she gave them what they wanted? Inaction weighed on her. She slid out her notebook.

"Mom."

"Yes?" Half-listening, she flipped the pages, looking over her notes.

"Do you remember me cutting myself, making little slices on my arms and fingers?"

Still distracted, she said, "That never happened."

"It did."

Vera pulled over a chair. "When?"

"In middle school. First year."

"I would not forget something like that."

Liza made an unpleasant noise under her breath. "So, I'm making it up?"

"No." *I want it to be untrue.*

"Sara Winter and her idiot brother Ray, they bullied and tortured me. Every day."

What a horrible mother she must have been. "When did it end?"

"Dad took care of it."

Of course. Vera sat quietly, tears seconds away. She snatched a tissue from the generic box on the tray next to the bed and pressed it onto her eyes.

"I've been thinking about my screwed-up life and attempting to figure out the why of things. I'm not trying to hurt you."

The tears escaped. She dabbed under her eyes and blew her nose in the soggy tissue.

"You always seem disappointed in me."

"I'm sorry." She failed Liza, she failed Penny, and evidently, she failed Charlie too, because look at the mess he ended up in.

"It's my fault too. Lots of bad choices," Liza said.

"You are still young."

"Young enough, I guess, to start over. I might move closer to Penny or to someplace warm."

"I love you."

"I visited Tampa, Florida once. Liked it."

"I truly love you."

Liza made a tiny movement of her mouth, a failed attempt at a smile.

Vera sucked in her breath. "Why Florida?" Not what she wanted to say. Liza disappointed her, but it shouldn't show. She shouldn't judge so harshly. And there was no excuse for missing bullying and self-inflicted cuts.

"A college buddy invited me down. Do you remember Kiki?"

Relieved that she did, Vera said, "Yes. Super tall engineering major?"

"That didn't work out. Nor did her marriage. She's divorced. Thought we'd hang out together and think about starting a business."

"Oh?"

"She's a headhunter, talent manager. It's hot right now."

The money Vera had lied to Liza about came to mind. Possibly dirty. Would the police confiscate it? "I will help you. Charlie left me some cash plus the insurance." It was not too late for either of them to do better, be better.

Liza's response surprised Vera. Perpetually money hungry and broke, Liza suspected Charlie held an insurance policy that Vera just confirmed.

"We'll see. Nothing's certain." She sank back onto her pillow and closed her eyes again. "Thanks, Mom."

***

For a long while, Vera sat and watched her daughter sleep. She forced herself to remember her children's life in middle and high school. Liza awkward, poor grades and neglected homework. Vera working full time, flat out and exhausted by the time she got home. Vincent still at the office. Dinner too often was pizza or burgers; all she could manage after a long day. Penny excelled. Quiet, she stayed in her room reading or listening to music. Only Charlie brightened the house. Beautiful, laughing Charlie. She pictured all his friends from elementary school. Justin, his best friend from next door. Who were Liza's and Penny's closest chums? Shame washed over Vera. *Do better, be better*.

"Mom?"

"I'm here."

Liza's smile seemed genuine this time. "I loved our family vacations at Cape Cod and Disney, my favorites."

"Mine too."

"Okay."

She closed her eyes again and slept.

Chapter 39

Dani

The Lavender driveway appeared as long as a football field and as twisty as the storied roads that hugged the California coast. Bright pink and purple impatiens edged the asphalt. Bursts of red and yellow roses encircled a dogwood tree. She parked her car. Pillars, like the kind you see in paintings of Greek temples, adorned the entranceway. The welcome mat in front of the double doors spelled out Lavender. Two brass knockers, one for each door, gleamed in the late-afternoon sun. Dani searched for a doorbell. Before she located it, one of the double doors opened.

A small Latina woman asked, "May I help you?"

"Hi. I'm from campaign headquarters."

"Oh yes." She put her hand out for the package.

How to get inside? "This is so embarrassing."

The woman cocked her head. "Pardon?"

My cell died, and I need to make an urgent call? I must have a drink of water or I'll faint? "May I use the restroom?" She gave an apologetic shrug.

The woman moved aside. "Of course, come in."

Dani stepped into the foyer. *Wow.*

The woman first scanned the hall toward the right. The east wing? *How many guest baths did they have?* She looked left. *Yes, please.*

She pointed toward the west wing. "There's a powder room a few doors down. I'm sure its unoccupied." She spoke in a soft and educated accent.

Dani handed the woman the package. She had to find Hugh Lavender's home office, the place Jim said Lavender conducted business. She trotted down the hall. Family photos decorated the walls leading to the bathroom. Hurrying past the gallery, she called over her right shoulder, "Are these the Lavenders' children?"

No response.

Using her peripheral vision, she searched for nearby access to the upper floor.

"The powder room is just there." The woman said, her tone impatient.

Dani slowed in front of a family grouping, two adults, three children and a Lab with the tip of its tongue poked out. "What a great-looking dog."

The woman seemed worried, or something akin. Her tone became agitated. "I have to prepare dinner." She disappeared into one of the zillion rooms.

The powder room was a large two-section deal. A long mirror and a fabric covered bench centered the outer space. A box of tissues, small-unopened bottle of Scope, cups, a hand lotion with a foreign name (French?), and a can of hairspray sat in a wicker basket on the counter just below the mirror. A toilet and sink occupied the inner space. Rolled cloth towels stacked in a matching wicker basket stood to one side of the sink on a marble shelf. A larger version of the towel and supplies baskets sat under the shelf.

Dani ran the cold water. She checked her watch. Four fifteen. She cracked open the door and listened to the distant roar of lawn mowers and leaf blowers. Inside, water splashed in the sink. Should she leave the faucet on in case someone came by? No. She turned it off, slipped out and, in search of his home office, headed in the opposite direction of the entranceway.

The corridor led to the library. A ladder, high enough to reach the uppermost shelf, rested against one book-lined wall. The room looked larger than Mirko's apartment. Dani kept going. Sofas, chairs, footstools, and small round tables filled the next room. A flat-screen television dominated one wall. She reached a carpeted staircase and bolted up. What would she say if someone asked her what she was doing? Jim Bayer trusted her. She'd never get another opportunity to get back here and search. Plus, he'd been so nice to her. He'd get in trouble. Not good. *"Think positive. Act with confidence."* Bogie's voice urged her forward.

Dani walked past multiple doors along the wide hallway. She dashed in and out of bedrooms, many with private baths. Two, three, four, five. *Geez. How many bedrooms and bathrooms did a person need?* Room six. She twisted the knob and gave the door a push. It swung open. Jackpot. A room twice the size of those she'd passed. Desk, executive chair, conference table with eight leather chairs around, cabinets, another TV, laptop, and a printer. Four eighteen. Sweat trickled down the sides of her face. Her blouse clung to her back.

She moved the mouse, and the computer woke from its sleep state; a photo of snow-covered mountains filled the screen. In the center appeared a spot to type a password. *Damn.* Remembering the computer at the campaign office, she typed "WINNING." No, a red alert instead. Next, she tried "Winning." Still no luck. One more attempt. "winning." The screen came alive, revealing the desktop cluttered with folders and files.

Four nineteen. She studied the folder labels. Bills. Family Photos. Campaign. Fundraising. Hudson River Project. Charities. Oak Lane. That was on the license plates of the cars involved in the accident and later at Javier's garage. She doubled clicked. Dozens of Word and Excel documents, far too many to look at now. Four Twenty. Her attention went back to the Oak Lane folder. A quick scan. Schedule. Repairs. Personnel. Her eyes flicked from the screen to the closed door, to her watch. Four twenty-one. She opened the personnel file, moved the cursor to print. The printer whirred awake. Several sheets of paper flopped onto the printer's shelf. Another folder in the Oak Lane file. Correspondence. Again, she double clicked. Her breathing became audible, a huffing pant. She continued to scan the files until a folder labeled Bigelow caught her eye — the name of one of baddies Erika mentioned. Dani dug into her front pocket and snagged the thumb drive she'd brought with her, shoved it into the USB port and copied the Bigelow folder to the drive. Four twenty-three. American Liberty Council. The name sounded familiar. She searched her memory but couldn't place it but, just in case, copied that file as well. Four twenty-five. She grabbed the papers from the printer, closed the computer folders, folded, and pressed the documents into her waistband under her blouse, stashed the memory stick back into her skirt pocket and bolted out the door.

Skip-walking, she retraced her steps. Down the stairs, down the hall, the powder room now just ahead.

"Who are you?"

A tall woman, her red hair tied back in a messy bun with escaping curls, stood in front of Dani, blocking her way.

"I got lost. This place is so mega."

"And you are...?"

Dani dried her palms on her skirt and extended her right hand. "Dani Gerrity from campaign headquarters. I'm an intern there."

"Why are you here?"

"Jim Bayer sent me."

The crease between the redhead's almost rust-red eyebrows eased. "The front door is this way." She flexed her wrist and pointed.

"Made a wrong turn out of the bathroom."

"It happens."

Dani and the redhead walked back towards the entrance. "I admire Mr. Lavender so much. Doing my best to help get him elected."

The woman stopped and offered her hand. "Bridgette Fitzgerald."

Dani pumped her hand. "Oh, Ms. Fitzgerald. Mr. Bayer speaks about you with awe." Dani grinned. People accepted lies that flattered them. "You must love working here."

A no-teeth smile. "I do."

"May I have a glass of water? Sorry." Dani flapped her damp shirt away from her bra. She hoped the outline of the papers didn't show. "I've been going non stop all day."

Bridgette's freckled pug nose and green eyes added to her attractiveness. "This way."

"Are these pictures of family members?" Dani waved her hand to take in the wall gallery.

"Yes."

Boy, this woman used as few words as possible. Dani tried again, stopped in front of a framed photo of a pudgy boy of about three or four. "Is this one him?"

She nodded.

"He looks kinda sad."

She seemed to study the portrait. "I don't think he experienced a loving childhood."

Longest sentence so far. "I'm sorry."

Red blotches crept up Bridgette's neck. "He's a fine man."

"For sure." *A racist, rapist, murderer, yet Bridgette liked him. What was wrong with her? Or did he keep secrets so well?* "I know why I'm supporting him, but I kinda wondered about your reasons."

"He cares deeply about under-privileged children." She peered down on Dani. Her voice took on a suspicious edge. "Why do you ask?"

"I'm totally glad he's running; wanted more ammo for when I'm talking to potential supporters."

"Have you met him?"

"Not yet."

Bridgette's frown vanished. "You have to hear him speak. He's passionate about making sure every child has opportunities."

This did not compute. "Can't wait." A thought. "Will he be home soon?"

Bridgette gave her the type of smile people give to precocious children. "No."

The same Latina woman who greeted Dani appeared at the end of the hall. "Sonia, please get us two glasses of ice water."

Sonia turned, but not before throwing Dani an inquiring look, as if wondering how she ended up with Bridgette.

Dani ignored Sonia. In a bright voice, she asked, "No photos of Ms. Lavender?"

"What do you do for the campaign?"

"Anything and everything."

Bridgette stayed quiet for several beats. "There are lots of pictures of Ms. Lavender in the east wing."

"And their children?"

"None."

They entered the kitchen. Spicy meat scents infused the air. Dani drank her ice water. She hoped the files she took revealed clues or even better answers. They could be nothing. Dani finished her water. She might need to get back here to search some more. "If I can help you, give me a call at the office. I'm good with computers and research. Want my number?"

Bridgette checked her smartphone. "Hmmm."

"Love all the charities the Lavenders support." She was taking random shots and in danger of sounding too eager. "And you've inspired me with his commitment to underprivileged children." An exaggerated sigh. "I'm an orphan, so I get it." That lie often played well.

Bridgette kept her eyes glued to her phone screen. "They're quite philanthropic."

"Which is so important image-wise and for the community. Loved their last bash." Uh-oh. She told her she'd never met the Lavenders. "I mean, I heard about it from Ms. Noble."

"I must return to work." Bridgette put her glass down on the countertop.

Dani did the same. "Better get back to headquarters." *Argh.* One more gambit. "Oh, I forgot to mention, I'm great with fundraising events. I do that for a living." A half-white lie. She'd worked at the party place for eighteen months, selling balloons, paper products and plastic serving-ware in bulk. More like a ninety-nine percent white lie.

Bridgette squinted at Dani. "Aren't you a student intern?"

"Gotta work too." She hoped Bridgette sympathized with tough times and having to do it all.

Bridgette's face softened again. "An orphan?"

She'd listened. "Grew up in foster care."

"We've got one coming up next Tuesday. We might need an extra hand."

Bogie wisdom: "Hum the tune as if you know all the words."

"Assist with the prep?" She didn't want to be in a house filled with guests. Or would that make it easier to skulk around?

"I can reach you at the campaign office?"

"Absolutely."

Chapter 40

Erika

Erika eyed Bigelow as he dropped the digital card in an envelope without looking at it, grabbed his cell phone, pushed open the sliding glass doors to the deck, and stepped outside. The cool morning breeze lifted the edges of her hair.

After several minutes, Bigelow re-entered the great room, his cell phone still in his hand.

"So that's that, right?" Erika asked.

"We'll see."

"You have what you came for; it's time to get the hell out of my house."

He didn't respond.

Cappy joined them. "We ready to roll?"

"What's your other partner up to?" Erika remembered the man with Liza's ex-husband, Sam.

"Huh?"

"Isn't Zeek, the guy with the ravished face, part of the gang of charmers?" She kept her tone light, amused, as if bantering.

"Wadda you know about it?" Chest first, he inched closer to her.

Cappy, up until now standing quietly off to the side, said, "Leave her."

"Butt out."

Just looking at Bigelow made her furious. *Fucking bastard, cretin.* She'd complied with all his shitty demands. "The three of you are part of some stupid conspiracy involving Lavender." *Take that, asshole.*

Bigelow made his trademark low growling noise, conveying unspoken menace. His fat gut stood inches from her face.

A mistake. With trembling legs, she held her ground and tried to recover. "Don't worry. Not my concern." One-shoulder shrug. "All I care about is both of you getting out of my house." She used the opportunity to put distance between Bigelow and her.

In her peripheral vision, she saw Cappy swing his gaze back and forth between Erika and Bigelow as if waiting for something to happen. He scratched his jaw line with dirt edged chewed nails.

"Why d'you mention Lavender?" Bigelow asked.

"Lavender?" She went into the kitchen. "Anyone else want something to drink?" How much trouble was she in?

"You looked at this." A statement, not a question. Bigelow followed her, the digital card now out of the envelope and in his hand.

"No." She pulled open the refrigerator door, its gleaming stainless steel marred with hand and fingerprint smudges. "I assumed. Forget it." She gripped the stem of a Coke bottle, tried to keep the tremble from her voice. "Where's Griff?" Bigelow's sour breath infused the air. If she hit him hard enough, could she run, get to her car? A quick pivot, swing with all her might, and smash the bottle on his chin, the highest she thought she could reach from her five-foot-two vantage. What would Cappy do? He'd just stuck up for her. Would he help her? Did Cappy have a gun too?

"Your piss-ant husband ain't here."

Damn it. With authority she asked again, "Where *is* he?"

"Phone sent him running." Bigelow put his hand on her shoulder and dug his fingers hard. "What'd you see, bitch?"

Cappy said, "Come on man, leave her alone. We got the goods. Let's bounce."

Bigelow tightened his grasp, digging deeper into her flesh. "Your high-and-mighty ways don't cut it with me."

"Nate, let's go."

The crushing pressure made her knees buckle. "Get off me."

"You need a lesson in manners."

His other hand came up either to hit her or strangle her. She had to stop him. Using all her strength, Erika twisted around until she faced Bigelow. With her right knee, she thrust hard into his groin.

He doubled over.

With two hands, she brought the bottle down on his skull. Shards of glass cut into his scalp and forehead, drawing blood. Several pieces nicked Erika's hand. Soda splashed and ran down his face and onto Erika's hair.

Bigelow wobbled, but he stayed on his feet, still bent from his waist. Before she could react, he came up with his right and swung. His fist smashed into her gut. The air whooshed out of her lungs. He landed a second punch to her left temple. Pain blinded all thoughts. She sank to the tiled floor in a haze of agony. His shoe smashed into her ribs. Blackness descended.

Chapter 41

Dani

Dani pushed open the door. Headquarters was empty of volunteers except for Marcus, who pressed his fingers to his lips. Jim must have cleared the place for the interview. Dani eased the door shut without making a sound.

In the middle of the room, Stephanie stood with her back straight. A few feet away, the two camerawomen arranged their equipment, including a dome-shaped light. Working together, the technicians moved their cameras and dome-light around, peering into the lenses every few shifts, until the heftier camerawoman nodded to Stephanie and offered a thumbs up.

Dani gave Stephanie the once-over. With some envy, she guessed Stephanie's dress was expensive. Not because Dani wished she had money, more because she desired to look all polished and pulled together. Cobalt blue chemise, not too tight but still outlined nice curves. She could see why Mirko found Stephanie attractive. *Mirko.* Dani's spirits sagged. She lifted a stick of gum from her pocket and popped it in her mouth. The surge of mint on her tongue perked her up a bit. Mirko's brand.

Stephanie's clear, well-modulated voice broke in. Looking directly into the first camera, she said, "We're here at Hugh Lavender's Westchester County campaign headquarters, speaking with his local campaign manager, Jim Bayer. Recent polls have the multi-millionaire up by twelve percent over the governor, who continues to struggle with lackluster fundraising." Her smile seemed genuine. "Welcome, Jim."

Unlike his usual rumpled attire, his dark suit, white shirt, and brick-red tie looked crisp and professional.

"Thanks for inviting me, Stephanie."

Ignoring additional niceties, she plunged in. "To what do you credit Mr. Lavender's latest surge in the polls?"

Despite his garb and twitchy-grin, Jim looked uncomfortable. His eyes flicked about. A sheen of perspiration covered his forehead. Probably more of an inside, behind-the-scenes guy.

"Our message for helping the middle class without scaring off business resonates throughout the state," Jim said in a stilted tone. "Hugh Lavender came from humble beginnings and understands what it means to work hard. He earned his way to the top, and he wants to help others do the same."

"Not exactly humble beginnings." Stephanie flashed white, even teeth. Her Mediterranean-brown skin glowed. "I thought he grew up in an affluent community, earned a BA from Columbia University, and an MBA from Cornell? Those are not middle-class schools."

"Columbia awarded him a scholarship."

"According to our sources, not one based on need but on his athletic skills."

"He worked his way through college."

Stephanie dropped the smile. "Admirable. What are the chances his likability ratings continue to climb once the public finds out about his dealings with felon Nate Bigelow?"

Dani almost choked on her gum.

Jim stood frozen in place.

"We understand that convicted felon Nate Bigelow and Hugh Lavender are business partners. Is that correct?"

Jim coughed, cleared his throat. Blinked too many times.

Dani knew little about public relations, but Jim sure sucked at it.

"Mr. Bayer?"

His tone a bit smoother, Jim said, "Hugh Lavender is a man of principle and generosity. His opponents try to discredit him with lies and innuendo." He pushed his mouth into an amused half-smile. "I'm surprised at you, Stephanie, falling for this kind of mudslinging."

Her expression stayed fixed. "So, they are *not* business partners?"

Out of the corner of her eyes, Dani saw the alarmed look on Marcus's face.

Jim said, "If anyone Mr. Lavender is working with is a felon, he and we are unaware."

"Don't you do background checks on all of your employees and associates?"

Jim's eyes started moving around again. His voice lost its confidence. "Of course, we do."

"Wouldn't prison sentences show up?"

Jim appeared crestfallen. "I'd appreciate some time to investigate your allegations, which I'm confident are either not true or have a logical explanation."

Ignoring Jim, Stephanie looked straight into the camera facing her. "Is gubernatorial candidate Lavender associating with a known felon? We'll keep you informed as this story develops. This is Stephanie Mack reporting."

The hefty camerawoman said, "And we're out."

Red-faced, Jim said, "I figured you were above ambush journalism."

"I have proof that they work together. FYI, we're running this at eleven-o'clock and a follow-up in the morning." Stephanie's voice remained cool. It reminded Dani of the way Erika managed things. Dani could learn to do that without relying on stories and lies. Always sound smooth and unruffled, no matter how upsetting things got. Maybe.

Neither Stephanie nor Jim paid attention to Marcus or Dani standing in the corner watching and listening, but now Stephanie smiled at them. "You might want to find a new candidate to support." She signaled to the camerawomen by twirling her finger. "Let's wrap up here."

"Please give us the courtesy of more than a heads up. We'd like to respond with the truth." Jim took a step closer to Stephanie. "What will you report?"

"Nate Bigelow is a three-time felon, incarcerated at Dannemora, served five years for armed robbery, and at Sing Sing for drug running and money laundering. Now he pops up here, running a car service for Lavender."

"People change. He paid his debt."

"Oh, so you're aware of his record?"

Sweat dripped from under Jim's scalp. "No, I'm saying give the guy the benefit of the doubt before humiliating him on the eleven o'clock news."

Stephanie zipped a glance at Dani. "He might have something to do with the murder of Charlie Moon."

Marcus coughed into his hand. His eyes huge.

Jim glared at him before swinging his head back toward Stephanie. "Get out now."

"So, for the record, that's a denial or a no comment?"

"You get the hell out of my office." He swept his angry glare over Dani and Marcus. "All of you. Get the hell out."

Chapter 42

Vera

Vera sipped her chamomile tea. It often calmed her. Not today. Her mind leapt from one worry to the next. From where did the twenty-thousand dollars she found in Charlie's safe-deposit box come? Hugh Lavender must have paid Charlie to keep quiet about the photos and a punishable crime. Did Charlie demand more? Is that why Lavender killed him? Charlie was not a greedy person. He lived simply. Perhaps he needed the cash to run away with Erika. That might make sense. Designer clothes, fancy jewelry; loving Erika might require more means than Charlie ever earned. But if he saw the racist photos, thought they had violated a woman, he would not attempt blackmail.

Erika's conniving ways popped back into Vera's mind. She tried to fathom what Charlie saw in her. Pretty, rich, polished, okay, but did that explain sneaking around with a married, white woman, who was devoid of a moral compass? A liar and a thief? Vera was an inclusive, fair-minded, forgiving Christian. Yet she was upset about something that no longer counted. Hugh Lavender, on the other hand, mattered a great deal.

She roved around the living room. Thought about the twenty thousand again. How could she spend money that came from a murderer? She promised Liza financial assistance. Would the insurance be enough to pay bills, get a new place, and help Liza move and start a business?

Vera walked into the kitchen. A bottle of Chianti, its cork jutting from the neck, rested on the counter. She promised Dani to stop drinking and she knew better than to drive after imbibing. Suppose she hit someone? Unacceptable. Half a glass, however, would not be enough to impair her.

Deep in thought, filled wineglass in hand, Vera returned to the living room. She agreed with Dani. They needed more facts about Lavender's involvement in Charlie's murder. The video and pictures were not proof of anything. She should have asked Dani about her plan. Vera took a sip. What was Sam's full involvement with Zeek? Sam might have useful information about Lavender or help her interrogate this Zeek person.

"Get a grip."

Brandy lifted her head, ears perked.

"No, dear heart, talking to myself."

Brandy ambled over, rested her snout on Vera's leg, soulful eyes looked up expectantly. Absently, Vera stroked Brandy's thick coat and dug in her pocket for a treat. She was tired of feeling worn out and discouraged. Make things right with Liza. Penny's plane landed tomorrow at noon. The three of them together again. Apologize. Do better, be better.

First, they had to solve the murder. Find out Dani's plan and contact Sam. She took another small gulp of wine and reached for her phone, but before she finished punching in Dani's number, the phone vibrated.

"This is Nurse Maura Johnson at Northern Westchester Hospital. Liza experienced a setback. You need to get here as quickly as possible."

Vera steadied herself by placing her hand against the living room wall. "What has happened?"

"We're not sure. She's in pain and asking for you. The attending physician is tracking down Dr. LaSalle."

"I just left her. She seemed fine."

"If she were my daughter, I'd get here as fast as I could."

Chapter 43

Hugh

Hugh Lavender loved this room. Tall French doors framed in walnut led to cultivated gardens, almost fully in bloom. The Japanese maple's intense red leaves, the irises just about to open; blushing peonies edged the walkway to the pond and miniature waterfall. Not that Hugh gardened. The choices and placement, however, bore his mark. Most times when he sat in this room, he faced the gardens. When he had visitors, like today, he let them enjoy.

A young woman with an unfortunate nose and a washed-out complexion sat across from him. She represented a down-county day school.

"Sixty percent of our children are on scholarship," she explained. "An investment of $25,000 would help one child receive a life-changing education."

Hugh already decided to give her the money. He'd discussed it with Kate, and she'd agreed. Still, he liked to look folks in the eye so he could witness their reactions. "You make an excellent argument." He beamed at her. "Mrs. Lavender and I will happily support your school."

He loved this part of his life. Their friends thought Kate drove the family's philanthropy, and he let them, encouraged it. Kate liked to throw parties, and she basked in the adoration. And yes, his generosity helped him with campaign fundraising and his likability numbers in the polls, but the kids mattered the most to him.

"Thank you for your generosity and kindness." She stood and offered her hand. "Do you have children of your own?"

Hugh frowned. It angered him when people asked that question. It was rude and impertinent. He smiled his fake smile and shook her hand. "We've not been so blessed." Kate hated the thought of motherhood. At first, they fought about it. Then, as his businesses grew, he'd put his desire for a family aside. "Supporting the children in our community more than compensates." And that was the truth.

To this day, thinking about all the children and families he helped brought moisture to his eyes. Adults do crappy things to kids. Hugh learned this through personal experience. Despite the narrative his campaign spun, he grew up in affluent privilege of the dysfunctional sort. Both parents found Hugh an inconvenience, and during their fights, he didn't exist at all. Nannies rarely lasted more than a year. Fortunately, his aunties Maddie and Pat loved him and stayed in his life. Pat's husband, Uncle David, stepped in as a surrogate father. They gave money to lots of causes, but mostly to support kids. Hugh saw that as his mission in life, to be like his aunts and uncle and save children in need — through charity and, if he should win, *when he won*, via legislation. Our youth required both.

He couldn't let this Charlie Moon business, or the American Liberty Council interfere.

Bridgette, her often unruly hair in a tidy bun, interrupted. "Sorry." She gave an apologetic smile to the guest. "Quite important." She waggled a cell phone.

Hugh excused himself.

In a low voice she apologized again and said, "It's an urgent call from Nate Bigelow."

It took concentration to fake composure. "No worries." He hustled down the hallway to the stairs that led to his home office. He waited until he reached its sanctuary before speaking to Nate.

"What?"

"We have it."

The damning digital card. Bigelow succeeded. Maybe Hugh could still overcome. "Who viewed it?"

"No one."

Not likely. "Give me the names of the possible list." Just a few more steps to safety, to keeping his reputation, to winning his big prize.

"Sure thing, boss."

"Starting with you."

Chapter 44

Hugh

The dark closet required navigating from memory. Kate's side reflected her passion for suits, evening gowns, shoes, and order, each organized by color, length, event, and date. Dresser drawers held bras, what advertisers now referred to as shapewear, stockings, and silk nighties.

It would be at least another hour before Kate came home. An hour of solitude. Callers might ask Bridgette where he'd disappeared to, his campaign managers for sure, but Hugh was entitled to peace and pleasure.

Moving to his side of the closet, he pulled out his special computer, the hidden one he used when he needed release. He sat on the cushioned stool and fired it up. The scent of the potpourri he kept in the drawers, a mixture of lemon and ocean, soothed him.

The first time he viewed porn in one of his father's stashed magazines, he wet himself, the excitement so intense it took a few seconds for him to notice. His parents were fighting again. He'd scuttled up the stairs, their screams following him even though he'd clamped his hands over his ears. His mother had thrown a teakettle at Quentin Lavender, a small man with close-set eyes.

Quentin slapped her hard with his open hand, staggering her. Cassie Lavender, tall and narrow, towered over her husband. Her right fist sprang forward, followed by her left and another right. One of the blows landed squarely on Quentin's jaw. He sacked her, knocking her to the floor where they wrestled. She bit his shoulder. He screamed and then punched her hard enough to draw blood from her nose. Hugh felt confused. He wanted to save his mother, but most of the time she beat up her smaller, less fit husband. Hugh ran to his room, shut his eyes, put on earmuffs, and pulled a knit cap over his head. The screams still reached him. Then laughter. Soon the other sounds began. Back then, he didn't understand them. Later, he figured it out.

Hugh tried to remember the first time he'd watched them have sex, first in horror and then with fascination that still made his face flush and his breath hot. Thirteen? Fourteen? By then he was buying his own porn magazines and videos. Although the fights' frequency and ferocity remained, his reactions changed. Instead of peeing in his pants, he started getting erections.

His parents had been at it again, kicking, punching, biting, and yelling obscenities. Hugh crept back down the stairs. His mother, on her hands and knees on the cold tile floor, hiked her skirt around her waist, her ass bare. His father's penis hung limp in his hand as he rubbed it without effect. "Come on, you faggot. Do it, you weak pussy. I'm married to a Nancy." He smacked her butt hard. "Yeah. That's it. Be a man." He hit her again each time harder. Red welts rose on her pale skin. His penis grew thick and long. Hugh looked away. "Do it, baby. Fuck the shit out of me."

Hugh headed for the closet.

***

Hugh slid the computer back into its hiding place, his orgasm satisfied if not transported. Sometimes he wondered if something was wrong with him, why he needed the violent porn to get aroused. With a warm washcloth, he rubbed his penis clean and then patted it dry with a hand towel. No, not twisted in anyway. Pleasure that hurt no one. The blackface incident was not the norm. That night, hanging out with business backers from the American Liberty Council, he got caught up, drank too much. They'd hired a prostitute who, for a substantial paycheck, agreed to the bondage and group fuck. The ALC guys pushed the blackface. The spanking, ass-fucking, others cheering him on. Remembering got him hard again. The monkey antics, not him. No one would understand or believe him. The ALC posed a different problem. Put the two together, and he was screwed.

The world judged. Period. No questions asked. The higher up you were, the more they wanted to see you fall. He took precautions. Kept his porn out of sight and his ALC backers at a distance. Except for once. He'd left a video out in error. Stupid. He waited for the shoe to drop. Nothing.

Last spring, however, he worried that Kate had discovered something or suspected. She acted cool to him. No sex, no intimacy, a troubled look in her eyes, a watchfulness. He wracked his brain trying to identify his offense. He asked her if anything was wrong. She shrugged it off. The thought flicked through his mind that she'd come across some troubling evidence. Then it passed, and things went back to normal. Until now.

Damn Charlie Moon.

At least he felt better, stronger, more able to reflect upon the conversation with Bigelow and decide what to do next. He'd given Bigelow instructions to clean up his mess. Who had viewed the video? Moon's mother and sisters? Sam? He owed Hugh a lot, so it shouldn't be a problem pressing him for verifiable information. Would he have to give Sam specifics? No.

Hugh got dressed.

Who else? Erika and Griff for sure. The young woman hanging around Moon's mother. Cappy, Bigelow, and Zeek, all possibilities. In Hugh's experience, a secret known by one other person meant twenty people knew. They'd want money. Everyone did. Threaten to go to the press. A shudder moved down Hugh's spine. If Bigelow couldn't uncover all the witnesses and then take care of things, Hugh had a plan B. Bigelow, and his goons, would not like its implementation.

He tied the laces of his Oxfords. He expected Kate home any minute. Time to get back to work. The campaign and the children required money. Things would work out. Hugh was adept at making circumstances go his way.

Head high, smile in place, he left his bedroom, hurried down the hall, and bounded down the stairs.

Chapter 45

Erika

Pain radiated throughout her body. Erika stayed as still as possible. Voices penetrated the haze.

"Why the hell did ya do that?"

Cappy's voice. The kitchen floor tiles cool against her bruised cheek. Erika licked her lips and took quiet breaths.

"You saw what happened."

Bigelow. Defensive. Change of roles? Wasn't Bigelow in charge of Cappy?

"Boss won't like this."

Cappy again, talking about Lavender?

"She deserved it."

Bigelow must have screwed up by hurting her. Why would that be a mistake? Breathing hurt. She suppressed a moan.

"He said no footprints, no path back to him."

Of course.

A shoe nudged Erika. She kept her eyes closed. A second nudge, this one harder. Fire rocketed through her body and bile flooded her mouth. She swallowed. Couldn't throw up. Let the assholes think she was out cold. For how long?

Bigelow must have squatted next to her because his foul cigarette breath filled her nose. "Wake up," he shouted into her ear. Another shove. "Wake the fuck up."

Erika opened her eyes. Bigelow yanked her to her feet and pushed her against the refrigerator door. He thrust a bottle of water at her. "Drink. It'll help."

With her lips curled tight, she gave him the meanest stare she could muster.

"Suit yourself."

Without moving her head, she scanned her surroundings. Bigelow and Cappy, their backs to her, stood in the breakfast nook, the unopened bottle of Poland Spring on the round table. Sunlight slanted down from the louvered blinds onto Bigelow's hairy hand. The combination of bottled water and sunlight created a rainbow on the polished tabletop. What a thing to notice.

She heard the door thud closed and Cappy's receding footfalls. Griff must be back. *Please let it be Griff.*

Bigelow swung around and glared at her. "This is your fault."

"Where's my wife?" His voice was loud enough for Erika to hear.

Cappy said, "Stop. Wait. Let me explain the situation."

She summoned her strength. "I'm here." Her voice came out a strangled croak no louder than a whisper. She forced the volume up. "In the kitchen." Her throat ached.

Griff strode into view. "What have you morons done?" He sounded furious, clear, and sober. His arms went around her shoulders and under her buttocks. He lifted and cradled her. "Baby look at you." He carried her into the great room. "Get out. Get the hell out. You have the device. We delivered. Now leave."

Bigelow growled. "Who else seen them pictures?"

"Erika, tell him." He eased her down onto the sectional couch.

"No one."

"She's lying," Bigelow said.

"No one, I swear."

"Satisfied?" Griff yelled so loud each word throbbed through her body. "Get the fuck out."

She closed her eyes again and listened to the breathing of the three men, bracing for whatever came next. Then footsteps, the front door opening and slamming shut.

Erika sat up. Each move sent shots of pain to her head and stomach. “Are they gone?”

“Yeah.” He no longer sounded angry. Instead, his tone threatened. “Who else saw the photos?”

“What do you care?” How come Bigelow listened to him? Before Bigelow controlled Griff. Her head and body hurt too much to think straight.

Griff brushed hair from her face. “Not that Moon woman or her friend?”

“Asked and answered.” She kept her gaze steady even though her heart pounded. She wasn’t sure why she lied to him, why she didn’t tell him about Vera and Dani, but something felt off.

“You keep a copy?”

She wanted Lavender to give them money. If Vera took the photos to the cops first, why would Hugh pay Erika? Griff could help her. They’d have getaway money.

“Did you?”

“Yes.”

“Good girl.”

Chapter 46

Dani

Dani banged on Mirko's door. When she left campaign headquarters, she worried about where to go. Vera's apartment made the most sense. But she had a lot going on. Dani thought about Javier. She couldn't go there. Solving this would also save him from the people intimidating him, the same people threatening Erika, no doubt. When Javier heard what she'd done, how clever she'd been... Even if she saved him, she still lied and disappointed him. Once she solved the crime and heralded a hero, she'd tell the press Javier played a key role. They'd interview him at his gas station. He'd like that.

Anyway, this was the only place she wanted to be.

Mirko opened the door.

Her spirits folded. He didn't look surprised. Not angry, not happy either.

"Hey." He stepped aside and ushered her in with the sweep of his arm.

"I'm not staying." Better to say it before he brought it up. She studied the room, half-expecting Stephanie changes. The apartment appeared as orderly as ever. Golf bag, bike, sleeper couch with Dani's decorative pillows lined up along the back. Opened next to a stack of papers on one side and a notebook on the other, his laptop glowed in the dark room. No signs of a Stephanie takeover.

Mirko switched on an overhead light. "You okay?"

"Great."

"S'up?" He crossed his arms, legs wide apart. Not too inviting or forgiving.

"We got the goods on Hugh Lavender." Dani dug the drive from her pocket and eased her backpack containing her laptop and the Lavender documents she'd printed onto the carpet. "I have the evidence here, and Stephanie is going to start the ball rolling on the eleven o'clock news." Although reluctant to say it, she knew she should. "Stephanie rocked."

Dani palmed the drive. "Can we check this out? I need your advice." She figured Mirko was still angry with her, done with her, after her big confession. Who loved liars? Still, it was worth a try. "Fresh eyes." She moved toward his computer. "I might see only what I want."

"I'm glad Stephanie helped you."

Dani bit her lower lip. "You asked her to?"

"Yeah."

"Thank you. She pinned Jim Bayer to the wall."

"She's special."

Not good. "Will she be over after the news tonight?"

"It's not like that."

Rather than press for more clarity, she decided to quit, and believe he meant they weren't together as a couple. Yet.

"Why do you lie?"

The way the question came out, it sounded like he'd been waiting to ask her, that he really wanted to understand.

"I don't purposely hurt anyone."

"Liars always harm others, whether or not they mean to."

Dani flashed back on the earlier conversation when Mirko told her his family kept secrets. "Did your parents lie to you about something important?"

A jumble of voices passed by Mirko's closed door, neighbors on their way in or out. Someone coughed-laughed. Mirko watched her face, his eyes unwavering. "Yeah." A faint scent of garlic and tomato sauce infused the air. The hallway noises drifted away. "My dad suffered from depression. Dark moods dogged him." Mirko sat sideways on his computer chair. "I asked about it all the time. They never answered. Phony smiles. Nothing for me to worry about."

Mirko spoke in a voice so low, Dani had to strain to hear.

"Then one day, I came home from school and he wasn't there."

"He left your mom?"

"He deserted us both. Killed himself."

"Oh."

"We had a one-car garage. He sat in his Buick with the engine running, seat slanted back, and a smooth jazz station on the radio."

"How old were you?"

"Fourteen."

"I'm sorry I lied to you and sorry you lost your dad and that your parents didn't trust you with their troubles."

"I asked my mother why. Even with my dad dead, she kept the truth to herself." He paused. Seemed to consider his next words. "Maybe she had no clue."

"Suicide note?"

"No explanation, no nothing."

Tears formed. "I didn't mean to cause you pain."

"I know. I wanted you to understand. And to thank you."

"Me?" Her eyes went wide.

"For leveling with me. Not easy."

"Hardest thing I've ever done. I confessed to everyone I care about — Vera, Javier, Bogie," she paused, "and you." Dani thought about Alice. "Almost everyone. Two more people to go." Her ex-landlords deserved an explanation, apology, and payment plan.

"That's good." He swung around, pulled his legs under his makeshift desk, and took a deep audible breath. "Let's see what you found out about our would-be governor."

Dani handed him the thumb drive and watched him slide it into the USB port on the side of his Mac.

She grabbed a chair from the kitchenette and sat next to him. Her mind flitted about. Mirko had shared the most personal information ever. He'd asked Stephanie to help her, and now the two of them were on Lavender's trail together.

She drank in his scent, smelled the lotion on his skin, took in his profile, the curve of his jaw and the tiny mole on his cheek. He'd cut himself shaving. A reddish-brown nick sat just below his left ear.

His voice pulled her back. "Where d'you get this?"

She was about to launch into her cloak-and-dagger saga, the danger she'd been in, the narrow escape. For the entire ride from the campaign office to Mirko's apartment, the story spun in her mind. Heads pressed together, they would read the documents and find damning evidence, be the team that solved the case. She stopped before the first words came out.

The first document opened. He'd been looking at the screen. Now he turned his gray-green eyes on her, his brow creased. "Well, where'd this come from?"

She swallowed and breathed in. "I stole it."

"From who?"

She told him the truth without embellishment.

"Stupid chance to take."

"Yeah."

"But kinda badass, too." He smiled at her before swinging back to the computer.

Relief flooded every nerve ending.

"Let's see what we've got," he said.

"We're looking for anything that links Lavender to Charlie Moon."

They examined dozens of documents — invoices dating back three years, requisitions for various building materials and car parts. One file appeared to be checklists for things all in code. Dani's bottom hurt from sitting so long. She got up and stretched. So far, nothing about Charlie.

"This is interesting," he said.

Dani sat back down and leaned in to see.

"I'd guess from this..." An Excel document filled the screen. "Lavender owns most of Oak Lane car service."

"They were in Vera's smashup."

He scrolled down revealing dozens of names and numbers. "And he passes major bucks through there. See?" Mirko put a finger on one line. "Money in from people or places in code and then cash out to my guess is the initials of various accounts."

"Different countries?" In the movies, offshore accounts ruled. "Money laundering?"

A skeptical look rippled across his face.

Dani squinted at the screen. "NB. Nate Bigelow? He's the top goon living in Erika's house."

"Who?"

Dani explained about Erika, Griff, Cappy, and Bigelow.

"Is Cappy his first or last name? Could he be FC?"

Did Erika share Cappy's actual name? "Not sure."

"Whoa. American Liberty Council. Lots of coded notations in their file."

"Who are they?" Dani paced, twitched, and walked in a tight circle. "The name sounds familiar, but I can't place it."

"White supremacists." Mirko moved his cursor to the browser and brought up their website. "Hate group."

"That ties into the photos and videos we found."

"He's a sleaze."

They perused the rest of the documents for another hour. Nothing that proved Charlie blackmailed Lavender. Nothing that would make anyone believe Lavender murdered Charlie or hired someone to do it. Next, they examined the papers she'd printed. Still zip.

Dani got up and paced around the small living room, edging around the furniture. She felt a mixture of frustration, disappointment, and anger. "He killed Charlie, and we still can't prove it."

"We got damning evidence — the blackface photos, possible rape, association with a white supremacy group, and possible money-laundering."

She sank onto the couch and banged her hands on the cushions. "Yeah, but does it add up to murder?"

"Lots of motive."

"I wanted to uncover save-the-day evidence about Charlie." They'd all forgive her and be proud. Love her. "I live in fantasyland." Bogie used to tell her that. He'd caught her in one of her many white lies. *"We all have fantasies, Dani girl. The problem is you say them out loud as if they're real."*

"Not nothing," Mirko said. "Clues to follow. This guy Bigelow works for Lavender. Together they have a business that might be shady, and that's what all those codes are about. They move in uninvited with your buddy Erika and her husband, they threaten them, and they all work for Lavender. There has to be more we can uncover."

He said *we*.

"What'd Stephanie find out?"

"That Nate Bigelow is a three-time felon who runs the car service."

"More pieces of the puzzle," Mirko said.

"Yeah." Except Dani wasn't the hero; Stephanie got to report the news. "Should I go back there? They're having a fundraising party on Tuesday and I volunteered to help." She watched Mirko from the corner of her eyes.

"No. Don't push your luck."

How could she explain, without sounding pathetic, that she needed to be the one who uncovered the evidence? Dani slumped into the chair, pumped her right leg. "May I stay to watch?"

"The news?"

"Then I'll go. Right after it's over." *Please ask me to spend the night*. "You're good at coming up with the *right* next steps to take."

This time he didn't hesitate. "Sure. Hungry?"

"Starving."

"I'll fix us something."

And just that quick, all was right with her world.

Chapter 47

Vera

Vera called Sam. Instinct or habit? No matter. Sam should be there. Penny too. She wasn't arriving until the next day.

It took Vera twenty minutes to get to Northern Westchester and hustle into Liza's room. She found Sam already there and Liza's bed empty.

"Where is she?"

Sam wore his bomber leather jacket, unzipped, with a pearl-grey T-shirt, jeans, and black Nike's. "They took her to radiology for a CT scan. She'll be back in thirty-minutes."

"On the phone, the nurse made it sound as if Liza might die any second." Vera heard the tremors in her voice.

"Sit," Sam said, grabbing her by her elbow and guiding her to one of the two metal chairs.

Vera covered her cheeks with both hands. "What did they tell you?"

"The doctor said she'd be back once she analyzed the scan."

She could not lose another child. Period. God would not do that. Vera gave herself a shake. Would not do that to whom? To Vera? Make her suffer more? Such hubris. Better to pray Liza healed and was not in pain.

"I told her."

Vera tried to re-focus. "Told her?"

"About my marriage."

"Oh." *Poor Liza. Bad luck dogged her.* "How did she take it?"

He lifted his shoulders, eased them down.

"I have not been the best mother to her. Working on making amends."

"Liza didn't make things easy."

"It is not a child's responsibility to be easy. It is a parent's job to love them anyway." Vera reflected on their last conversation. Liza owned her missteps. Tremendous progress. Vera had to own hers. "Thanks for coming."

"Glad to help." He scooted the other chair closer to Vera and reached for her hand. "I care about you guys."

"Liza loved you, loves you still."

"I'm worried for her."

Something in his voice made Vera stiffen her back. "*For* her or *about* her?"

"Both."

She waited. Lord, she longed for another drink. She had gulped down the last of her Chianti before grabbing her keys and dashing to the hospital. Just enough to smooth her frayed nerves. Unfortunately, its medicinal effects wore off some time ago.

"You and your pals are poking around Hugh Lavender."

Her unease quickened.

"Zeek filled me in."

Was no place safe from Lavender's reach?

Sam offered an obviously fake smile. "I'm hoping you're not in over your head."

Vera pressed her fingers to her forehead. "Is he a client of yours?"

"He's managed a few projects for me, like I told you."

Vera dropped her voice, peered around in case someone was listening. "Not that creepy, slithering-Zeek. Are you involved with *Lavender*?"

"I provided legal assistance for a couple of his properties."

"He paid you. You do not owe him anything."

"He's going to be the next governor; there will be plenty of new opportunities."

"For a lawyer?" she asked.

"I have many talents."

"He is a murderer." The minute she said it, she regretted the statement. "He *may* be one," she amended.

"That's a hell of an accusation." Sam leaned close to Vera's face. His voice hissed. "You can't go around saying that."

"Why not, if it is true?" She thrust out her chest. "What do you know about him, about his *character*?"

"Who do you think he murdered? Charlie?"

"Lavender has secrets."

"This is nuts." His forehead puckered.

Vera could not stop now; words gushed out. "Charlie was...maybe...blackmailing him, threatening to reveal damning secrets. Motive." Something flicked across Sam's face. Recognition? An insight?

"These are powerful people. Back away." He jumped up from his chair and thrust his hands in the jacket's slash pockets. "Now, before it's too late."

Vera was an excellent judge of character, understood a person's values, and yet Sam just threatened her. Or warned her. Either way, why associate with Zeek and Lavender?

Her cell buzzed in her purse. "I have to take this." She faced the wall and kept her voice low. "Hello?"

"It's Dani. Watch the eleven o'clock news tonight. Make sure. The reporter, Stephanie Mack, is going to expose Lavender. Remember, I told you about her?"

Vera stepped into the hall, her heart banging. She whispered into the phone. "You found proof?"

"No," Dani said, her tone deflated. "Not yet. But lots of dirt, clues, white supremacy and money-laundering things."

"Nothing about Charlie?" Her tone mirrored Dani's. She did not think Dani had a chance of finding incriminating evidence and yet disappointment washed over her.

"It's going to take him down a little, and it could lose him the election, or at least get the ball moving in that direction." Dani's voice got small. "I'm sorry."

"We will keep trying. Do not worry." She put a bit of optimism into her tone. "Thank you, for all you have done. I mean it. You've been great." She knew how much Dani craved praise.

"I have another shot. I plan to go back and get more dope on him."

"No." Vera swung her head. She located Sam on his cell, his back to her. "It's not safe."

Dani made a non-committal sound.

"Where are you?"

"With Mirko."

That made Vera smile. "Tomorrow's agenda is the police and the reporter you mentioned. My daughter Penny is flying in. Everything will be okay."

"Do you still plan on meeting up with Erika?"

"Yes. I have to."

"Then I do too."

"It's unnecessary. Stay with your boyfriend."

"No. I'm coming."

Vera's smile broadened. "You are a good friend." She clicked off, slipped her phone into her bag, and walked back toward Sam. He still held his cell in his right hand. Squinted eyes glared down on her.

"You haven't answered me. Why link Lavender to Charlie's murder?"

"I misspoke."

Sam worked his mouth. "What d'you take from my house?"

"Evidence." Sam would not intimidate her. If Dani could be brave, then so could Vera. Her hands squeezed into fists. "Be careful with whom you keep company, sir."

"Did Erika Noble show you something?"

Vera's breath caught in her throat. "Like?"

"Don't play dumb. I'm trying to protect you and Liza."

"Are we in danger from you? From Lavender?"

"I can help you, but you have to tell me what you learned. This is a very *precarious* situation."

Dear God. The video cost Charlie his life, and now she and Liza were in jeopardy. Dani and Erika too. Well, she intended to uncover the facts, turn it over to law enforcement, and see justice prevail.

"We do not require help." *Not from you.*

***

By the time they wheeled Liza into her room, Vera had fallen asleep in the chair. She jolted awake.

Liza lay pale on the gurney.

"On my count," the nurse said to the two others surrounding Liza. "One, two, three." They hoisted her onto the bed, straightened her sheets, and took her vitals.

"When will the doctor be back?"

The nurse, her skin like black satin, gave Vera an encouraging smile. "In fifteen minutes or so. She's reading the CT scan."

"Is there anything you can tell me?"

"Dr. LaSalle will be in shortly." She gave Vera's hand a pat and left.

Vera hated feeling powerless. When she found the photos and the money, she enjoyed a sense of control. But now — a shudder traveled through her body. She stared down on the face of her sleeping daughter. No one was going to harm another of her children. No one. She should have told Penny not to come. Why put her in danger? She thought about Charlie's gun in the box. She had to hang tough. Tomorrow, everything they uncovered, learned, and guessed, went to the police. Then what would be would be.

She climbed into Liza's narrow bed and lay beside her. "Mommy's here now. I've got you."

She closed her eyes and prayed.

Chapter 48

Hugh

Kate and Hugh Lavender munched a late-evening snack and talked over the campaign.

"How confident are you?" she asked.

Until recently, Hugh felt terrific about his chances. Charlie Moon, from his grave, changed everything. "Polls look good." He took a bite of brie and cracker.

"You seem more worried than usual."

"A little." An understatement. Only perception mattered. He wasn't a racist or a rapist. They'd paid the hooker well. Said she liked group fucks, the sting of the whip, and dicks up her ass. The blackface was a go-along-with-his-supporters kind of thing. Meaningless.

Bridgette strode into the kitchen. "Sorry to interrupt." She nodded at Kate and then spoke to Hugh. "Jim Bayer asked to see you, says it's important."

Bridgette's competence and loyalty impressed Hugh. She assessed situations with deftness and managed most things without Hugh even knowing about it until after the fact. A smart hire and deal. She lived on the grounds rent free in a two-bedroom carriage house, with a full bath, powder room, kitchenette, living and sitting rooms, private deck, and yard. The arrangement worked well. Most days it allowed her to arrive at the house as early as seven and stay as late as eleven at night. From what Hugh could tell, she had few friends. No family came calling except for a sister who lived in Connecticut. Working for him left little time and energy for a life. Too bad. Not beautiful but pretty, with the white, almost translucent skin of the Irish, upturned nose sprinkled with freckles and huge green eyes.

Kate frowned. "At this hour?"

Hugh's Rolex read nine forty-five, late for guests and especially for Jim.

Kate pursed narrow lips colored with coral lipstick now faded to pink after a long day. She'd made it clear she didn't trust Jim. "He's second rate. No record of consequence. Anna agrees with me."

Most times Hugh listened to these two smart women. Anna Vernon, Hugh's savvy campaign advisor, often agreed with Kate and they were almost always right. Politics was new to Hugh, so he had no stable of old hands eager to help him. Finding the best people for each campaign office across New York state proved difficult. Thank goodness for Rake Ratchette, Hugh's tough strategist. He, at least, knew competent people in many of the major markets — Buffalo, Albany, and Syracuse upstate, and Yonkers, Manhattan, and Brooklyn downstate. Westchester County represented small potatoes in terms of votes, but a big deal for campaign contributors. Besides, the Lavenders lived in the county. A donor recommended Jim Bayer to Hugh.

Leaving Kate, Hugh climbed the back spiral-stairs to his second-floor office and waited. Within a few minutes, Bridgette ushered Jim in. He looked ragged, with tousled hair and bloodshot eyes. Hugh watched Jim chew his lower lip. Let him sweat. He preferred to keep his people on edge. Made them sharper. They sat across from each other, Hugh behind his oversized desk and Jim in an upholstered chair on the other side.

After listening to Jim's pathetic tale about the reporter's interview, Hugh asked, "Why did she dig into Oak Lane?"

Jim fidgeted. "Not sure. She set it up as a puff piece." His head dropped to his chest. "She ambushed me."

"Tell me word for word what she asked and your responses."

Jim replayed the encounter, this time mining his memory for the exact words. Bridgette, her wild red hair pulled back and tucked, took notes on her iPad. Although late in the evening, she still wore her green suit, a fitted jacket and skirt. Only her pointy-toed pumps disappeared for a pair of ballet flats.

"At the end..." Jim coughed into his hand. "Sorry. At the end," he said again, "She made a crazy statement."

"I can't wait."

"That they, the station higher-ups I guess, suspect you might have something to do with Charlie Moon's murder."

Hugh heard Bridgette suck in her breath.

"The guy killed a few months back. That's when I kicked her out."

Hugh almost smelled his rage rising from his core. The barely visible tie between Hugh and Charlie remained buried. An unsuccessful photographer killed, and they draw a straight line to Hugh, one of the wealthiest and most successful men in the state? Were political enemies worried about losing spewing muck? According to Sam, the Moon woman believes Hugh killed her son. What evidence did she think she uncovered? And now the reporter's station thought so too? He could not afford to have the press digging into his connection to Charlie Moon.

"Who do we know at channel twelve? Who owes us?"

Jim glanced at his watch. "It's too late for that. The reporter said it would be on at eleven."

Bridgette said, "It's already ten."

Hugh pushed back from his desk, stood, and paced. "Any of their sponsors on our list?" Things were spinning out of his control. "Bridgette, thoughts?"

"I'm searching our contacts." Her head was down as her fingers scrolled the tablet's screen. "No one stands out."

"Jim?"

He shook his head. "I'll make some calls." It came across as a question.

"Do it."

Hugh felt his life fraying at the corners, or worse, being ripped right down the middle.

Jim said, "The reporter plans a follow-up piece in the morning as well."

Hugh faced Bridgette. "Get Anna and Rake here."

"They're about an hour away."

"It's a rinky-dink local station, but the *Times* might get wind of it, or another, bigger player."

"They will," Bridgette said.

Hugh stared at her, hard. She picked up her phone.

Chapter 49

Hugh

The doorbell rang.

"What the hell?" No way either Anna or Rake made it that fast.

Bridgette said, "I'll go."

Hugh paced until Bridgette returned. Late-night visits always spelled bad news.

Bridgette announced, "Nate Bigelow is here."

Sweat beaded on Hugh's forehead and nose. "Take him to the library."

Bridgette snatched up her tablet and cell and headed for the door.

"And Bridge..."

She stopped, pivoted, her emerald-green, A-line skirt swirled at her knees.

"Alert me the minute Rake and Anna arrive."

"Will do." She spun back around and hurried out into the hall, her devices in her hands.

Hugh grabbed his jacket from the back of the desk chair and shrugged into it. *Dress the part, be the part*. He said to Jim, "Stay here. Keep working those phones." Not that he had any hope they could pull the plug on the story.

Nate looked like hell. An angry gash swelled above his left eye and curled into his scalp. His jacket, unable to cover his gut, stippled with what looked like blood spatters, hung open.

"What happened to you?" Bigelow was an unavoidable evil, and one that Hugh would soon boot out of his life.

"Griff's bitch hit me."

Suppressing a grin, Hugh imagined Erika hitting Bigelow over the head. No doubt he deserved it. *Good for her*. "And?"

The library was one of Hugh's favorite rooms. Well, one of *many* favorites. He loved this house. This room ranked among the top three. The smell of leather and walls of books, shouted education, discernment, a lifelong learner. He usually brought potential campaign investors here. They'd sip cognac, talk politics, and make deals. Tonight, Bigelow's arrival at Hugh's door forced him to use it for their nasty business.

Bigelow, his buck teeth flashing, proffered his right-hand palm up, the digital memory card nestled in the middle.

Hugh's breaths quickened. He pressed his lips tight, drew in air through flared nostrils. He hated that Bigelow might smell his fear, see his relief. One shoulder roll. He lifted the device and stared at it. *Finally*.

When Griff first came with Charlie's demands, Hugh insisted Charlie tell him to his face how he got the photographs. Stowed in Hugh's concealed video camera in the master bedroom walk-in closet, not even Kate knew it existed. Not a snooper, she lacked curiosity, or she trusted Hugh. The time last year when he worried that she suspected flashed in his mind. Could she know but not care enough?

Kate enjoyed being rich, and Hugh enjoyed having her as a partner. Much younger, attractive, easy to be with. Like his house and this room, she said something about him. The sex, fun but infrequent, kept him happy enough. They understood each other. Anyway, if she'd found it, she'd tell him. Kate was straightforward. Besides, even if she discovered his secret, why give the device to Charlie? Once the blackmailing started, whenever their paths crossed, he searched for signs of chemistry or conspiracy. Never saw a hint.

After days of trying to puzzle it through, Hugh figured out that during the shoot for *Westchester Magazine,* Charlie must have come across the high-end Hasselblad. Hugh's over-confidence resulted in carelessness. Normally he stowed the camera in a locked drawer. As he thought back, he remembered he'd used it early that morning while Kate worked out at her spin class. Worried about all the things that might hurt his chances, he reviewed the group-fuck video. It pleased him to view it on the big screen, projected from the Hasselblad. The computer didn't do it justice. His masturbation was powerful and satisfying each time he watched it. That day proved especially sweet.

Late for a campaign event, he'd pushed the button to send the screen into its hidden slot in the ceiling, shoved the camera into a corner, and threw clothes destined for the cleaners on top. Stupid, costly mistake. Charlie must have been sorting through various spaces for the best shots. The master suite was a natural. Kate invested plenty of time and money in making it a sanctuary. His-and-her bathrooms, each with sunken Jacuzzi tubs, double-head shower stalls, bidets, and vanities. The closet spread across the width of the bedroom.

Why would Charlie take the digital card unless he'd watched it? What about Griff? Both had visited that day — Griff, earlier for an Oak Lane meeting and Charlie for the magazine shoot. Seemed less probable that Griff poked around the closet and checked the Hasselblad's contents.

Griff swore he was only the messenger, no inkling about what Charlie found, but Griff knew. He said Charlie refused to meet with Hugh. Hugh pressed, but Griff remained adamant. No Charlie meeting. "He's not used to your kind of power. Trusts me to stand firm." Through Griff, Hugh paid Charlie $250,000 by the time his head got cut off. What portion of the money landed in Griff's hands?

"Who else viewed this?" Hugh asked Bigelow.

Bigelow, stinking of beer and cigarette smoke, said, "Erika swore she didn't."

"She might have made a copy."

"Not on her home computer. I checked."

Hugh rubbed the back of his neck, trying to ease the tension gripping his body. "Did she have time to do it somewhere else? FedEx, CVS, the Moon woman's house?"

"Possible. She went out."

"What about you, Cappy, or Zeek?"

"Erika and me, we're the only ones that touched it. No one else."

"And you weren't curious?"

"No, boss."

"It's payday, Nate. You've done an outstanding job." *Yeah, if I don't count the stupid car crash and your subsequent fuckups.* "As agreed, I'm going to transfer funds into an offshore account for you, and a little less for Cappy and Zeek." Whom else would he have to pay off? "It will come in a series of payments from various shell-corporations I've set up in the Caribbean. Trust me, the funds are *untraceable.*" He paused to let that to sink in. "If for any reason what's on this card surfaces..." He waggled the tiny electronic device under Bigelow's nose. "No matter whose fault it is, payments stop, and hell rains down on you."

"When's the first one?"

"In a couple of days. Gives you and your *colleagues* time to pack up and vanish."

Bigelow crossed his arms. "I like it here and I'd like my money now."

Hugh eyed the gun-bulge under Nate's ill-fitting jacket. "I have a long and wide reach. I know people everywhere." Again, he paused for effect. "In *every* line of work." *How dare this imbecile, this gnat, defy me*? "Unless you plan to shoot me now, you will *never* be safe again."

Bigelow blinked hard. Blinked again. Hugh's scrutiny never left Bigelow's face.

Finally, Bigelow spoke. "Are we doing anything about the Moon woman and her daughter?"

Hugh continued his stare-down. He wanted to watch Nate's right hand and the gun, but he kept his glare on Bigelow's eyes instead.

"They probably know something," Nate said, his tone now conciliatory.

"What makes you say that?"

"Been following the mother. There's another one too, a girl."

"What girl?" No word from Sam, yet. His assignment was to suss out information the family uncovered.

"Name's Dani Gerrity. Saw her license plate. A buddy at the DMV did some digging. Got her address but she's not living there no more."

"And..."

"Trailed her to an apartment building on West Street. She might be shacking up with a guy."

"Give me the info."

"Oh yeah, and this gas station guy, Mexican or something. He and the girl talk. I gave him an immigration scare, so we're safe from him."

Bigelow dropped his arms and appeared to relax. He dug into his back pants pocket and eased out a tattered wallet. "Want me to do anything about 'em?" He handed Hugh a slip of paper. "Got the gas station guy's info on it too."

Hugh tried to work it through — the interview with Jim, trusting Bigelow and company to be greedier than stupid, taking care of Erika and Griff, and now these women, a boyfriend, and a gas jockey. What the hell? "No. I'll deal with it."

Not sure how, but Hugh knew all loose ends had to knot.

Chapter 50

Erika

Erika stared at the front door, now shut behind Bigelow and Cappy. Good riddance. Her face, gut, and ribs still ached. Breathing hurt. She shifted on the sectional couch, back against the cushions, trying to get comfortable. The silence, so different from the recent occupation of Lavender's minions, comforted her. All day they'd watched baseball, golf, reality shows, and those judge programs. The house smelled of their sweat, beer, and cigarettes. She planned to arrange a thorough cleaning. They'd cancelled their maid service at Bigelow's insistence. Erika cleaned the master bath and kitchen, but that was all. Let them either clean their spaces or live in their filth.

Carrying an icepack, Griff came back into the great room. He reminded her of the man she'd married. Clear-eyed, clean-shaven. He'd gotten a haircut. The silver locks were now shorter, smoothed back. "Nice hair."

He sat next to her and handed her the ice.

She took it trying to decide which ache required the remedy more.

Griff leaned in and kissed her, first on her cheek and then on her lips. Erika rested her head on his chest.

"It's good to have you back."

He frowned, as if not sure of her meaning.

She chose not to explain. "And the marauders gone."

A rough almost laugh. "Time for us to re-locate."

Funny, that was Erika's thought too. "Where should we go?" Griff dreamed of Brazil, but not Erika. Europe for two or three years.

London or some-place in Spain or the Netherlands. Australia held a lot of appeal. From there an easy hop to Asia — Hong Kong, China, Singapore, Japan, and Vietnam. Lavender couldn't track them down if they moved around, stayed low profile.

Griff said, "We'll need get-away money."

Despite their opulent lifestyle, Griff and Erika were broke. Griff's habits kept them in debt. In addition, to be honest, Erika's clothing, charity work and entertaining all cost a lot. "We'll make a nice profit on the house."

"Take too long. We gotta leave now." His face scrunched in concentration or determination. "Tomorrow. Lavender's gonna fund us."

Lots of things still bothered her. Like the new clean and sober Griff. His newfound control over Bigelow and Cappy. What changed? Not that she had a complaint, but still. "How did Charlie get the video in the first place?"

Griff twisted around, gave her a hard stare. "Why?"

"Curious."

"Lavender owns a Hasselblad H50."

"So...?"

"It's a forty-five-thousand-dollar camera, not something Charlie got to hold, much less use. He stumbled on it and couldn't resist examining it."

"And the photos were still there, not moved to Hugh's computer?"

"Evidently."

Erika thought about Charlie's plans to run away with her, get her to leave Griff. He knew about her expensive tastes. Was she his blackmail motive, his murder her fault? Would she have left Griff for Charlie with no money? She said yes, but...

Griff's frown deep, he seemed to read her thoughts. She changed gears. "How will we get Hugh to pay us?"

"Where are the copies?"

"I emailed them to myself from Lavender's campaign headquarters using my private address, not the main one. Wanted to throw the thugs off the scent in case they stumbled on it, so I called it ladies' luncheon."

Griff slid off the couch. "Show me."

"Going back to Hugh is chancy." Not that she had other ideas for financing their escape, but now her plan to insist on a million dollars worried her as reckless. "Bigelow might ooze back into our lives." Just the thought of it sent spasms down her back. "Let's just pack up and go. We'll be okay."

His tight smile didn't reach his eyes. "One more foray."

"He killed Charlie."

Griff's eyes, moments before sharp and clear, now clouded. "He won't kill me... us, once we tell him we have copies in a safe place. Happy to keep our mouths shut and disappear. For two million. Then he gets the video, pictures, and our silence guaranteed for life."

Two million? Greed often backfired. Only a few days ago, Erika would have grabbed this chance. Made Lavender pay. She touched her bruised face. Not anymore. "We take our savings, leave town while the house is on the market, and once it's sold, it will go fast in this neighborhood, we head overseas."

She heard the pleading in her voice and shifted. Her tone strong and confident, she said, "It's the only sensible thing to do. Don't blackmail Hugh." She bit back the last word. *Again.*

"Have to. The house is our only asset."

A darkness crept into Erika's being. She'd been holding things together for the past three months, on edge all the time. Charlie, the car crash, the thugs threatening their lives, Griff's drugging and gambling, Erika having to sneak around, lie to Vera, and lie to Griff. Unable to grieve. Bigelow's beating terrified her. Tears seeped out and down her cheeks. "Don't confront him." The pleading was back in her voice.

Griff eyed her. Through the haze of her tears, she tried to fathom the meaning behind his expression. His features smoothed out, and this time his smile appeared more genuine.

"Don't be afraid. We'll get some sleep. Tomorrow we'll check out the photos and decide. You pack up the house while I visit Hugh."

"I'm going with you."

He sat back down and put his arms around her waist.

She winced.

"Sorry, baby." Gently, he poked her ribs.

She groaned. “Stop.”

“We’re taking you to the emergency room. They might have cracked your ribs.” He scooped her up, careful not to touch her ribcage again. “Tomorrow we wrap it all up. It’ll be fine.

That’s what she’d told Vera and wanted to believe, but dread suffused every thought.

Chapter 51

Dani

Dani sat next to Mirko on his couch, his arm draped across the back, his fingers touching Dani's neck. Not quite a hug, but still. Dani eased closer until their hips touched.

He searched for channel twelve, the Westchester County local station where Stephanie worked. The clock on Mirko's computer read ten fifty-five. A woman with sooty eyes and a smoky voice discussed male sexual dysfunction. Then the GEICO gecko told them how they could save.

"I know you said don't, but if I do more snooping at Lavender's house..."

He cut her off. "Go to the cops."

"With what?"

"All your suspicions, all you've uncovered so far."

Laughter seeped in from under his front door. A dog barked.

Mirko faced her. "It's their job to solve this crime."

If that were true, why did she feel like a failure?

Mirko shifted back to the television screen. "It's starting."

The news came on. A grim-faced man with windblown hair reported that a storm was brewing just off the coast, with dire predictions of record rainfall; more to come later in the broadcast. The anchor thanked him and then introduced Stephanie, "with breaking news."

Stephanie, elegant and professional, set up the piece with the anchor. The tape rolled next. Jim squirreled about, his face flushed and damp with perspiration. Stephanie asked her damning questions. It ended in under three minutes.

The male anchor said, "We'll continue to follow this developing story. With the election still six months away, many things can change."

Six months, still time enough to nail him. Stephanie's last question to Jim about Charlie's murder didn't make the report. No proof. Probably slanderous. Dani propped her head up with her hands, her elbows resting on her thighs. She had to uncover evidence that tied the murder to the photos.

Mirko switched off the TV and took another pull on his beer. Foam clung to his upper lip.

Still down on herself, Dani said, "The story probably hurt Jim more than Lavender."

Mirko licked the foam away. "I've been re-thinking things. We can't give the police the papers you took."

Even though she liked that Mirko said, "we," again, she felt caught. Guilty of being dishonest — which she wasn't.

"Then I have even less to show them. I thought you said we'd give them everything."

"They'll ask you how they came into your possession."

Dani clamped her mouth shut before the words came out. *I'll make something up.* "We saw suspicious stuff in those papers. Isn't there a way?"

"Hmmm."

Dani waited.

Finally, he said, "Reporters don't have to share their sources."

"Excellent, we'll ask Stephanie to help us again." *Not really.* She still didn't understand Stephanie and Mirko's relationship. Were they just school buds helping each other out? Besides, that would make Stephanie the hero. Not Dani. Again.

He rose, hooked up his Beats portable speaker to his iPhone and tapped a jazz playlist. Dani preferred dance music, electronic, crazy loud, but Mirko's music was okay by her. He returned to the couch. If only this could last, and they found a way to be a couple again.

"Mirko?"

"Yeah?"

"You can trust me."

He peered at her from the corners of his eyes. "I want to."

Dani nestled into the crook of his arm. "You can. I promise."

Chapter 52

Vera

Emotionally exhausted, Vera stepped into her entranceway. She switched on the overhead light. Brandy bounded into her, slobbered, and energetically wagged her tail. *Almost time for the news Dani mentioned.*

The apartment's stale air born from closed windows and days old dust twitched her nose. She pulled at her shirt and sniffed. She smelled stale as well. Take Brandy out, shower, catch the news report Dani told her about and then bed.

"Come on, girl." She slipped on Brandy's leash, shoved a plastic bag to pick up poop into her right pocket, grabbed a flashlight and rape whistle, and checked her left pocket for her house keys. "Quick walk around the block to do your business. No leisurely sniffing."

With one hand on the deadbolt, she stopped. *One sip of wine, just enough to get through the next few hours.* She left a half-full bottle of red on the counter earlier in the day, its cork poking up, waiting for her to pull it. Brandy yanked and yipped.

She promised Dani she would stop drinking. How could she hold Dani to no more lies if she kept boozing? What about her promise to herself? She walked to the counter, gripped the cork, and tugged. Her hand shook. She concentrated until it stopped. Then she poured the wine down the drain, leaving behind swirls of burgundy against the white finish.

To face the next day, she required rest more than a drink. Sleep and time to re-charge. She left Liza sleeping. Dr. LaSalle's assurances about

Liza's recovery offered a measure of comfort, but not enough. They were not sure what caused the latest scare, but the CT scan revealed nothing worrisome. *Thank you, Lord.*

"Okay, girl, now we can go."

The elevator, for once, worked. It jerked down to the first floor. Vera snapped on the flashlight. The whistle and keys were in her jacket pocket. Brandy's rumble and swishing tail signaled her happiness. These last few days, Vera left the dog for long stretches of time. Well, it was almost over. Tomorrow she, Dani, and Erika would review their evidence and go to the police. Penny's arrival would lift Liza's spirits, help her heal. Perhaps Dani could arrange a meeting with the reporter tomorrow afternoon.

With her left hip, she pushed opened the door.

The man slouched against a parked, midnight-blue Ford stood up the minute she came through the door. Vera's heart stuttered. Brandy whined and pulled hard to the right.

"Hello."

Zeek.

He approached her, hands in his pants pockets. "Mr. Lavender wants to see you."

Brandy barked, tugged, and then lurched.

Zeek backpedaled.

Vera jerked Brandy back.

Zeek's voice lost its intimidating tone. "Can't you shut it up?"

Brandy bared her teeth and growled. Did she recognize him, remember him hurting her from the night of the murder?

Zeek took another step back. "Mr. Lavender just wants to talk. Make you an offer."

She shone the flashlight directly into Zeek's eyes. "Tell Mr. Lavender to call at a respectable hour, and if he wishes to speak with me, he has to come here. I am not going to him." She hoped she sounded indignant and unafraid.

Zeek appeared to regain his composure. "Lower that light."

She did not.

Shielding his eyes, once again he stepped closer. Brandy snarled. Zeek stopped advancing. "I'll give him your message."

Vera lowered the beam.

"It's a good thing he's trying to do for you and Liza. Best to cooperate."

"If it is so beneficial, why send you to scare me in the middle of the night?"

"Not my intention. The matter is urgent is all."

"The morning will be fine. I am usually up and able to receive visitors by nine." *Liza.* "Ten," she amended to give herself enough time for a visit to the hospital. "I'm overly stressed and tired."

"I'll tell him."

"You do that."

Zeek got into the car, revved the motor, and pulled out into the quiet street. Vera watched the receding taillights until they became tiny specks in the distance. She patted Brandy.

Although her legs wobbled, she walked Brandy to the curb. "Sorry, girl, I cannot go any farther." What did Lavender want with her?

Chapter 53

Hugh

Hugh, Bridgette, Kate, Anna, and Rake watched the channel twelve news. Jim Bayer left before Anna and Rake arrived. His calls were unsuccessful.

Hugh paced in front of the set. Relief flooded every nerve in his body. Yes, it was bad, but no one mentioned murder, or incriminating video, or his association with the white supremacist group ALC. On the other hand, the anchor promised a follow-up on the morning news.

"They're trying to make a big deal about Bigelow being a felon," Hugh said.

Anna said, "We've got damage control rolling."

"We can contain this," Rake added, although to Hugh's ears he sounded less confident.

Kate rubbed her face and stretched her arms over her head. "It's late. I'm going to bed. We should tackle this first thing in the morning."

"I agree. I'm bushed." Anna stood. "We checked into the Tarrytown Marriott. We're only twenty minutes away."

"You could stay here..."

Hugh cut Kate off before she finished her sentence. "Let's regroup around lunchtime. By then, you guys will know how the morning news and papers are spinning it, and you can work up a plan."

He needed them all out of the way, since he expected visitors that he didn't want Anna and Rake to meet.

***

Thursday morning brought the downpour predicted by every local news show. Rain pounded the windows. Excitement in their voices, the weather professionals warned of two inches with flooding sure to follow. The temperature rose to a balmy sixty-two degrees. By noon, it would be close to seventy-five, well above normal for May in New York. Probably thunder and lightning too.

The driveway alarm beeped, alerting the household a car was approaching. Hugh stood in the foyer. He'd set his expression on neutral. Sam Davis was a lightweight. He barely figured into Hugh's plans but still represented an avenue requiring closure. In fact, there were far too many, and Hugh worried he couldn't shut all of them down.

The front doorbell chimed, and Sonia, his household assistant, opened the door.

Sam's baseball cap and windbreaker dripped. He gawked at his surroundings until his eyes rested on the crystal chandelier that hung from two stories up — always a showstopper. He snapped his mouth shut as if embarrassed. With vigor, he wiped his feet on the mat before stepping onto the tiled floor.

Hugh didn't approach him. "Thanks for coming on such brief notice."

"Sure." He tugged off his wet jacket, slipped his hat off, and handed both to Sonia's outstretched hands. Tiny puddles formed on the floor.

Hugh said to Sonia, "He's not staying. Don't take those far."

Having worked for Hugh for years, Sonia understood. Instead of hanging them up, she waited nearby for Hugh's signal.

Sam seemed confused. *Good.* "What information do Liza and your mother-in-law possess?"

"Nothing."

Hugh waited. He'd mastered the art of intimidation at a young age. He understood the importance of having a posse at the ready and, as a last resort, how to use violence to end trouble in his life.

"There is one thing," Sam admitted under Hugh's punishing glare. "For some reason..."

"Yes?"

"They said you know who murdered Charlie Moon." He thrust his hands into his pants-pockets, jiggling keys, or change. "They were hoping whatever they found, whatever you've been searching for, proves you killed him or had him killed." Sam pulled on his nose. "I totally denied it."

Hugh's breath felt hot in his mouth. An ache plagued his left shoulder, but he resisted the urge to knead it.

"I warned her not to cross you."

"Wise counsel." Hugh loved pauses laced with menace. It made him a great debater. On today's political circuit, candidates filled pauses with bombast, lies, and innuendo. He switched strategies and used his withering glare instead. "Did they share the *evidence* they *think* they have?"

Perspiration bathed Sam's face. "No."

Fabrication or fear? "You failed to ask, or they wouldn't tell you?"

"Please don't hurt them."

Fear. "Why would you ask that?"

"The crash. It wasn't an accident."

Hugh's rage, until now only simmering, bubbled up. How insufferable that all these insignificant people knew his secrets and suspected him of others. He forced his anger to stay in check. He kept his eyes trained on Sam.

"They're harmless, really. Vera is a decent person and Liza is ill."

"They held that stupid rally, made a scene. Not so harmless."

Sam swallowed. His Adam's apple bobbed.

"*Did you* ask to examine their evidence?"

"Yes, but no luck." Sam's voice gained punch. "It can't be much since they've not said anything to the cops."

"Do you know this, or are you guessing?"

Sam appeared to sag. "I'm fairly confident."

For a fraction of a second, Hugh had welcomed Sam. He'd pulled Sam into his outer circle. They'd met two years ago through an introduction from Hugh's long-time corporate lawyer. Since then, Hugh and Sam's paths crossed frequently. Hugh found Sam useful when Bigelow's crew required legal advice, which happened more often than Hugh expected. Sam helped Hugh keep them at arm's length from the campaign and Hugh's other businesses. In January, Hugh included Sam in a luncheon for lesser acquaintances. Not friends or partners, but people whom Hugh liked well enough. Over beers, Sam mentioned his divorce and upcoming marriage. Although Hugh wasn't the least interested, Sam volunteered info on Liza's money woes and poor fiscal skills. Hugh planned to use that insight now.

"How is Liza covering her medical expenses?"

"I've been helping. Her mother too, I'd guess."

"Must be difficult."

"Yeah, kinda."

"What if I take care of that? Give her a little re-launch cash?"

Sam stayed quiet, as he seemed to weigh Hugh's words. Did he want money for himself? Hugh couldn't pay off the whole damn town. "Plus, a bit for you, of course. If that were the situation, might Vera and Liza move on?"

"Could work with Liza."

"And the mother?"

"She's tough."

After the botched crash, Hugh had expected Vera to shrivel away. Dropped calls, windows rattling, one of Bigelow's idiots following her, all part of his goal to shake her up, force her to relocate, allowing him to tie up one more loose end. Instead, she became a stubborn thorn in his side. "She must want *something*."

"I'll talk to her."

Hugh thought about Sam's offer. So far, Sam had proved an unreliable investigator and messenger. "Never mind, I'll take care of it." Without shifting his gaze, Hugh signaled Sonia. "Mr. Davis is leaving."

On cue, Sonia materialized. Sam snatched his jacket from her.

Hugh sensed Sam had more to say. "What?"

"If anything happens to them..." Sam cleared his throat. "Should another incident occur, I'll tell the police everything."

Sonia's eyes widened. She handed Sam his hat.

Hugh mustered his best constituent smile. "No need for threats. There's no truth to their suspicions and, of course, they're safe." He paused and counted to five in his head. "Just as you and your fiancée are in no danger."

Sam made a funny sound, low, guttural.

Exactly, you idiot, who do you think you're fucking with? Hugh stepped forward and put out his hand. "You and I will continue to make money together, yes?"

At first, Sam did nothing, his hands loose at his sides. Hugh kept his right arm extended. The heat subsided. *Back in control.*

Finally, with a limp, damp hand, Sam shook Hugh's.

"Yes?" Hugh asked again, gripping Sam's hand hard.

"Yeah."

Hugh let go. "Thanks for coming by." He turned on his heels before Sam could say anything else and left him standing in the foyer.

This screw-up was getting worse by the hour. "Sonia," he said over his shoulder, "send Bridgette to my office."

Chapter 54

Erika and Hugh

Rain battered the roof and windows. A gust of wind upended a lounge chair on Erika and Griff's deck.

"Let's view the digital card after breakfast," she said. Did he hear the weariness in her voice?

They were sitting in the breakfast nook, her private laptop, the one she kept in the safe, at the ready. Finishing Griff's famous scrambled eggs and roasted potatoes, creamy with melted cheddar, Erika tried to remember the last time Griff cooked for her. "One more helping, then we can watch."

Ignoring her, Griff reached over and woke up the computer.

She typed in her password and opened her email.

Watching the horror show again left Erika queasy. She lowered her eyes and sipped her coffee.

"Damn," Griff said. "Wow."

Although Griff's surprise sounded genuine, Erika believed he'd seen the video before. She suspected Griff and Charlie had partnered in blackmailing Hugh. Not Charlie's style or expertise. Charlie enjoyed gambling and performing occasional favors for acquaintances who paid well. Even a motive like running away with Erika wouldn't have sent him to Hugh's door. No, Griff hatched the plot. That had to be why Lavender involved Griff in the car crash and invaded her home.

The two men knew each other from high-stake poker games. Perhaps Charlie let it slip he'd found the photos, or he owed Griff and offered the video as payment. If that were the case, why hide them? She wanted to confront her husband, ask her questions. She decided not to. Not yet. Get the money and get out of town before Vera blabs to the cops and press. Then seek answers from Griff.

The video ended. "This has to be worth at least two million," Griff said.

"I have savings. We pack up..."

He cut her off. "No. I confront him. Demand our due."

"He owes us for something?"

Jaw muscles visibly clenched, Griff glared at her. "I'll make it clear."

"We will, together."

"No," he said again, this time with more force.

"Getting people to cooperate is my wheelhouse. Plus, with two witnesses, he's less likely to hurt us."

They argued for several more minutes, but Griff grudgingly agreed. "Get dressed. We leave in twenty."

"We should record the meeting," she said, scraping plates and placing them in the dishwasher. "More insurance against future harm."

"Good idea."

Griff's new sobriety appeared to be sticking. His words remained clear and crisp.

"I'll take the lead," Griff insisted.

"Fine." Not really, but she'd won all the points she could with the newly sober Griff. Under the influence, she manipulated him with ease. Now, she had to claw and grapple for every point. "Your meeting, your way."

***

They drove to the Lavender mansion in silence. Rain blurred the road ahead, the windshield wipers barely able to keep up with the downpour. The canvas top of her electric-blue convertible shimmied under the onslaught. Last night, they'd spent several hours in the emergency room. Now, with her ribs taped and painkillers in her system, she was ready to face Hugh.

They pulled into the circle at the top of the Lavender driveway and parked. Umbrella in hand, Griff pushed open the passenger door and climbed out. Rain swept in. With his elbow, he slammed the door shut.

Erika struggled out as well, careful to miss any puddles. She'd settled for riding boots, skinny jeans, and a close-fitting T-shirt. A red raincoat, patent-leather shiny, topped the outfit. The boots, not designed to take a lot of punishment, would wilt if muddy. She pushed the button to her self-opening umbrella and dashed to the covered portico, Griff a step ahead.

He rang the bell. Erika heard its chimes reverberating throughout the house. They waited. Nothing. He pressed again. Still no response. They let several more minutes pass, the wind-driven rain pounding their backs.

Either no one was home, or Hugh didn't want to see them.

The drumming rain drowned out all other sounds, including an arriving car and subsequent door closings.

"Erika."

She swung around. Dani and Vera made a dash for the sheltered porch. Water dripped from Dani's scalp onto her face. Vera looked disheveled, as if she'd climbed out of bed, put on her raincoat, and left home with no attention to her appearance.

Griff said, "Let's go. We'll come back later."

Erika ignored him. Instead, she spoke to Vera and Dani. "What are you guys doing here?"

Dani said, "Lavender sent Zeek aka Florid Face to threaten Vera last night and demand she meet with Hugh."

What the fuck?

"I told him no. Lavender had to come to me." Vera's well-worn rain boots squished as she moved closer. "Then Dani called, and we came together to face him down."

Griff said, "Bad idea." He tugged on Erika's arm. "We're leaving."

"You should go too," she told the two women. "It's not safe."

Griff pulled on Erika's arm again. "Or smart." He leaned close to Erika's ear. "We don't want an audience. We'll come back in an hour."

One of the double doors swung open. Erika tried to place her.

Dani said, "Hi, Bridgette."

Bridgette took several steps back and gestured with her left hand; her right held the door. "Come in."

Dani, Vera, and Erika stepped into the foyer. Griff heeled his way back to the car. "Erika, let's go."

"Give me a few minutes." Dani and Vera might need her help. "We can speak with Hugh after, or I can ask Vera to drive me home."

Griff slammed the car door shut.

***

The driveway alert warned Hugh of arrivals, but he told Sonia to wait until the bell rang. Thanks to Zeek, Vera Moon and her sidekick were heading his way. Good. Get them out of the way before Rake and Anna showed.

"It's Miss Erika and Mr. Griff," Sonia announced. She watched them through the peephole.

Damn. Hugh blew out a puff of air. *Let them stew.* "Wait."

Griff rang the bell again. Getting antsy. Let him. Hugh preferred to keep his adversaries off kilter. *Give it another minute.* The Nobles provided another opportunity to cut off trouble and send it packing but their timing was poor.

Crap. Vera Moon and that hang-on-girl arrived and joined the Nobles.

Get this over with, one at a time. Not all together. First Moon and the girl. Probably wouldn't take much money to keep them quiet. They're obviously poor and desperate.

Griff and Erika posed a genuine threat. Had they teamed up with Moon and the girl? "Sonia, brew a fresh pot of coffee."

Behind him, he sensed Brigette's presence. She wore a signature scent, fresh with a hint of spice. Should he ask her to stay and record the sure-to-be blackmail demands? No. She was loyal but a straight arrow like Anna.

"Bridgette."

She joined Hugh. "Yes?"

"Let those fools in. Bring them to my office. Then leave us."

Chapter 55

Hugh and Vera

Vera and the girl fidgeted and gawked. Not Erika, of course.

Hugh asked, "Where's Griff?"

"In the car."

Chicken shit. Let his woman do his dirty work. Probably drunk or high. This might be easier than Hugh first thought.

"He'll join us soon, after Vera and Dani conclude their business."

Erika had introduced Vera Moon and Dani Gerrity, the girl Bigelow investigated. Lightweights. Inconsequential. "And what business is that?"

"You summoned us… me," Vera said.

The women sat on the leather couch in Hugh's office. Vera and Dani side by side. Erika perched on the end, angled toward Hugh. Seated in a matching leather chair, Hugh positioned himself at the center, across from the threesome. The earthy aroma of hot coffee scented the room.

He used both of his superpowers — silence and the glare.

Vera coughed as if clearing her throat. The girl's entire body quivered; her legs pumped up and down. Hugh waited.

"Why are we here?" Vera asked.

In his constituent voice, the one that relayed "trust me. I'm sincere and transparent," Hugh said, "To clear the air. Set things straight. Help you and your daughter find closure."

***

"Closure." Vera's baggy pants clung damp against her skin. A chill traveled through her body. "How will we do that while my son's murderer walks free?" She stood up and took a step toward Hugh. "Why did you kill my Charlie?"

"I didn't."

"Was keeping those photos and video secret worth a life?"

Christ. He shot a look at Erika. No surprised expression. He returned to Vera. "I'm trying to help you."

"He was a decent, loving, and kind man."

Erika made a throaty sound.

"I'm offering you life-changing money."

Vera heard a vacuum cleaner's rumble from the floor above. The rain let up; the grayish light from the windows became brighter. She tried to damp down her emotions. She craved an explanation and a full confession, not a payoff. Even though Dani made her practice, she couldn't remember anything she agreed to say, to ask; it all left her as soon as she saw his face. The man who killed her boy. "He blackmailed you and you wanted it to stop, so you killed him."

"Please hear me." Hugh leaned in. "Are you listening?"

She nodded.

"I did not kill your son. Period."

"Then you had him killed. That Zeek person or one of the thugs you planted in Erika's house." Her hands shook. *Steady. Breathe.*

"No."

Vera flinched from the ferocity of Lavender's voice.

He stood up, towering over her. "You will *not* say that to anyone else ever again. For your sake and Liza's, never again tell that libelous tale."

His face muscles bunched. A vein throbbed at his throat.

"I will help you..." He swung his gaze toward Dani. "All of you. That said, should you repeat your baseless accusation to anyone, the consequences will be beyond your greatest fears."

Dani leapt up. "You can't terrorize us."

Vera said, "You are guilty. We know your dirty secrets."

"You are in way over your heads."

Vera's rage overwhelmed her. "You are a murderer. Admit it. You killed because you are a hatemonger and a rapist."

For several beats, only the thrum of a vacuum cleaner filled the air. "For your sake and your family's..." He faced Dani this time. "Not to mention that guy you're living with and your gas station pal. Doesn't he have a wife and baby?"

Dani's body, usually in constant motion, seemed to freeze.

"You might not go to jail, but the governorship is out." Anger, new and sharp, surged through Vera. "Last night's news report stained you. I will get out the African-American vote for the sitting governor, use those photos and videos and hints of your other wrong doings like..." she swung her head toward Dani.

"Money-laundering," Dani said.

"... to galvanize the Black community." Vera heard the high volume and pitch of her voice. *Good.* Let him realize the strength of her determination.

"You are an inconsequential woman. No one cares what you say."

Her rage became a terrible pain in her head, almost blinding her. Her heartbeat rocketed. "You cannot control all of us."

Erika said, "Wait."

Dani said, "We scored documents, too, proof."

He glared at Dani. "Proof?"

"About your corrupt car service and work with racist hate groups."

"I am *not* a racist. Look at all I've done for the Black community."

Vera said, "We saw you in blackface and your antics. We know about the ACL."

Hugh advanced toward Vera.

Vera stood her ground.

With his right hand, he grabbed the fabric of her sweatshirt at the throat and lifted her until she balanced only on her toes. "You listen to me, old woman. You will not tell anyone."

With all her strength, she screamed, "I will." Spittle sprayed his face.

Dani ran forward, pounded her fists on his arm. "Leave her alone."

Erika cried out, "Hugh, come on, we can talk this through."

He shoved Dani hard. She hit the floor.

Dangling, her entire body shaking, Vera screamed at him again. "You cannot kill us all."

His expression moved from purple rage to a hard, controlled mask. Slowly, he lowered her and released his grip. A tight smile lifted the corners of his mouth.

Her heart still raced at an alarming speed. He had to confess. He had to say it. "You murdered him to save your reputation and your ambitions. Admit it."

He rang a bell that sat on a small table. "Sonia will see you ladies out. Take the money when delivered and shut up, go away, disappear... or live to regret it."

"You cannot win," Vera said. "Justice will hunt you down and convict you."

He took out a cloth handkerchief and wiped his face and then spoke to Erika. "Fetch your husband."

Chapter 56

Hugh

Shaken to his core by the Moon woman, he met with Griff and Erika in the foyer. Usually, deal making gave him a rush, even with amateurs. It left him high. Similar, he imagined, to a potent drug. A euphoria almost but not as transporting as... He didn't finish the thought. In his ordered world, private things and business stayed separate. Instead, he felt almost crushed, exhausted. No matter. He could fake it. *Shoulders back, head high. Look them in the eyes.*

"What do you want?" he asked Griff. Better to deal with the greedier Griff than crafty Erika. Besides, Erika saw the earlier Moon debacle. That left him at a disadvantage, but previous encounters with Griff gave Hugh an edge. Whenever he hit the right number, Griff's eyebrows shot up — a tell, as gamblers called it.

"Two million. Off-shore account. Today," Griff said.

"Five-hundred thousand. More than fair."

Erika said, "No, we..."

Griff jumped in. "One-point-five and we'll call it square."

Hugh said, "No." One million was his best offer, but too early in the negotiation to reveal.

Erika said to Griff, "Let's take what..."

"Shut up."

Hugh watched them squabble. His confidence grew. "Seven-fifty."

Griff said, "One-point-five, and we vanish. You won't have to worry about us ever again."

Hugh was done. Emotional exhaustion drained him of his motivation. "One million, last offer. Leave town, now. Otherwise, go to reporters or whatever you plan to do."

"Deal." Griff stuck out his hand ready to shake.

Hugh turned on his heels. "My people will be in touch to make arrangements. See yourselves out."

***

The storm kicked up again. At noon, Rake and Anna arrived with dripping umbrellas and squishing shoes. Bridgette returned as well, her damp hair sagged against her scalp and her face shined as she shucked her raincoat.

Sonia brought in more coffee, water, hot tea, warm scones, and raspberry preserves. A glass dish contained chicken salad, and another held miniature grilled cheese sandwiches with tomatoes. A bowl of fresh fruit sat in the middle of the table. Cups, saucers, glasses, flatware, and large cloth napkins completed the service.

Five of them sat around the low coffee table in Hugh's office — Hugh, Kate, Bridgette, Rake and Anna. He didn't want Kate there, since the topic at hand might upset her, but she insisted. He agreed because she too had excellent political instincts.

"How's the spin going about Oak Lane and Bigelow?" Hugh asked, his voice betraying his weariness and something else, a new emotion — fear. He had to shake the morning off.

"Not bad," Rake said. "It's this other thing that's got us worried."

Anna sat ramrod straight. The napkin across her lap covered the pencil skirt of her tan suit. Crumbs dotted it. "I don't see a way to contain a scandal with so many people involved."

Rake nodded his agreement. "How many know, ten, more?"

"It's not a secret with that many people aware." A grim expression spread across Anna's face. "One whispers it to a lover who only tells her best friend, who shares it with her husband."

Hugh, his fingers intertwined into a fist against his lips, listened to their death knell. "Your thoughts, Bridgette?" *Are you going to pile on too and abandon me?*

Anna asked, "Can't you tell us the secret? We can't advise you without the facts."

Bridgette said, "Photographs and a video." Her blush almost matched her red hair.

"Of?" Anna tossed her napkin onto the table. "Hugh, what the hell is this about?"

"They'll say it's rape and racist." Hugh paced. His coffee sloshed in his cup. "Which it is not. It's play-acting. Candidates survive worse." The sense of exhaustion tinged with fear threatened to overwhelm him. He set his gaze on the face of the grandfather clock in the corner. Forced himself to stay focused.

"Are there children involved?"

The horror and terror in Anna's voice sent a chill through Hugh. "No," he said with force, training his eyes on Anna's. "Of course not. How could you ask that?"

"You're not giving us any information. What kind of sexual play-acting and racism?"

Monumental cluster fuck. He was the right person at the right time. New York needed him. Rebounding from a tumultuous year, the ravishes of the pandemic, domestic violence at an all-time high, racial justice reckoning, economic uncertainty on one side and boundless opportunity on the other. He'd make a great governor. He understood the issues facing people of color and supported reforms in policing, healthcare, and economic opportunity zones. Painting him as a racist was unfair.

Kate spoke for the first time. "Leave the gubernatorial race."

"I'm not a quitter, never in my life."

Kate lowered her porcelain cup. It clinked onto the saucer.

"Anna and Rake have the Bigelow thing under control," Hugh argued. "We can maneuver around this other thing too. We've always powered through."

With a primness she usually saved for public occasions, she dabbed her mouth with the cloth napkin. "I'd say this time is quite different."

"My God, the people forgave drug addicts, thieves, and confessed sexual predators and elected them."

Kate's mouth moved, her voice so low that he stopped pacing and listened. Her usually unlined face was now tight crinkles, her mouth a hard, straight line. She spoke between clenched teeth, like a patient still in pain from extensive dental work. "We'll go to our summer place in Maine, plan a trip abroad, and come home when it dies down."

Ah, she knew. His suspicions had been right. She'd discovered something last year but chose not to confront him. Now, he wished he'd pushed harder, pressed her to tell him what she discovered. He could have explained and helped her understand.

Rake said, "Things *will* simmer down."

Kate spoke to Rake. "Tell the press I've taken ill. The campaign trail, lack of sleep, daily stress, proved too much for me. Hugh's only choice is to care for his wife."

Anna and Rake faced Hugh in expectation. If it were possible, Bridgette appeared whiter than usual. Kate's back was straight, her gaze just over his shoulder.

Face it. It was over. The pictures were enough to slam the door on his political ambitions. The mood of the country had changed. Racial missteps were no longer tolerated. Somehow the Moon woman and the girl believed they have proof about his financial sleight of hand. Were they in touch with the reporter? Thanks to her, rumors flew about Oak Lane, Nate Bigelow, and Hugh's connection. If she dug into the car crash involving Vera and Liza, how soon would it be before the press speculated about Charlie's murder? Bigelow and his minions had screwed that one up. Hugh ordered them to scare Vera with phone hang-ups, strangers following her. The rally worried him too. Stirring up trouble. He thought she'd run upstate to visit her daughter or check into a motel. If she had the memory card hidden in her apartment, they could comb the place once she vacated. Either way, they'd have unfettered access to the apartment. He'd tasked Zeek with searching Sam and Liza's house.

The idiots had tripped up every step of the way. Instead of the non-headline-grabbing scare-tactics Hugh had ordered, they staged a car crash on Main Street. Stupidity was a dangerous flaw, and Bigelow had more than his share. The earlier meetings with Vera and the girl and then with Griff and Erika came back. *Damn*. At what point had he lost control?

Anna said, "What are you going to do?"

No, "*we*" anymore. Time to bring in his lawyer.

"Bridgette, get Michael here as quickly as you can."

Bridgette sat silent and still.

"Did you hear me?"

"I believed in you," she said in a small voice.

Christ. "I've done nothing wrong."

Kate smiled at Bridgette. "It's a misunderstanding. All will be well."

"I've been so honored to serve, but now..."

Kate rose and faced Bridgette. "You're right to put your faith in him. I do too. We must help him out of this mess. We're the only ones who can."

Smart. Kate was skilled in managing sensitive situations.

Bridgette stood visibly trembling.

Kate put her hand on Bridgette's arm quieting her agitation. "He needs us."

Building on Kate's strategy, Hugh said,"*I* need you."

A loud silence followed. Hugh pressed his lips together to keep from speaking, begging. Finally, Bridgette said, "Okay." She bit into her lower lip. "Yes."

In unison, Kate and Hugh said, "Thank you," Hugh in a voice filled with relief, Kate's tone more confident.

With the decision made, Hugh had no time for handholding. Again, he spoke to Bridgette. "Once we're gone, close up the house. Rake, see to the press and campaign offices. Pay the staff. Close it down."

"What about the donors?"

A problem. Many people had invested in him, people he'd need again, people his business counted on as well. "Anna, can you manage that? Play up Kate's illness; assure them I'll be in touch."

Kate said, "The doctors aren't sure what's wrong with me. I'm in a great deal of distress, can't be out; they're worried it may be life-threatening."

"I'll take care of it over the next few days." Anna cleared her throat. "Then I'm moving on."

Disdain colored her words. Loyalty with short strings. “Sure. I understand.” *And will remember*.

Rake scratched his stubble. “How do we reach you once we’ve shuttered it all?”

“Cell phone. You have my private number.”

Hugh thought about the getaway plan. *Maine? Was that far enough away?* “Kate, investigate additional locations. Not on the East Coast. Bridgette can help you.”

Kate sounded cool, ticking off items as if she’d thought all this through before. “Bridgette, please keep Sonia, the housekeeping staff and the gardeners on. Continue our contracts with pool cleaners and, in case this lasts longer than expected, make sure the snowplow firm is still on retainer. Provide everyone with a substantial bonus. Tell them we’ll be gone for a while, and under no circumstances are they to speak to anyone about our situation.” Kate stood next to Hugh. “Please be quite firm about that. One whiff, and their paychecks vanish.”

Damn Charlie Moon.

With a slight quaver in her voice, Bridgette asked, “Do you want to make a statement, announce a press conference?”

Hugh opened his mouth to respond, but Kate preempted him. “No. He’s too distraught about my illness. At the right time, once he’s sure I’ve recovered, he’ll be back in touch with the fine people of New York.”

He admired Kate’s command of the situation. Impressive. Should he still write those silence-inducement checks? He *had to* pay Bigelow and his boys, and he’d committed to paying the Nobles. What about Sam, Liza, Vera, and the girl? Hugh was a thorough man. Or that gas station guy? Hugh believed in insurance. He’d transfer the funds and write the checks today, withdraw from the race, hold an emergency board meeting, and they’d be on the road in two days, three tops. Hopefully, before the vulture press descended. Or the police.

Chapter 57

Dani and Vera

Instead of April showers, May downpours pelted them. The storm that started on Thursday continued into the weekend. Saturday morning, several days after the scary meeting with the murdering Hugh Lavender, the skies stayed dark and the rain relentless.

Dani stood in the middle of Mirko's living room, her bags packed and at her feet.

"Where will you go?"

He'd taken the day off to study, he said. Was that really the reason, or did he want to say goodbye? "I guess I'll head west and stay with my brother for a while. Like I planned." *How long ago was that?*

Rain cascaded and streaked down the windows. The apartment was warm, the air close.

Mirko stepped forward. "Will you be safe from Lavender?" He came closer until he was right in front of her. "I'm worried about you... and Vera."

She didn't want to live with Bogie. She wanted to stay here, forever. But clearly that would not happen. "Yeah, sure. We'll be fine."

They stood so close that she smelled his skin and breath, sweet from lotion and toothpaste. "I guess I better get going."

He leaned in, his lips touching her cheek. She turned her face so that his mouth rested on hers. They kissed. At first a chaste brushing, and then he slipped his tongue into mouth. She sank into him.

He pulled away and ran his hand down the side of her face, her neck, her arm. "Why don't you leave your things here while you go to your meeting with Stephanie and Vera?"

She held herself still, not allowing her feet to jump up and down or her mouth to say something pathetic. "Okay. Thanks."

He kissed her again.

***

Dani and Stephanie sat in Vera's apartment. Plates of chocolate crumbs from the cake Vera baked that morning lay on the snack trays next to them.

A low, Brandy-rumble followed each rub of Vera's hand. The storm delayed Penny's flight until late that day.

Stephanie, her notepad, and pen still in her hand, said, "Lavender has quit. Claims his wife is ill. There's nothing more to do." She shut her tablet.

"But we didn't prove he's a murderer." Dani pumped her right leg. "He gets away with it."

The way Stephanie snapped her notebook closed reminded Vera of Officer French. They'd gone to the police department directly from the Lavender house and shared all their suspicions and evidence. Stephanie met them there, showed Officer French and Detective Monroe the information Dani had swiped and gave to Stephanie. Stephanie claimed she received them from an anonymous source. The police officers listened, asked questions, read the documents, and watched the video. In the end, they said there was nothing more they could do but promised to give the papers and video to the detective squad. Said yes, plenty of suspicion but unfortunately, no facts. Case closed.

Stephanie's station refused to air the video. They weren't sure about the identities of the participants. Lawyers would review and get back to them. They had to track down the woman in the video, to find out if it was rape. The blackface was damning by itself, but the other individuals had rights. The higher ups said they would investigate.

Stephanie said, "With Lavender ghosting, I doubt my managers, or the police will have the appetite to pursue this." She shrugged. "Sorry."

Vera said, "You were great. Really. Thank you."

"I promise to keep digging for a connection to Charlie's killing."

Vera doubted her. Not that Stephanie lied. She meant well. The news cycle, however, moved at crackling speed from the election to the latest natural disaster to shootings and wars. In the words of Officer French, Charlie's murder was now a cold case. "We have special county detectives assigned to these crimes. Sometimes it takes years, but they eventually solve many." Translation: *This is no longer my responsibility. Good luck. Do not hold your breath.*

The rain picked up again. It peppered the roof, a fitting coda to their work. "I am sorry, Dani." Vera walked over to Dani and pulled her into a hug, at first stiffly, then a full-on embrace. Vera stepped back and smiled. "It is time you got on with your life."

Dani asked, "What will you do?"

"Take care of Liza while she heals." Vera thought about the seventy-thousand dollars. *Could Charlie's life be worth so little?* "And move out of here. Like you, get a fresh start."

Tears ran down Dani's cheeks. "Are we still going to Erika's this afternoon?"

"I cannot decide if Erika is friend or villain."

"People make mistakes."

"This from you?" Vera chuckled. "I thought Erika was on your enemy list."

Dani let out a swoosh of air.

"You're right," Vera said. "They do. And God expects his people to forgive."

Besides, she promised Erika to return the box of photos, the one's Charlie took of Erika. The request surprised Vera since Erika and her husband were moving. Why take the pictures with her? More disturbing, she asked for Charlie's gun. Vera did not want it, but why would Erika? The explanation she gave, that the beating she received from Bigelow left her feeling vulnerable, did not ring true. *Forgive. Be generous.*

"Erika?" Stephanie asked. She'd packed up and stood by the door, one hand on the doorknob. "Noble?"

"Yes. Do you know her?"

"She's married to Griff, right?"

"Uh-huh. She assisted us with our... investigation."

"The husband was in your accident."

The crash. One more unanswered question. Another cold case, or completely forgotten, not important enough for further inquiry? Liza still in the hospital, Vera still on edge. "Do you have pertinent information?"

"Nothing for sure." She gave them a half-smile. "He has a reputation."

"For what?"

"I don't deal in rumors. Just be careful around him." She paused. "Perhaps I'll stumble onto new clues. Keep in touch." Stephanie faced Dani. "Mirko has my info."

"Come on. Let us get over to Erika's. It is time we put all this behind us." As if Vera ever could.

Chapter 58

Dani

Dani liked organization and cleanliness. It fell to her, therefore, to divvy up the labor and get the three of them focused on the packing at hand. Just as Dani had done, albeit on an entirely different scale when she left her apartment, she now created piles. Take, donate, trash, and they began sorting.

Katy Perry, Rhianna, Beyoncé, and Estelle's voices filled the house. Dani, Vera, and Erika were in the Noble's bedroom, the king-sized bed covered with stacks of clothes. Dozens of pairs of shoes lined the far wall, all waiting for a decision.

Erika held up a lemon-colored suit and pressed it against her frame. "This is a great statement piece."

Vera frowned. "What is it saying?"

"Look at me. Take notice."

"In that case, remind me to never buy one."

Dani and Erika chuckled, the first laughter of the afternoon. Until then it had been a somber party, despite the music, the wine Erika offered (Dani and Vera declined), and the canapés she provided – stuffed mushrooms, smelly cheese and a French baguette, water crackers smeared with whitefish and salmon spreads.

Dani asked, "Did you and your husband work things out with Lavender after we left?"

"Yesterday our banker assured us we're set."

Vera said, "A courier arrived with three envelopes. One for Liza, one for Dani, and one for me."

Dani said, "We don't want his filthy money."

The man had knocked on Vera's door, short and fat with protruding teeth but dressed professionally. He handed Vera the envelopes. "What is this?" "A gift from Mr. Lavender. He said you comprehended the consequences of undesirable behavior, and in exchange he'd like you to have this symbol of his appreciation. Told me to ask you if you understand." Vera had nodded her assent.

On and off, for over an hour, Dani and Vera stared at the white envelopes, most of the time quietly. Vera got up and went to the bathroom. When she returned, Dani had the envelope with her name on it in her hand. "It's kinda flimsy." She held it up to the light. The opaque envelope revealed nothing. Vera said, "If it is a check, you need it, honey." Dani could use money for sure, but not from that murderer creep. Assured that it wasn't cash, money they could donate, they flushed their envelopes containing the checks down the toilet without even opening them.

Dani watched the papers swirl away. How much? Enough to pay her back rent and get a new place, enough to send some to Bogie and help Javier? She had stood there until it disappeared, feeling both proud of herself and sorry. "Will Liza be okay with you flushing her money away?"

"Yes." Vera paused. "I hope so. Charlie left me a considerable amount of cash, and I will share it with her."

Dani said, "We told the cops, so we didn't even earn his blood money. Wait until he figures that out."

Now, pointing at the yellow suit, Dani asked Erika, "Donate or take?"

"Take." Erika tossed it to Dani.

Dani knew she should mind her own business. The question popped out anyway. "How much did he give you?"

"Dani." Vera's tone scolded.

Erika said, "Less than we asked for, but more than enough." She gave Vera a wistful look.

"I do not blame you." The *take* pile was enormous. Vera moved a mound of clothes to make room for more. "Will Lavender try to hurt you once he finds out we told the police everything?"

Erika gave Vera a disappointed look. "I wish you hadn't done that." She hiked her shoulders and lifted her hands, palms up. "No matter. Griff and I are keeping our end of the bargain. Besides, it's too late. We've moved the money."

Eyeing the growing pile of clothes on the bed, Vera asked, "Where are you going again? Will your next place be as large as this one?"

Dani loved the house. Not as palatial as Hugh Lavender's, but Dani liked it better with its spacious great room, floor-to-ceiling windows, and glass doors on one side leading to the deck. Their bedroom suite included a walk-in closet and his-and-her bathrooms.

"I could house-sit for you until the place gets sold, make sure no one comes in and steals anything." Despite her seriousness, Dani said it in a joking voice. She had nowhere to go. Things were good with Mirko, just not move in good. He said she could stay tonight, but what happens tomorrow?

Earlier, she'd gone to see Javier. She brought him up to date, talked about Lavender's withdrawal from the governor's race. Their relationship wasn't the same. Not like they had been before her confession. Javier said he was glad to see her, but no warm hugs or joking. He asked lots of questions. He told her he too received a present from Hugh Lavender with a promise to never discuss him or Oak Lane with anyone. The messenger threatened deportation and harassment of family members if Javier reneged.

Dani fretted. Would her visit to the cops with Vera end up hurting Javier again? With Lavender ghosting and the police and television station not believing they had enough to pursue, maybe not. She warned Javier anyway. Full disclosure. He'd thanked her but said he was glad he took the money. He and his wife were shopping for a condo.

Dani felt happy for him. They promised to get together again soon. She had to make a trip to her old place, make things right with Alice, her former landlord. Explain. Apologize. Amends still left her with no place to live and no money to pay for anything.

"Are you serious?" Erika asked Dani. She eyed a leather coat.

"Would that help?"

She added the coat to the "take" pile. "Let's talk about it after we're finished."

Did Dani want another handout? Wasn't it time for her to be independent? Deep in thought, Dani went into the walk-in closet. They'd folded most of the clothes on the bed or placed them in donate bags. Empty hangers hung from the rods. Several boxes, stacked one on top of the other, stood ready for inspection and decisions. Dani opened the first one. Receipts, bills, and lists filled it almost to the top. Best not to snoop; let Erika go through them. The next box had other miscellaneous items — cufflinks, a stopped watch, a jumble of old chargers for out-of-date phones. Crumpled in a corner, Dani spied a photograph. Curious, she picked it up and smoothed out its edges.

Geeze. Her heart flip-flopped. Erika and Charlie posed like the photographs Vera found in the box in Liza's basement. Except, black and red XX's striped their likenesses. A thick red line circled Charlie's neck, and another X covered his crotch.

"You can't take all this shit." A man's voice in the bedroom. It must be Griff. "Two suitcases. Three at the most."

Dani shrank against the closet wall. She stared down at the photograph. Erika's doing? Did she get mad at Charlie for something? Dani looked at the red circles and XX's. She peeked out and watched Griff move toward the door.

"I bought packing boxes from Staples. I'll bring them in." Over his shoulder, Griff added, "Meanwhile, fill up those trash bags. We're traveling light."

Dani waited until the door slammed shut. What should she do? The photo seemed important, damning in fact. She stepped into the bedroom.

Erika, her arms crossed against her breasts, stood tapping her foot, mumbling to herself.

In a shy voice, Dani said, “I found...” She held the mangled picture out toward Erika.

Erika shrieked.

Vera came into the room, her arms loaded with towels. “What is going on?”

“Where did you get this?” Erika’s voice shrilled.

“In the closet.”

Vera said, “Let me see.” She moved closer to Erika. “Oh, no. Dear God.”

Chapter 59

Erika, Vera, and Dani

Air whooshed out of Erika's lungs. She stared at the disfigured photo from that day, their getaway. They'd been so happy. Griff suspected, had accused her in fact, but she thought her denials convinced him. She shook her head, trying to clear it. No. Griff couldn't take a life. Even as she thought it, she realized she might be wrong. Boozing and drugging stoked his temper. No. He couldn't have done this.

She replayed their conversations. The blackmail. Griff alone? Had he set up Charlie so Lavender would kill him? Had the truth been right under her nose all this time?

With arms filled with flattened cardboard boxes, Griff strode back into the room. "Start putting the crap you're not taking in these. We can stash them in a storage facility." He dropped the cartons onto the bed and swept his gaze over the three women. "What's wrong?"

Erika stomped toward him. She thrust the photo in his face. "You used Lavender to get Charlie killed?" She stared into his eyes, hoping to detect truths or lies.

"Of course, not." His tone contradicted the unclouded coldness glaring back at her.

"Did. You. Do. This?"

"No." A sneer crept across his face. "You have to admit, though, you gave me cause." He jabbed the mutilated photo. "You think I don't hurt? It's fine with me you fuck all the lowlifes in town?"

Tears streamed. "He was a good person."

Spittle foamed at the corners of Griff's mouth. "And you're a whore." With his left hand, he grabbed her wrist, "But you're my whore."

"Let go of me." Erika yanked, trying to free her hand.

Griff's hold tightened.

"You're hurting me."

Vera stepped forward, still holding the box of photographs she promised to return to Erika. "Were you and Charlie blackmailing Lavender?" Her often trembling hands were now steady and her voice strong.

"Your weak son had no clue how to blackmail anyone. I struck all the deals with that pompous asshole Lavender. I pulled the strings and now it's payday. Be smart, ladies. Take your money and run. That's what we're doing." He looked down on Erika. "Isn't that right, baby?"

With the back of her hand, Erika wiped her cheeks and then her running nose. She never sensed danger from Griff. *Before*. Her heart banged against aching ribs.

Vera asked, "How did Charlie come by a safe deposit box of cash?"

"How am I supposed to know? He gambled. Me too. Sometimes we won."

Was Charlie stashing winnings to take her away? She said aloud what she hoped wasn't true. "Did you do the killing yourself?" *Please, say no. Tell me you goaded Lavender but didn't think he'd go that far.*

Griff twisted. Pain shot up through her arm.

Silent up until now, Dani yelled at Griff. "You're hurting her. Let go."

Instead, he circled Erika's torso with his right hand, pressing into her fractured ribs.

She groaned. "Damn it."

"You better stop." Dani picked up a tall, solid-glass candlestick from the donate pile and hefted it like a baseball bat. "I'm not kidding."

Out of the corner of her eye, Erika saw Vera reach into the box still in her arms and pull out Charlie's gun.

"No." Erika screamed at Vera.

Griff let go of Erika and spun around.

Feet apart, knees slightly bent, with two hands, Vera leveled the Glock and aimed it at Griff's chest. "You murdered my son. I am placing you..." She paused as if considering. "Under citizen's arrest."

"Ha. You stupid cunt. Did you see me do something? You can't arrest me." As if she were a naughty child, he shook his finger at Vera. "You're going to hurt someone. Give it to me."

"Why kill him? Why not divorce?"

Erika begged Vera, "Put it down." She almost said, *"He's not worth it,"* but she swallowed the words, hoping for de-escalation. This was getting out of hand, screwing up everything. "Why don't we all take a seat and talk this through?"

Vera held her aim steady, her eyes locked on Griff's. "Tell me why you killed my boy."

"He was fucking my wife. Not enough reason for you?"

Oh God, he just admitted murdering Charlie. This can't be right.

"No," Vera said.

"Yeah, well, the sap planned to send the video to the media and the chair of the board of Lavender's company. Take him down. Aware of my connection, he asked for help." As if speaking to himself, Griff added, "Lavender's a rich prick who treated me like shit."

The chuckle that followed sent chills through Erika.

"There you go. Two birds, as they say. Kill Charlie, milk Lavender. Boom. Done and done."

***

The words, *Boom. Done and done*, bounced around in Vera's head and shuddered through her body.

Openly crying, Erika said, "Shut up." She swung her body towards Vera. "Please put down the gun. Let Griff and me walk out of here. You'll never see us again."

"Listen to the lady."

"Step away from him," Vera said to Erika. "He's a killer. Didn't you hear him?" *What was wrong with her? No matter.* Vera raised her voice and kept her eyes on Griff. "You are under citizen's arrest for the murder of Charlie Moon," she repeated.

Still hefting her candlestick, Dani spoke from behind him. "Get on the ground face down."

Ignoring Erika and Dani, he advanced toward Vera with his right hand extended. "Don't be stupid."

"Stop." Vera's voice came out loud and clear. "Do not come one step closer." Every lesson Vincent taught her, every practice session, straightened her back and steadied her arms. She kept the Glock trained on his chest, a direct line to his cold, murderous heart.

Erika said, "They'll put you in jail. Let us go."

"Dani," Vera said, "dial 911."

Dani seemed frozen with indecision, the candlestick-bat still in her hands.

"Don't call the fucking police." Erika snuffled up mucus. "Let's all take a moment to think this through. Griff, Vera, take things down a fucking notch, okay?"

Griff didn't seem to hear. He took another step forward. With a swift movement Vera barely saw, he grabbed for the Glock and caught her arm. She struggled to hold on to it, her finger still on the trigger, but he was strong and tenacious. He held both her hands. The gun pointed up.

Bang. A shot flew into the ceiling. Bits of plaster fell to the floor.

With a final wrench, Griff wrested the weapon from her. The back of his left hand swung and slapped her hard.

Erika and Dani cried out.

Her face aching and blood oozing from her mouth, Vera stumbled and landed with a thump on the floor.

Griff aimed at the center of her forehead. "You dumb Black cunt. "I'm going to kill you, just like I wiped out that wimp son of yours."

***

Remembering her stance from her softball days, Dani stepped forward, cocked her arm, and swung with a smooth, clean arc. The oversized candlestick landed on his back just below his right shoulder. The gun flew from his hand and skittered across the floor.

At first, he staggered, then righted himself, spun around and faced Dani. "Then I'm coming for you."

On all fours, Vera scrambled and grabbed the Glock, then rolled onto her back, holding the weapon with both hands. "You're under arrest," she shouted for the third time.

Griff lunged forward.

Vera fired.

Erika screamed.

"Fuck." He looked down at the blood spurting from his left thigh and then raised his eyes to meet the now standing Vera's, his expression incredulous. "What the hell did you do?" He took a halting step toward her.

Dani swung and the candlestick landed on his neck.

He howled but kept moving.

Bang. Vera fired, this time hitting him in his left shoulder. The shot spun him around before he sagged to the floor.

"Do not move," she said. "Or the next one goes straight to your corrupted heart."

Chapter 60

Dani

A few minutes after Dani called 911, three patrol cars rolled up. Cops jumped out. Hands above her head to assure them she was neither armed nor dangerous, Dani met them at the front door.

"The woman holding the gun is Vera Moon. She's the good guy. The perp is on the floor bleeding." Dani knew they might misunderstand the situation, a Black woman aiming a weapon at a white man could get shot. She signaled the way to the master suite.

Next, an ambulance wailed up the driveway.

A police officer asked Dani, "Who else is in the house?"

Dani told him and explained everyone but her was in the bedroom.

They didn't seem to believe her because they fanned out and checked every room while the EMT's tended to Griff's wounds.

A female copper led Vera into the great room. She looked awful. Her eyes appeared opaque, her skin ashen, and her right cheek swollen and bruised. Blood crusted her lips. She swayed on her feet until the officer steadied her. Grabbing the other side, Dani and the officer eased Vera onto the sofa.

"Thank you, Officer French," Vera said.

Dani remembered the name. A copper Vera liked and trusted.

French peered at Vera. "Are you okay? Do you need a doctor?"

"I'm a little lightheaded," Vera said. Tears rolled down her cheeks.

"Understandable. You've been through a traumatic experience. You shot someone."

"Yeah, but the guy in there," Dani said, "killed Charlie Moon, and he was going to murder us."

"The detectives are on their way," the cop said. "You can explain everything to them. Right now, I need your names and addresses."

There was something comforting at first by the routine question until Dani remembered that she didn't live anywhere.

***

The lead detective gave his name as Monroe. Tall and thin but with a potbelly, Vera appeared to recognize him, just as she knew the woman named French. A compact detective with flaring ears, Monroe introduced as his partner, Liz Torres.

The most unusual part of the bizarre scene was Erika, who Dani thought of as an icy diva, sobbing and snuffling. Rain drummed on the great room's skylights, and police car strobes colored the windows – all adding to a movie-like quality to the unfolding action.

Except, a drama with a tragic ending. Would the police arrest Vera and take Dani in for her part? Would Griff get away with murder? Not if Dani could help it.

The paramedics wheeled Griff out of the house along with a pole and bag of liquid feeding into his arm. Two uniforms followed.

"We need to get you out of those bloody clothes," Detective Monroe said to Vera. He turned to Erika. "Can you provide a change for Ms. Moon? She'll need shoes as well."

"What's going to happen to my husband?" Erika asked.

"They're taking him to Northern Westchester."

Erika nodded as if she either agreed or understood. "There's crime tape blocking my way. The clothes are in my closet."

Another female cop said to Erika, "I can take care of it. What am I looking for?"

Erika eyed Vera as if assessing what in Erika's wardrobe might fit. "A caftan and slippers or flip-flops."

The woman disappeared into the bedroom.

Officer French approached Dani. "We'd like to take your statement at the station."

"I can't leave Vera. She needs me."

"It's okay," Monroe said. "Once we've got her clothes sorted, Detective Torres and I will bring her there as well."

"She did nothing wrong," Dani said. "She saved my life. He said he'd kill us." Dani moved to Vera's side. "I have to tell you something. It's super important."

Stepping between them, the Detective shut her down. "Let's talk about it at the station."

Chapter 61

Vera

The rain finally stopped, leaving the air sweet, washed, the way a spring shower perfumes the night. Dani and she sat in a booth at their favorite diner, side-by-side.

Dani said. "We solved it."

Vera patted Dani's hand. "Indeed."

"You were so brave, not even scared."

"Terrified, in fact. Where did you learn to swing like that?"

Dani grinned. "Played high school softball. Even won a trophy."

Vera gave Dani's hand a squeeze. Then she touched her aching cheek. At seventy, the cost was high for all the physical abuse she'd suffered – first in the car crash and then at the hands of the heinous Griff.

"Hurt?" Dani asked.

"Not so much," she said, trying not to worry Dani.

Right after the shooting, which felt like a long time ago, the police took Erika, Dani, and Vera to the station on Green Street. Erika's lawyer arrived. After a tough conversation, Sam arranged for a lawyer for Vera, a stout woman with dyed blonde hair named Laura Peach. Vera assured Dani that Ms. Peach was available to her.

Detectives Monroe and Torres questioned each of them separately. The scariest moment for Vera was when Monroe read her rights.

Despite that grim moment, Vera told the unadorned truth. Sam said Ms. Peach would be there soon, but Vera had nothing to hide. She shared Griff's confession, explained why she had an unlicensed gun with her, and told them about Griff's assault and death threats.

"Any word how Griff is doing?" Dani asked. "Have they arrested him for the murder?"

"According to Detective Monroe, Griff will survive his injuries and he's in custody in the hospital."

"And you're fine, right?"

"So far," Vera said. Detective Monroe had contacted her at nine this morning, but Vera didn't answer. She knew it was him because she'd finally enabled caller ID. Silly. But she didn't have the strength to face whatever came next, not yet. Laura Peach called as well. Vera planned to return the calls after the visit with Dani. Soak up Dani-energy and optimism. Fortified, she'd face the consequences.

Larry, the waiter, brought them refills for their tea and Diet Coke. "Can I interest you ladies in pie?" he asked, raising his eyebrows.

They smiled their thanks but declined.

Dani asked, "Your husband taught you to shoot like that?"

"I hated it. He insisted. Said the ability to protect myself, should it ever come to it, was important." Funny, but from the time she found the Smith and Wesson Glock in Sam's basement, and despite the obvious danger, it never occurred to her to keep it close.

"Ever use it? I mean before?"

"No. We practiced at the range until I adjusted to the recoil and hit the target with consistency. Then our first baby came, and we got rid of it."

"Like riding a bike?"

Vera managed a small smile. "I guess." Did she fire in rage seeking revenge? The scene spooled in her head on a loop. No. He intended to harm them, said so, attacked verbally and physically.

Muffled voices from other customers and the rumble of cars along Route 117 played in the background. Vera thought about Erika. Such a complicated woman. "I think Erika still loves her husband and might deny he attacked us."

"Right. And you beat up yourself."

"I shot him. I admitted it."

"He's a killer. Done for."

"We still do not have proof. Our word against theirs."

"Nope."

Vera sensed Dani's confidence. "You think she told the truth and corroborated our version?"

"Yup. After she heard about the recording." Dani's grin spread across her face. "You remember how I like making copies. Didn't your lawyer tell you?"

"You captured what happened?"

"On my cell. Not from the beginning, but I've got him confessing and threatening to take us out. I tried to tell you at the house, but your Detective buddy stopped me."

"You are an amazing and resourceful young woman."

Dani's eyes shone. She looked happier than Vera could remember.

Chapter 62

Erika

Erika folded her clothes into two large Tumi suitcases. Her suit and blouse from the day of the shooting lay heaped in a trash bag. She never wanted to see them again. The skinny jeans, boots, and fitted sweater worked well together. A go-to outfit for traveling.

The police held her for questioning for hours. Poor Vera. If they kept Erika that long, it had to be hell for the older woman. When they finished with Erika, they told her to stay in town. *Fuck that.* One million dollars from Lavender in a numbered account in the Cayman Islands waited for her plus, three-hundred thousand in cash, the get-away money she'd saved for this moment, a fiasco that might materialize. She was getting out of Dodge. *Catch me if you can.*

In a third suitcase, she put toiletries and clothes Griff asked her to bring. They had him manacled to his hospital bed with a police officer standing guard. Their lawyer was working on next steps, but Dani's recording was damning. That surprised Erika. It never occurred to her that Dani taped them, her phone in her pocket and the record button on. That not only sealed things for Griff, it helped Erika decide about splitting. She'd drop off Griff's stuff and then hit the road.

Griff. She stopped packing. The tears flooded again. *Shit.* Grabbing a tissue, she swiped them away.

Erika believed in plans A, B, and C. Sell the house and use the money for Griff's defense. The rest belonged to her. She'd earned it. *Thank you, fuck-shit, Hugh Lavender, for coming through, and good luck. May our paths never cross again.*

With the heel of her boot, she crushed her phone. No tracking her. Everything important she saved to her laptop. She'd buy a throwaway along the way.

Without a backward glance, she locked up the house, loaded her car, and sped down the driveway.

Chapter 63

Vera

Charlie. For the first time since the murder, Vera thought about him without crying. "Charlie was innocent of wrongdoing" she said to Dani. "From time-to-time, I let doubt creep in, but in my heart, I knew the truth."

"You did right by him."

So much for not crying. Vera pulled out a tissue from her purse. "I am not worried. It is going to be okay." She dabbed at her tears. "Detective Monroe was more than kind."

After leaving the diner, Dani and Vera went to her place. First, she phoned Monroe and then Laura Peach. The news lifted her spirits. Next, she called Penny.

Now Vera and Dani sat in Vera's living room, Brandy curled at her feet.

"What did your lawyer say?"

"Your tape took care of everything. The District Attorney will not press charges. Self-defense."

"And you caught a murderer."

"That probably helped." She smiled, remembering her conversation with Laura Peach. "Even though I used an unlicensed gun."

Laura Peach made a strong case to the District Attorney who was up for re-election. "Two men after her – Lavender because of his despicable behavior and deception, and Griff because Dani stumbled onto the truth about Charlie Moon's murder. And you're going to blame this woman, an African American senior citizen, a pillar of her church and community, a grieving mother, because she used an unregistered weapon? Thank God she had the fortitude to defend herself and the other two women in the killer's crosshairs."

"So, we're both in the clear?"

"Apparently so."

"Heard from Erika?" Dani asked.

"She left a message on my cell that she is heading for parts unknown."

"Wow. Leaving Griff to his fate alone?"

"He murdered someone she loved."

Dani snorted. "I think she mostly loves herself."

Vera's endless nightmare needed to end. Reality beckoned. No more fretting about crazy people, thieves, liars, and killers. Too many good things to look forward to. Top on her agenda was repairing her relationships with her daughters and becoming a devoted grandmother.

Vera thought about her own lies, her own mistakes. She should have reached out to Penny long before and brought her up to date on Liza's prognosis, ask how things were going with Archie and the kids. Penny had called several times, but Vera, swamped with worry, responded with quick text messages. It was only when Liza relapsed, gave everyone a scare, that Vera asked Penny to come. Yesterday, Vera shared the news of the shooting and solving Charlie's murder. Penny wanted to come back right away, but Vera told her to wait. *I need to plan that visit now.*

Her mind turned to Liza. They made progress in their relationship, but still lots of repair work to do there as well.

Plus, she must find purpose outside of herself. Time for giving back again. Reconnect with the Women's Ministry of her church and help feed the homeless and hungry every Saturday. She'd not participated in anything ever since she'd lost Charlie.

"And you?" Vera asked Dani. "What is next?"

"Not sure."

"Are you and Mirko getting back together?"

She lifted her shoulders and eyebrows. "I've stopped lying and apologized, trying to make things right with everyone I wronged. Mirko has let me stay with him for now, but I don't think he's ready for me to move in, to trust me completely again."

"It will take time."

Dani nodded. "I called Bogie."

"How did that go?"

"I told him everything and he said I could still come and stay with him."

Stroking Brandy's head, Vera waited.

"He loves me. Always has. I can fix things."

"I appreciate you. I am profoundly grateful."

Dani dipped her head.

"I've been thinking," Vera said.

"About?"

"You living with me for a while, until you find a job, and get on your feet."

"Really?" Dani's right leg pumped.

The joy in Dani's voice made Vera's heart clutch. "The court will probably summon us to testify if Griff does not take a plea deal and I could use a hand finding a new place, plus Liza requires post-op care. You would be doing me a big favor." She reached over and rubbed Dan's jackhammer leg. "What do you say?"

"You honestly need my help?"

"Absolutely. We are a great team."

"You got to be right with yourself before you can be right with anybody else."

— August Wilson

Acknowledgements

With gratitude, I thank Black Rose Writing, Reagan Rothe, and his team for giving me this opportunity.

Thank you to my early and final readers for their keen eyes for details, patience and encouragement: my husband, Robert Osborne, Sr.; my son, Robert Osborne, Jr.; my friends and fellow writers Marianne Haggerty, Willa Hograth, and Dorin Hart.

Thanks to my cousin, Robert Johnson, Retired Squad Lieutenant, NYPD, for his expertise.

I am most appreciative to all the friends, readers, and reviewers of my first novel, *Getting It Right*. A special thank you to Cheryl McKissack. Without you, there wouldn't be a second one.

An extra and special thank you to my husband of fifty-three years for his extraordinary support and to my family for their love and encouragement: Alicia, Bob Jr., Suzy, and J.P. Osborne and Adam, and Aidan Quallo.

About the Author

Creating stories to entertain her friends since she was a girl in The Bronx, NY, Karen always wanted to write. At sixteen, beneath her high school graduation picture, read Ambition: Writer. Marriage, children, and career sidelined her passion. Her novel, *Getting It Right*, Akashic Books, debuted June 2017.

Retired from The Osborne Group, an international consulting firm, Karen lives in Florida with her husband, Robert. She serves on the state board of Easterseals Florida.

Note from the Author

Word-of-mouth is crucial for any author to succeed. If you enjoyed *Tangled Lies*, please leave a review online—anywhere you are able. Even if it's just a sentence or two. It would make all the difference and would be very much appreciated.

Thanks!
Karen E. Osborne

CPSIA information can be obtained
at www.ICGtesting.com
Printed in the USA
LVHW041109021221
705079LV00014B/607

9 781684 337323